MW01107358

BUYING TIME

A Jaunt In Time And Space

Mondo Fax

the Singing Judge

Author's Edition

Buying Time
A Jaunt In Time and Space

Every morning we wake up (for the most part) with 24 free God-given hours to live as we please. But what if one morning we didn't get this time for free? What if we had to *earn* it? In *Buying Time*, humorously slanted at the huge Fantasy/Science Fiction market, a kookie quintet of disparate LA Subway riders finds itself in that predicament. There is sex, mystery, action, suspense, space-chase, love, friendship, and, most of all, revelation. Pearl, Makeba, Nardo, Norma and Jake experience their earthquaked subway car falling through a crack in time and space. As they reach the huge pink glowing gas planet that supports its surrounding floating islands, they are outfitted with R.O.'s (ReadOuts) to calculate the time and credits they must now earn. Needing twelve credits each to return to their Plane of Origin, the great digression begins. Each discovers his/her best talents to make the team go ever forward. Earning full credits, they return to the L.A. Subway car only nano-seconds from whence they started, and remember nothing. Forever changed, now they are sitting next to each other, relating and planting the seeds for the best of friends.

"First time novelist Mondo Fax, the Singing Judge, spins his story through a cavalcade of characters and situations. His observant eye has never missed or forgotten anything. He writes with an entertaining style that makes you sit back, relax and enjoy."

John-Michael Howson
Books and Authors

". . . highly imaginative, well-written, very amusing, compassionate, inspirational, wonderful characters . . . a great read!"

Michelle Anderson, Publisher,
Hill of Content Publishing Pty Ltd.

BUYING TIME

A Jaunt In Time And Space

Author's Edition

MONDO FAX

The Singing Judge

Mondo Fax Publishing

Copyright 2001 Alan R. Glasser pka Mondo Fax

Buying Time
A Jaunt In Time And Space
By Mondo Fax, the Singing Judge
(Author's Edition)

Mondo Fax Publishing
P.O. Box 2904
Santa Clarita, CA 91350

www.mondofax.com
info@mondofax.com - e-mail

All rights reserved. No part of this book may be reproduced or
transmitted in any form or by any means, electronic or mechanical,
including photocopying, recording or by any information storage and
retrieval system, without express written permission from the author,
except for the inclusion of brief quotations in a review.

Copyright 2001 by Alan R. Glasser pka Mondo Fax, the Singing Judge

Printed in the United States of America

Library of Congress Cataloging-in-Publication Data

Fax, Mondo.

Buying time / Mondo Fax, the Singing Judge. – 1st
ed.
p.cm

1. Science fiction.   I. Title.

PS3556.A9955B89 2001   813'.6
                    QBI01-700359

ISBN 0-9710095-0-3

Library of Congress Control Number 20011116829

To Steve who makes time priceless.

About the author:

MONDO FAX ™ (AKA Alan R. Glasser) was born in New York City, but spent most of his time growing up in Southern California. He was confirmed and Bar Mitzvahed in Southern California after ten years of Jewish and Hebrew School. His parents were both dancers in New York (his father danced with Major Bowes Radio Show at Radio City Music Hall). He studied music and began writing songs at the age of five, playing a variety of instruments including guitar, piano, violin and flute. Mondo was a dancer with the American Folk Ballet for eleven years as a child, and was a principal dancer with the Yovail Folk Dancers in Europe and Israel.

Mondo studied at UCLA and graduated in Music and Political Science before studying for an advanced degree in Ethnomusicology. He also minored in Theater Arts, and was repeatedly chosen to study acting in the exclusive UCLA Theater Arts Department Acting Specialization program. After these studies, Mondo performed as a guitar player/singer for Olivia Newton-John and for John Davidson and at age twenty-five became the musical director for the Jim Nabors and Natalie Cole shows. Mondo toured with his own successful cabaret show group, performing everywhere from the Plaza Hotel in New York to the MGM Grand in Las Vegas.

After touring, Mondo returned to UCLA School of Law and graduated at the top of his class, serving as a member of the *UCLA LAW REVIEW* and writing for the *FEDERAL COMMUNICATIONS LAW JOURNAL.* Afterwards, Mondo became an entertainment attorney, working for Walt Disney Pictures and Television and Saban Entertainment. He has a law practice in Southern California and currently serves as a *Judge Pro Tempore* in both the Superior and Municipal Courts for the State of California, County of Los Angeles, which he has done for the past eleven years.

Mondo is prolific in his music. He recently released four CD's of original irreverent social song parodies that have become staples on MP3.com and Amazon.com. One song, *"Eat My Shorts,"* became a national hit recorded by national radio personality, Rick Dees. Mondo wrote and produced his one-explorer musical, *Christopher Columbus, The Live Album,* premiering in Hollywood, California. Most recently, Mondo's song "*Saving Hanukkah For Monica*" has been number one on the MP3.com satire top 40. Mondo also recently released his first World/Folk/Calybossa CD entitled *Aquamarine.* He is currently releasing another comedy CD, *OKLAHOMOPHOBIA!* and an original children's CD, *Songs For The Thoughtful Child* as a solo artist.

Mondo is a member of the Academy of Television Arts and Sciences, and serves annually as a judge for the Prime Time Emmy awards. Mondo recently completed a second play entitled *So's Your Whole Family,* which chronicles his years in Southern California with his maternal and paternal Jewish Grandmothers who lived in a walk-up duplex across from each other. Mondo's first fictional novel, *Buying Time* is due to be published within the year. He has most recently starred in his own show, *Anarchy and Angst, An Evening With Mondo Fax, the Singing Judge* ™ being featured at the Melbourne International Comedy Festival, with coverage in all major Australian papers and radio shows and, over time, has received multiple rave reviews from the *Los Angeles Times* and several other publications.

Author's Note

Time, like the other senses, places humanity slap dab in the third dimension. As we touch, taste, see, hear and smell, we also perceive the change from one moment to the next. This sixth sense, like the others, is malleable. In other words, as sight is changed by focus, and hearing is filtered by human brains, so time stretches and shrinks depending on our circumstances. Minutes can turn into interminable epochs, and years can "fly by."

One thing is certain. As humans, we are gifted twenty-four hours each day for "free." In *Buying Time*, I demonstrate how things would be if we had to "earn" each minute, and each minute was used as currency. Further, I tackle issues such as diversity and life choices, as our five diverse characters digress from Earth time, and set out on a jaunt that will forever change their personalities. Bon voyage!

1 - RETRO RAIL

Pearl Pelzman stretched her lower lip and internalized a big shivering "yiechh" as she descended into the Downtown station of the Los Angeles Metrorail. It was "Retro-rail" as her ten-year old grand-nephew Efram called it. "It's only been heah [here] less than a few yeahs [years] (no "r"s for Aunt Pearl)," she kvetched to herself, "and already it looks like God-knows-what South American country." Of course, Pelzman was formerly spelled with two "n"s at the end, but changed for Americanization. It was originally changed to "Peltsman" but Pearl's Rabbi made them change the "ts" back to "z" as a tribute to Israel when Pearl married Maury Peltsman.

It wasn't like the New York subways of the 30's and 40's when she was a little girl. Now those were subways. Exciting, fast, crowded . . . but people were going somewhere. People *had* to take the subway . . . "regulah persons," she thought as the Mid-Wilshire bound Metrorail pulled in. "Nowadays, be glad they have tracks," she continued as she contemplated her eventual transfer to a filthy city bus to take her into the Fairfax district. "I oughta give the drivah a drug test."

Whoosh. The doors to the car pulled open. The interior of the car was already starting to show signs of city wear. Each and every advertisement had "Chaka" scrawled on it in some kind of

Castillian calligraphy. What did it all mean? "I don't know and I don't wanna know from that!" Pearl answered her own question.

She noticed that the car wasn't too full. "Good," she thought. "Big people, big smells," she mused as she positioned each of her shopping bags one on each seat beside her. "That'll keep 'em away."

Good again. Because schlepping down the aisle was that same ol' obese black woman wearing much too much gloppy gold jewelry, a blousey African print schmate, belted, but you couldn't see the belt under the rolls of fat, with black spandex stretch pants and black patent leather heel-slapper pumps. On her head was some kind of turban (did this woman tell fortunes?) made of the blouse material, with a big wooden chopstick speared through the knot to hold it together. "Oh well. Live and let live." Pearl smiled to herself as she echoed Anita Bryant's immortal words.

"Fock! Lookie dat fat white bitch she takin' up three spaces. Who she thinks she is?" Makeba grabbed the back of the seat in front of her to line her ass up with the seats she planned to take. Plop. She didn't take into account that there were only four people in the car, she just didn't like the "white bitch" taking up three seats. And with good reason. "Lookie she. Two shopping bags full o' de shit fo' de white lady and no job for de black lady." Makeba always mentalized her thoughts in her own version of a West Indian bastardized ghetto talk, though she was perfectly capable of speaking impeccable English, having been thrown out of Berkeley mere weeks before her matriculation as an honor student during the Free Speech Movement in the mid-to-late Sixties. "I should have killed that asshole Mario Savio." Her English perfected as her anger level rose. She was a black belt in Tai Kwan Do. Her hands had to be registered as lethal weapons. She looked disapprovingly at her nails. The French Manicure had long since faded into Plaster of Paris.

She visualized her long-forgotten would-have-been diploma.

"The Regents of the University of California, Berkeley, hereby bestow upon Mona Lisa Edwards ('I should have blowtorched that birth certificate!') the degree of Bachelor of Arts, SUMMA CUM LAUDE. Makeba had changed her name during the Black Panther movement to something with several clicks in it, but reconsidered and settled on "Makeba" after her favorite folk singer.

In fact, Makeba was a singer herself. In the tradition of Odetta and Miriam Makeba, Makeba fancied herself the new "Gospel, African, Folk" messiah. Although she had done an admirable job in several local church choirs, she had a long way to go. And peppered in with the singing was a penchant for African dancing. She had resolved to learn all the cultures from the Mother Land in order to be prepared. Prepared for what, she wasn't absolutely sure.

Makeba took a compact from her shoulder bag. She wouldn't put any makeup on, but she was grateful that her skin, a golden tan, was still smooth and unwrinkled. "Good Black Don't Crack." Thank Allah this was only a short ride.

Nardo turned his head toward the subway car window and rested his forehead on it. He was crammed in the back seat, hiding and sipping his extra large Coke, easy ice. "Same people all the time," quickly raced through his head as he recognized Pearl and Makeba going through their predictable paces as they climbed onto the same car, the same time, sat in the same seats every day. His eyes caught a bushy-bearded homeless person with his blanket spread out on the subway station floor, taking in the view. He was a "same person," since he was there every day when they took the train downtown to work and every night when they returned to Mid-Wilshire.

Nardo's eyes glazed over and the homeless man's blanket turned into rice. Rice spread on the narrow two-lane highway. Rice drying on the side of the road as the small cars and trucks sped away from Manila, artfully swerving to avoid the food of the peasants. He would like a mango now. He would like to reach up as the mango reached down to him suspended from its willowy lone branch. He would like to be speaking his native language.

Leonardo, shortened to "Nardo", had worked all the drag clubs in Manila. Not a big circuit. Mostly travelers stopping in Manila were on their way to some more exotic port. Nardo wasn't short in Manila. But he was short here, back in the U.S.A. He was all of four feet eleven and weighed a whopping seventy-six pounds. He had the face of a beautiful island woman, and no one guessed that he was over forty. Nardo in drag had turned the eye of many a straight man, and he had been beaten within an inch of his life several times, even if they knew he was a man when they propositioned him.

He worked only part time drag now. He couldn't afford the costumes, the field was over-crowded, and he didn't have the drive to make it big in LA. By day, he worked at Canard & Sons, a high-end fabric store, filled with pretentious queen decorators flailing bolts of cloth to and fro. He liked it, you know. Got the job just by chance by giving good blow jobs to an older, graying white gentleman who turned out to be the showroom manager for thirty years. Also, people were used to quasi-hermaphroditic sprites selling fabric, and he felt accepted. The pay was pretty good. He could afford a one-bedroom in an older building in Silverlake, mostly gay.

Jacob Silver's contact-blue eyes peeked out through his "Bushman of Borneo" beard, as he pulled himself up on his blanket and stared at the people loading onto the Metrorail car. Where were they all going? Why would anyone want to go anywhere? There was plenty of food here in the trashcans. People just waste food. They throw whole Cokes out, entire hamburgers, French fries. He especially liked it when they just lit a cigarette when the train pulled in. Then they'd have to put it out in the ashtray, he hoped, and don't break it. Ugh. Why do people smoke

4

these ultra-lites? They don't taste like anything.

It was warm here, down under. A good place to sleep. He'd only been arrested for vagrancy twice, and then got pretty good food in jail, and a place to sleep and shit. He had a place to shit here, too. A restroom, fairly clean. Wow. His language had really gone down the toilet in the last year. He never used to say "shit." But that's what it was, and why not call a toad a toad, quoting Kermit.

Jake didn't need to wear colored contacts because his eyes were already a handsome blue, but he got the contacts in his former life when he was a waiter/actor. That's a person who's waiting to act. His agent told him it was a "good investment." He never understood why he needed blue contacts for a black-and-white 8 X 10 glossy entitled "Benjamin Warren". But he spent his last dime and got them. His agent, a woman with a no-filter Camel voice nicknamed the "Brooklyn Buzz Saw", looked after him quite well. At her insistence, he invested all $5000 he came to California with on "cold reading classes," "commercial workshops," and "pay to play" gigs she got him. Thanks to her, he went broke, started drinking and taking drugs, lost his day job, his car, his girlfriend, his apartment, and became homeless. By the way, his agent dropped him. She wrote him a letter stating that she just didn't feel the relationship was "working out" and "good luck with his career." Of course, Jake never received the letter at his new, more floating, address. The agent has since changed agencies six times, and professions twice.

How could a gorgeous Jewish boy who had enjoyed the three "B's" (briss, bar mitzvah and Bachelor of Arts) have ended up here, on the edge of survival. Oh well, he didn't care. His mother and father would care, but not before they gave him that all-knowing "I told you not to go into acting, you screwed up" look, a look that he would rather starve in the streets running away from than face.

5

Jake pulled a glossy out of his biodegradable "paper or plastic" plastic bag. The composites had seen better days. Jake always kept his glossies with him, just in case. "You never know who you're sitting next to" his agent used to tell him. As long as it wasn't her, he didn't care.

At once, Jake made a decision that would change his life. He would take the subway today, a change of scenery. He shoved the glossies back into the overstuffed plastic bag, crunched up his blanket and labored into an upright position, making several futile attempts to zip up his "California Surplus Mart" jacket. Was it originally brown and faded to army green, or vice-versa? Jake fixed his gaze toward the train doors.

As he bumped into the door, the "door close" electronic beep sounded and the aluminum doors practically crushed him. He then yanked on his blanket which had become lodged in the slamming panels, and, when the blanket released, stumbled back, throwing himself directly onto one of Pearl's prized packages.

"Yiecch," spake Pearl. This time it was audible.

"I'm awfully sorry," salaamed Jake, and Pearl nearly passed out from the smell of his breath. Now the train started with a jolt (you'd think that after spending a billion dollars on this verchochte train, it would at least start smoothly), and Jake, shaking from (1) the booze, (2) the need for a fix, (3) his recent fall, (4) the motion of the train and (5) generic LA palsy began "Susie Q"ing his way down the aisle.

Makeba's big brown eyes sternly met Jake's blues and he knew instantly he would not be sitting next to her. Nardo was shrinking in horror in the back seat.

"You can sit next to me. I don't mind." The light voice had an eerily mature ring to it, but upon turning, Jake looked down into an invitingly pretty golden-skinned face, albeit a little too much make up for a girl of sixteen-going-on-seventeen.

Norma Jardines was on her way home from babysitting, helping out at a day care center. An honor student, she was getting college credits for it, although she was a senior at Fairfax High, but her boss was paying her a little under the table. Norma's parents were very poor, and she lived in a three bedroom apartment with them and her three remaining brothers. Her oldest brother had been shot to death by gangs at her school, her youngest brother was lost to drugs, and her middle brother was forced to join the Army to escape the danger and squalor of the family's LA life. Her mother cleaned houses and her father stood amongst the illegal aliens near the paint store hoping to get picked up for some day labor and not by the INS. They were all bilingual. They were all U.S. citizens. Thanks to the amnesty, that is.

Besides being pretty in that East LA way, Norma had a natural gift. She sang like a bird. She sang as if she knew the secrets of the Aztecs, the pain of the Native Americans, or whatever they call themselves now, and the ecstasy of the best sexual intercourse in the universe. Norma had never been out of LA, and she was still basically considered a virgin, honest. That's natural singing talent.

But Norma was like a beautiful ice-princess. There was something dark and forgotten behind those almond eyes, something sinister and foreboding. On the surface, Norma was like a calculator, everything in its proper place, nothing less than an "A" on a test, doing things for everyone else, thinking of others before herself.

Jake couldn't believe that Norma was actually relating to him as a person. The only people he had spoken to in a year were either other bombed-out homeless or the police. Everybody else avoided him like the Bubonic. Even so, Norma asked about him, mostly. Jake could not pry even the most superficial detail from Norma about herself. He immediately put it off to shyness. But something inside him nagged that there was a hidden ghost in Norma; a beautiful swallow with the dark secret of an eagle.

"Do you take the subway often?" Norma was naive. Jake was not paying for this ride, but Norma didn't seem to mind his smell even though it had been weeks, no months, since he last bathed. Nardo could smell it, though. Nardo buried his nose in his shirt where the smell of "Gendarme" just ever so barely covered up the "Eau de Last Month" Jake was wearing.

"Hardly ever. In fact, this is my first time."

"Oh, really. I've got a month-pass. They buy it for me at school, since I'm working at a job and getting college units for it."

Pearl craned her neck disdainfully and once again the lower lip stretched. "Why doesn't he just go home?" she Marie-Antoinetted, extremely unhappy that he was talking to such a young girl, even if she was Mexican. "Anybody who looks and smells like that has got to be a sex maniac." She flinched as she tried to remember the last time she had sex with her husband, Maury.

"What college are you planning to go to?" Jake asked, thrilled that he was having a conversation about something other than wiping the ink off his fingers at the Rampart Division.

"L.A. City College if I don't get a scholarship to UCLA. And then Cal State LA in two years after I get my AA." Norma let some information go.

"I went to UCLA," Jake said, and Norma looked puzzled.

The lights went out in the car. Pearl thought it was normal. In New York, this happened all the time. The non-New Yorkers, however received lumps in their throats. So did Pearl when the sound of the electric motors stopped, and there was no station in sight. Suddenly the car jolted. There was a split second when everybody was waiting for hopefully nothing, but unfortunately something.

No lights, the sound was deafening. As if God had seen fit to tear these five little lives apart, the car began to hurtle back and forth, Pearl's Hadassah glasses went flying along with her packages. Nardo was shrieking, holding on for dear life, Makeba was getting very angry, and Jake instinctively put his arms around Norma's head, cradling it to protect it . . . earthquake.

Then came a deadly silence with only sounds of whimpering. The whole world was this car. The car was ominously shaking intermittently, as if to warn that the worst was yet to come.

Without warning, a second wave slammed the car up until it hit the roof of the subway tunnel, throwing the LA Brigade on the floor without regard to race, creed, color, gender, age or sexual orientation. Then, strange. The car began to tilt forward as if it were falling off a steep precipice. Slowly the car leaned further and further. Makeba grabbed the back of the seat in front of her as she felt her weight fall against it. Still total blackness. She felt her turban tumble forward. Soon, all were laying on the back of the seat in front of them. The car was completely on its end and beginning to travel at a remarkable rate of speed. They were in free fall.

The G-Force began to build. It was hard to breathe. The cheeks of Nardo's butt were pinching as tightly as they could. He was scared to death.

Then, slowly but deliberately, the G-Force began to lessen, like after a jet has taken off. Eventually, they all felt like they were floating, but there was, strangely, normal gravity in the car.

After several minutes (but you couldn't really tell how long it was), a strange salmon-colored glow filled the car, and everybody could see for the first time since the quake. Norma looked outside the window, cautiously pulling her head from the safety of Jake's arms. Out the left side of the car, the entire window was filled with a pink glowing substance. She couldn't tell if it was enveloping the car or how near or far to the car it was.

Pearl was anxiously looking around. "Oy my God." She started the conversation. All barriers were down now.

"Is everybody all right?" Jake asked loudly.

"I think so," answered Makeba, speaking for the masses. Nardo peeked over the back of the seat. He was still scared shitless. "Are you all right?" Makeba asked Nardo, making great effort to turn around in her chair to face him.

"Thank you. I am." Nardo said shakily, still hiding in his seat.

"What the hell happened?" Makeba was still mad at the inconvenience of the whole thing.

"I think it was an earthquake," ventured Nardo, happy that everybody still seemed alive.

Norma was transfixed on the glowing substance. All of a sudden it became clear as the edge of the substance approached and a black arc began moving in from the direction of the front of the car. Mixed in the coming blackness, stars.

"We're in space! We're passing by a sun. It's a kind I never studied. It's like a glowing planet, and we're passing by it! We're in space!" Norma had studied astronomy.

Pearl's lower lip was full tilt now. She certainly didn't wanna know from this. She had enough problems mastering the few square miles that she and Maury had confined their life to, let alone space. No, Pearl did not wanna know from this. "Oy mein Gott in Himmel."

Jake got up and walked towards Pearl. "Are you all right?" This time Pearl was happy for his company but wasted no time in offering him a breath mint. She lunged for her purse and stabbed her arm into it hoping for a lucky hit.

"Take two. It's vitamin foatified." Pearl was very hopeful. Jake smiled. His teeth were in surprisingly good shape considering what they had been through in the last year. Underneath, he was still the guy in the glossies. Pearl could not see this "inner beauty" yet, however. A yarmulke and a tallis might have helped.

"Are you hurt?" Jake's natural instincts had come back to him. Considering his state on his initial approach to the subway car, the adrenaline generated during the earthquake had bestowed upon him an "instant straightness" for which he was grateful.

"Thank you very much, but no, I don't think so. I'm all right. Oy." Pearl looked at the contents of her packages spread all over the floor. Two of the Pic-n-Save tchachkes were definitely beyond repair. On second thought, Pearl repented by reasoning that, if they actually were in space, maybe she wouldn't need the tchachkes after all.

2 - ORIENTATION DAY

All eyes were now transfixed outside the left side of the car. Indeed, they were floating through space, or hurtling. In that environment, they had no idea how fast they were going. There was still gravity inside the car, and the car seemed to be upright.

Makeba had lunged over to the left side of the car, her ample behind thrust into the aisle, as she squeezed into a seat and pressed her nose against the window. Pearl was balancing on the bars on the seatbacks, as she leaned over and squinted through her Hubbell-thick rhinestone glasses to drink in the sights. The lower lip had not changed position. Nardo had stolen out from his hiding place, peeking tentatively over Pearl's hairdo to see, his mouth open wide. Norma and Jake were turned in their seats, with their faces against the glass.

The sight outside the car was splendid, and Jake thought it far surpassed any "Star Trek" or "Star Wars" mattes, mock-ups or computer generated animation. Centered in the midst of the black and diamond backdrop was a huge apricot-colored glowing sphere which sent out a salmon-tinted corona around it one-half again the size of the sphere. Orbiting around the large globe on a flat plane like the rings of Saturn were several what appeared to be darker "moons", but oddly shaped. They were not round, but more random-disc shaped, with a top and bottom. It was almost like five or six islands, floating in a flat, rose-colored sea.

Nary a word was being spoken in the subway car, as the car began its own circle around the glowing orb. The passengers could now sense that they were circling nearer and nearer to the planet or sun or whatever it was, and as they approached, the islands took on their particular shapes.

Now they were moving past and over one of these moons, and as they looked down, they could see webs of lights, as if they were in a plane flying over a large city at twilight. It was a spectacular sight, with the light from the orb throwing constant dusk over each moon, as if day were forever breaking.

Pink islands or no, Pearl needed a pill, though surprisingly she didn't feel tired or achy or any of the physical discomforts she was feeling when she first sat down in the subway car that day. But she felt obligated to take a pill. This was a trauma. She *must* feel bad. She clamored for her purse in the salmon light and again thrust her hand down in. Retrieving a pill bottle, she held it up to the light of the orb. She had at least eight kinds of pills in there, all prescription. She had uppers, downers, even sideways pills. She was so confused, she didn't even know which one to take, but decided that this must be a dream, so she must be sleeping, so she should take an upper to wake her up. She threw the pill down with no water. By the way, the pill had absolutely no effect on her, whatsoever.

The car was still circling the orb, and drawing closer. They had now reached the other side of the orb, which they could not see at first, and saw that the moon-island they were approaching seemed larger than the others, and was completely studded with lights. This moon was flat like the others, but oblong and odd-shaped, with the lights displaying the shape quite clearly for the onlookers.

Makeba looked longingly at Pearl's codeine pills. This was the woman whose color she had so completely despised not one hour ago. Was it only an hour? Now, suffering from "in time of crisis, let's all be brothers and sisters" syndrome, she boldly asked, her English quite straightened out, "That's not codeine, is it?"

She knew very well it was, having partaken of both the prescription and black (you should pardon the expression) market varieties more than once.

Pearl's 5000 year old fear of schwartzes partially evaporated. Pearl was happy to have some conversation that resembled what she was used to in her Hadassah circle. "Double strengt." Pearl also left many "h's" off the end of her words, like "strengt" and "healt". "Help yuhself." Pearl handed the bottle to Makeba. "It's the big white round one."

"Thank you." Makeba also took the pill with no water. Likewise, it was to have no physical effect. However, a bond was formed - formed between this black woman born in the early fifties and this Jewish woman born in the late-thirties. They had common ground. They had pills.

All passengers were staring out the window at the awesome sight. Even Nardo had crept out of his hiding place, although his hands were still planted firmly in front of his eyes. They were drawing near to one of the island-moons now, and could clearly see the outlines of big city lights at dusk. Streaks of light leapt from the island to the other island-moons from time to time. But by now, the passengers knew they were going towards the city. They still did not know how fast they were going.

Without warning, the subway car lit up like a giant flash-bulb. Nardo shrieked. Pearl gasped "Oy!" Then they all slowly blinked their eyes open, as if they had just gotten out of a "four photos for $1" booth. The floating feeling had stopped. They became acutely aware of the babble of voices from outside. Jake pressed up against the window and looked.

They looked to be in some kind of outdoor yard. There were

all different types of what Jake guessed to be "vehicles", ranging from extremely "organic" looking alien craft to old bi-planes, balloons, saucers. "Star Trek meets Jules Verne" thought Jake to himself. He felt afraid, and turned to look at everyone else's expression.

Nardo's face was very blanched, and he looked like someone had just ripped the Wynonna Judd drag wig off his head. His best two drags were Wynonna Judd and Melissa Etheridge, although the olive skin was a little dark for a blonde Melissa. Pearl was shaking her pill box, while her eyes were transfixed on the scene outside the subway car, as were Makeba's, although Makeba's hand was cupped and palm up waiting for another codeine. Norma, who was standing next to Nardo, was probably the calmest. In one hand she clutched the crucifix around her neck. Her other hand slowly felt for Nardo's, and without looking at him, she took it. Nardo turned slightly toward her, mostly in disbelief that anyone would take his hand so, while the color returned to his face.

The chaotic bustle outside was becoming apparent now. Fear slipped away and curiosity took over. Makeba broke the silence. "What's going on out there?" There was no longer any hint of ghetto English. More important issues had superseded.

"It's gotta be some kind of hallucination," stated Jake being an expert on the subject, having had to hallucinate his way through many a night on the chilly Los Angeles streets with only Mr. Sterno for company.

"Maybe we're in the Bermuda Triangle," piped in Norma.

"I was in Bermuda once . . . with my sister-in-lore," said Pearl, mostly to convince herself that this illusion really did have something to do with and/or was near Miami.

"Well, we can't stay here forever," said Makeba, clearly the most adventuresome of the lot. "Let's go outside."

Nardo shivered. "Maybe we can't breathe outside. I learned it on Star Trek. Maybe this isn't a class-M planet. Oxygen-Nitrogen atmosphere." Nardo was a huge Trekee. He was positive that drag queens were well accepted throughout the galaxy, on all Class M Planets other than Earth.

Pearl was not obsessed with breathing for now. Momentarily, her New York mouth took over. "I got on the train on Wilshire Boulevard and now I'm on God-knows what moon of Uranus. Everybody's walkin' around out deah. If we can't breathe, so we'll come back inside. Right now I feel very stuffy and closed in."

"Me, too," said Makeba. "We should find out what's happening." Makeba went to the door of the car. She attempted to pull it open.

"Wait!" yelled Jake. "The little man's right. What if you let all the air out?"

Nardo's antenna went up, and the squawk box sounded. "I may be little," he squeaked, "but I'm . . ."

"Okay! Okay! I'm sorry." Jake pleaded. "I just didn't know your name."

"Leonardo. Mr. De Los Santos to you."

"Alright." Jake was sorry. He didn't have time for this now. "Look. Leonardo . . . " he looked at Nardo for approval. Nardo nodded slightly, and then went back in his shell. "Leonardo is right about this. We have to be careful."

"Well, what do you suggest, Einstein?" Makeba didn't take no shit from no one.

Norma broke in. chanting in her "East LA" style, "Come on, you guys. Stop making a big deal. It's time to think."

"Well . . . I don't know, exactly. Is there some way to test it?" Jake was out of ideas.

"Does someone have a straw?" said Norma.   Nardo, still limerant from Norma's affectionate hand clasp said, "Yes. I have one from my Coke."

"Well, if we forced the straw out through the rubber gaskets on the door, and held it with our finger, no air would escape, and then someone could breathe through the straw once and see if the outside atmosphere was all right." Norma had just an ever-so-slight Maria Montez accent, and coupled with her beauty and the scientific analysis, she made quite an attractive package.

"Great thinking sister!" yelled Makeba. "Leonardo, baby. Lemme' see that straw." Nardo pulled the straw out of his half-empty Coke with a little "squeak" and as he handed it to her he said "call me 'Nardo'."

Jake went up to the door. "I'll push the gasket back and you shove the straw through. Be careful not to bend it."

"It's a Flex Straw," whispered Nardo, still miffed at the "little man" comment.

Whoosh. The door was open. Everyone was taken by surprise. A woman in overalls swung herself up onto the subway car platform and stepped into the car. She looked like a janitor. "Boy. You guys are slow, slow, slow." Her lips seemed to move a little out of synch with her mouth. She began handing out what looked like nametags but they had liquid crystal digital readouts on them. These said in big numerals "12:00", and in the upper left hand corner "CO". "Pin these on," lip-synched the janitor lady, "and don't lose 'em or you'll have to buy another and that'll costya time. These are your R.O.'s. Caution. Your caution bought you some time, so I guess that's okay. Okay, listen up. I'm only gonna say this once. For your collective exercise of caution and your teamwork, you got twelve hours starting from the time you

18

leave the car. And that's a pretty good deal if I do say so. Personally, I wouldn't give ya' more than seven, but everybody working together to get the door thing happening, and all that. Anyway, during that twelve hour period, you'll have to find a way to buy yourself more time, and so on for each additional minute you earn. There aren't any days or nights here in most places and situations, and you don't sleep, usually — thank stars, what a waste of time. Not unless it's part of your task."

Confused, Makeba didn't know where to start. She blurted, "Buy? How do we get . . . what?" Makeba was not afraid of janitors.

"Look. I suggest you buy yourself an Explanation from one of the Information Brokers on the way out. Look, I gotta go. A Mental Block from Timeoid parsec was sighted, and I've gotta meet it."

With that, the overalled tomboy pulled out of the door and bolted. "I've gotta Mental Block," asided Pearl. "And them pills ain't woikin'. Well. What now?"

All the passengers turned toward each other with blank stares. What were they doing here? Where was here? What did the cryptic message from the janitor lady mean? Caution bought us time? Twelve hours? R.O.'s? Just what the heck was going on?

Jake broke the dumbfounded silence. "Well." He pinned his R.O. on. "She said to buy an Explanation from one of the Information Brokers. Let's do it!"

"But what do we pay with? Is our money good here?" Norma was scouring the bottom of her purse for change.

"We'll never know until we ask one of these guys. One thing I learned on the streets: If you ask enough times, you'll eventually get what you need. Yep. The ultimate weapon is persistence. You've gotta be there to win if you're gonna win." Jake was all go.

Slowly poking his head out of the subway door, Jake craned left and right. People were moving by, all with their own agendas and, by the way, all donning their R.O.s. Well, actually they weren't all people. It was more like something from a Princess Leia hologram. Some had strange faces, most, if not all were bipeds and walked upright. "How convenient," thought Jake. Wouldn't Spielberg love this. You could use all real actors, at SAG minimum. Lots of savings on the animatronics.

"I guess the phrase is 'follow me,'" announced Jake, sticking his head back inside the door.

"We should take our stuff, shouldn't we?" Nardo offered.

"I'm not leavin' this heah. I paid a foah-chun [fortune] for this poahslin [porcelain]," kvetched Pearl, grabbing the unbroken tchachkes.

"I don' know what good that's gonna do you here," mumbled Makeba, as she swung her bottom (and center of gravity) out of the subway. Norma collected her purse and beckoned to Nardo, who sheepishly followed. Soon they were all standing on the ground outside the subway car. The R.O's, now each pinned to a respective chest, started to count backwards. 12:00:00, 11:59:59, 11:59:58. Time, or whatever it was, was a'wastin'.

Jake pounded his foot on the ground. "Concrete," he thought, but he wasn't sure. Looking around, he tried to make some sense of this place, but he couldn't. It was like a huge parking lot, with all these strange vehicles parked in it. Still, every now and then, a flash bulb.

"Information! Information! We sell Explanations cheap. Information!" A man dressed very much like a Roman-Catholic Cardinal swinging an incense burner and dressed in a sandwich sign saying "INFO" spotted the klan. "Do you desire an Explanation? Only fifty-one minutes."

"It takes fifty-one minutes for the Explanation?" asked Norma.

"Oh, no. No. It *costs* fifty-one minutes for the Explanation. Each that is. Fifty-one minutes each. The Explanation only takes three minutes and thirty-four seconds. A full and complete Explanation of all important rules and regulations concerning Chronos. You all come this way." Well. That seemed easy. Anything you could do in three minutes and thirty four seconds should be easy enough.

Not knowing what else to do, Jake turned toward the subway crowd and shrugged his shoulders. "Okay. What've we got to lose? Let's go." The group began following the Cardinal, wending its way this way and that through the lines of strange vehicles and beings. Noises, flash bulbs. Where were they going? 11:48:33, 11:48:32.

After rounding a large metal structure, which looked too big to be a vehicle, neon lights met their eyes. "INFO." "Explanations of Life and Time." Some were blinking. Some had tracer lights. Tiny little store fronts were set up in booths, with rows of benches. It this had been a carnival, one would have expected to have seen ring toss, goldfish ping pong, shooting galleries, and the like. But here, it seemed only information and explanations were for sale . . . on benches.

"Come. Come. My children. Do not tarry. Time is not cheap." The Cardinal was hurriedly ushering the subway crowd past all the neon lights into a less lighted area. "First, payment. Now, you all must have some time credit for getting here. What did you get. Eight hours? Ten hours?"

"Twelve hours", said Jake, not even thinking that divulging this information could be harmful. The Cardinal was visibly taken aback.

"Well...well." He wished he wouldn't have offered the Explanation for fifty-one minutes...each. He probably could've gotten more...a lot more, if he had just waited. Well, let's see. One, two, three, four, five times fifty-one minutes. He would make four and a half hours. That's not bad. Maybe he could get more later from this group.

Our Subway Brigade stared longingly and hopefully at the Cardinal, waiting breathlessly for the Explanation. "First, payment. Each of you raise your right hand, and place it on your head. Do you each solemnly convey sixty-one minutes of your . . ."

"Hey, I thought you said fifty-one minutes," injected Makeba, more than used to having people think her stupid because of how she looked.

"Sixty-one," stated the Cardinal.

"Hey, guys. It's our first intergalactic rip-off. Let's get outa here." Makeba was on her feet, and none too spryly.

"Okay, okay, o-kay!" The Cardinal paused while the disgusted "failed con-man" look disappeared, and the supercilious "holier than thou" false prophet ambience poured over him like sugarless pancake syrup. "If . . . if there was a . . . a misunderstanding, I am willing to give the explanation for fifty-one minutes each. Now, we're wasting time. Raise the right hands and place them on your head. Do you each solemnly convey fifty-one minutes to I, his grace, Cone Walden Albany Haven III, Registered Channeler and Information Broker License Number Zero One Eight One Two Zero Four?" Silence. "Please signify by saying 'I will' . . . out loud so the universal transcriber can record it."

"I will" collectively sounded with the exception of Pearl who said "Voos is das?" which is Yiddish for "Vats dat?"

The syrup evaporated from Cardinal Haven's demeanor. "I must have unanimity" he exasperated.

"Come on, Pearl" said Makeba. "Say 'I will' or we'll never get out of here."

"I will, I will," whined Pearl.

His Grace rubbed his hands together like a mustachioed landlord villain about to foreclose a mortgage. No one noticed that the R.O.s each showed a loss of fifty-one minutes. 10:52:46, 10:52:45. "All right. Listen carefully."

What followed was a verbal blur, you could make out some of the words and phrases at first like . . . RECITAL . . . INSTRUCTIONS . . . UNDERSTAND . . . SIX SECONDS . . . I DID NOT UNDERSTAND THAT INSTRUCTION' . . . REPEAT . . . ONE HALF . . . ORIGINAL . . . SIX MINUTES . . . EXCEPTION . . . STOPPED . . . ABEYANCE . . . REVIEW/ APPEAL . . . RULES AND REGULATIONS . . . PLANE MONITOR . . . TIME ALLOTTED . . . YOU WAVE. After that, nothing was understandable in the a flurry of unintelligible words, a patch of white sound which lasted for about thirty seconds. Most of the brigade sat with mouths agog, wondering what the hell was happening. The only clear words at the end were "ONE, TWO, THREE, FOUR, FIVE, SIX" and an Andy Kaufman-esque "TANK YOU BEDDY MOCH" and His Grace was off and had disappeared into the crowd, ne'er to be seen again.

"What was that?" marveled Jake. "Did anybody get any of that?" The blank stares were deafening.

"We've been had. Dogged. Ripped off. Whea dat muddafaka?" Makeba's ghetto sound emerged. "I be rippin' him." Her face became even more colored. She started through the crowd when Jake physically stopped her. Fortunately, he was as tall as she was wide, and he outweighed her.

"Calm down!" He persisted. "Calm down. Hold on. Now, did anybody understand any of that?"

"How could dey, de white bastud." Makeba started through the crowd again only to be stopped by Jake.

"I think I got most of it, but I might have missed a few words." The crowd turned toward the lark singing from the back of the group. It was Norma. She was holding up a steno pad, completely filled with strange marks, and a pen. "I'm actually over two-hundred words a minute now, but I'm trying for two twenty-five." Once more all mouths were agog. Their first super-hero turned out to be a slight, pretty Hispanic girl who, studying to be a secretary, among other things, was able to take down the entire speed-o-log, probably without an error. Jake smiled.

"Go, girl," bellowed Makeba, who walked right up to Norma, and put her arm around her shoulder.

"So if she knows what they said, shouldn't we listen to it slow and find out?" Pearl was becoming impatient. Also hungry, she thought. She looked deep down into the tchachke bag. There, wrapped in tin foil and then in plastic wrap was one of her famous marble sponge cakes. It was to have been a gift for Winnie, but Winnie hadn't shown up to the Senior Center that day. However, there was never a doubt in Pearl's mind that the cake would be shared. Everybody must be getting hungry. Pulling the cake out of the bag, Pearl said, "Are yuhs hungry? Maybe we could eat the cake while Normer translates the story."

Everyone agreed that this was a good idea. Nardo piped in, "I saw a tree. We could sit by that." People were beginning to feel that Nardo had the best sense of aesthetics in the crowd. Jake actually had a problem with Nardo. He didn't think homosexuality was normal, and mostly didn't want to think about it, but he knew a fag when he saw one. He had been approached many times by slimy sleazy producers and whatnot in the entertainment business. The thought of being intimate with Nardo physically repulsed Jake. How could any man stand that, two hard creatures coming together? Lesbianism made more sense, Jake thought. Two soft creatures being intimate.

But for now, Jake was forgetting his phobia. He thought to

himself that he had never realized that aesthetics, like sitting under a tree, could actually enhance or degrade a situation, other than in the retelling of the incident. But he pictured the idea of them all sitting under the tree in the pink twilight, eating cake and going over the notes, and he got a good feeling from that picture. And these days, good feelings were hard to come by, especially for Jake.

When they all got to the tree, they tiredly arranged themselves in a semi-circle with Norma in the center. Pearl asked if anyone had a knife and they did. It was Makeba. She carried a large Swiss Army knife for protection. So much more subtle than the switchblade she used to carry in the Sixties. Anyway, now it had a definitely new and useful purpose . . . to feed the hungry masses. Pearl began cutting the cake and passing it, piece by piece, down the semi-circle. Nardo offered the remains of his giant Coke and passed it down the line. It was a little warm, and the straw was worse for wear after the attempt to shove it through the door-gasket, but it would help wash down the sponge cake. Jake realized that Nardo's vision of the tree conclave had, indeed, created a "moment." "Norma. Please begin," Jake said softly, not wanting to break the mood. The drone of the crowd seemed faraway, and the flash bulbs were only flickering reminders of the chaos that had just passed.

"My name is Cone Walden Albany Haven III, Registered Channeler and Information Broker License Number Zero One Eight One Two Zero Four. I am required to give you the following information. The minimum time I must spend on stating this information is three minutes and thirty-four seconds. Such three minutes and thirty-four seconds may not include this introductory paragraph. The following sentence shall be delivered at a minimum of 158 decibels higher than the average decibel level of the remainder of the recital as analogous to twenty four point bold print all in capital letters: "IF AT ANY TIME DURING ANY OF THE RECITAL OF THESE INSTRUCTIONS AND/OR EXPLANATIONS YOU DO NOT UNDERSTAND, WITHIN

SIX SECONDS YOU MUST STATE IN A LOUD AND CLEAR VOICE 'I DID NOT UNDERSTAND THAT INSTRUCTION' AND I AM REQUIRED TO REPEAT THAT PARTICULAR INSTRUCTION AT ONE HALF THE SPEED OF THE ORIGINAL RECITAL. IF I FAIL TO DO THIS, YOU WILL HAVE SIX ADDITIONAL SECONDS FROM THE TIME YOU STATE YOUR OBJECTION TO STATE "EXCEPTION". AT THAT TIME, THE ENTIRE EXPLANATION WILL BE STOPPED AS TO THAT PARTICULAR BEING AND YOUR MINUTES CREDITED TO ME SHALL BE HELD IN ABEYANCE UNTIL RESOLUTION OF THE DISPUTE BY REVIEW/APPEAL. I AM NOT REQUIRED TO RECITE REVIEW/APPEAL RULES AND REGULATIONS. YOU MAY OBTAIN SUCH REGULATIONS FROM ANY PLANE MONITOR. IF YOU DO NOT COMPLY WITH THESE REQUIREMENTS WITHIN THE TIME ALLOTTED, YOU WAIVE ANY AND ALL RIGHTS TO DO SO."

Norma looked a little perplexed. Makeba, however, understood completely, having worked at legal aid after receiving her J.D. from University of the World, College of Law. Remember, she couldn't get into any major university having already been kicked out of the University of California system. Although she never passed the bar, she was well-practiced in getting through mumbo-jumbo legalese. "In other words we got the shaft, big time. We never had a chance."

"Where is the dignity?" Pearl muttered, although under her breath, heard by all. And all of the brigade tacitly agreed. Here, once again, was some kind of technical requirement that seemed to have long-since lost its meaning. If the policy was to afford "beings" an opportunity to question, or to challenge the quality of the explanation, why was the requirement permitted to be delivered in such an unintelligible manner? "Sounds like my moahgage company," reflected Pearl, as she sliced a sliver of pound cake, ate it and washed it down with the final gurglings of Nardo's Coke.

"Well, since Norma was the only one who could have possibly understood that, in case we need any more Explanations, let's elect Norma as the designated 'objector' to slow down any explanations. Is that okay Norma?"

Norma nodded. "I should have done it this time, but it sort of took me by surprise."

"Well, of course, girl," laughed Makeba. "That's the whole idea. But, listen up girl. You better not blame yourself. You're not responsible for someone else's intentional act to trick you. That's one of the first legal concepts you learn in law school."

Pearl was listening intently. She was trying to get what everyone was talking about, but she couldn't. Maury handled this stuff. If you wanted the lowest price on cottage cheese, Pearl knew. If you wanted the latest on Gladys Rebemeyer's fatty tumor, ask Pearl. But quasi-high consciousness legal concepts, no. Customarily, Pearl would let it drop. In one ear and out of the other. The "Hadassah Bypass" she called it. But this whole mischigas (event) wasn't customary. So she said, "Wait. Wait a while. I don't get it. I don't know from that. What does it mean?"

Makeba, assuming the role of teacher, and asserting the pill bond with Pearl pontificated, "Sister, it means that when someone is trying to cheat you, you can't blame yourself when they succeed. It means that a cheater always has the upper hand, because he relies on your trust in order to effect his dirty work."

"Doity voik?" Pearl was just beginning to grasp. "So we shouldn't trust no one no moah?"

Now Jake spoke up. Pearl was exactly like all of the older Jewish women in his family. He understood her planet, and instinctively knew how to approach her. "We should basically trust, but we should beware. Any time we are in a new situation and don't know the rules, we should proceed cautiously."

All nodded in agreement. "Yeah!" exclaimed Pearl. Her re-education had started. She had her first lesson in how not to be a schlemiel.

"We should really get on with these instructions and the Explanation." Norma was scanning her notes and looked concerned. This says that we get counted off for every minute we spend here.

"Counted off what?" said Nardo, now feeling a little more comfortable and participatory.

"Let's read 'em. Go 'head Norma." Jake was back in the Presidency.

"Well, let's see. We just learned that we gave up our right to object to not being able to understand the . . . oh, yes. Here we are. 'The following are the rules regarding time and chronology. Each instruction and rule set forth applies to each of you individually:

DEFINITION OF TERMS:

UNIVERSALLY CONSTRUCTIVE - a result that produces a positive net effect.

POSITIVE NET EFFECT (PNE) - a result of any act that creates more positive results than negative results.

SUSPENSION - the cessation of time.

TIME – that sense which permits perception of change.

THE FIRST INSTRUCTION:

YOU WILL LOSE ONE MOMENT OF TIME FOR

EACH MOMENT OF TIME THAT PASSES.

THE SECOND INSTRUCTION:

YOU WILL LOSE THAT AMOUNT OF TIME WHICH YOU AGREE TO GIVE AWAY IN EXCHANGE FOR ANYTHING YOU BELIEVE TO BE OF VALUE TO YOURSELF.

THE THIRD INSTRUCTION:

YOU WILL LOSE THAT AMOUNT OF TIME THAT YOU AGREE TO GIVE AWAY FOR NO VALUE.

(The above instructions are cumulative and not mutually exclusive. Therefore, for example, for this Explanation, you will each lose the fifty-one minutes you agreed to give, plus the three minutes and thirty-four seconds it takes to explain.)

THE FOURTH INSTRUCTION:

YOU WILL BE CREDITED ONE MOMENT OF TIME FOR EACH MOMENT OF TIME SPENT PERFORMING AN ACT WHICH IS UNIVERSALLY CONSTRUCTIVE.

THE FIFTH INSTRUCTION:

YOU WILL BE CREDITED FOR THAT AMOUNT OF TIME WHICH IS GIVEN TO YOU IN EXCHANGE FOR ANYTHING YOU GIVE IN GOOD FAITH TO SOMEONE WHO BELIEVES THAT THING TO BE OF VALUE.

THE SIXTH INSTRUCTION

YOU WILL BE AWARDED ONE CREDIT FOR EACH CHRONOLOGICAL ADVANCEMENT AWARD EARNED (to be explained later).

THE SEVENTH INSTRUCTION:

YOU WILL BE AWARDED THE FULL TWELVE CHRONOLOGICAL ADVANCEMENT AWARD CREDITS (OF YOUR CHOICE) IF YOU SUCCEED IN THE GIFT LOTTERY (ODDS, THE NUMBER OF BEINGS ENTERED IN THE GIFT LOTTERY TO ONE) (to be explained later).

Norma stopped. She looked a little perplexed. So did everyone. "What is this all about?" was the general consensus. "Keep reading," barked Makeba, listening intently to what was being said. "Let's go through the whole thing first, and then we'll try and figure out what it means."

"Okay," agreed Norma, continuing.

"CHRONOLOGICAL ADVANCEMENT AWARDS (CREDITS): IN ORDER TO PASS THROUGH SUSPENSION ON CHRONOS AND RETURN TO PLANE OF ORIGIN, YOU MUST EARN THE EQUIVALENT OF TWELVE CREDITS IN CHRONOLOGICAL ADVANCEMENT AWARDS. THE AWARD CATEGORIES AND RESPECTIVE CREDITS ARE AS FOLLOWS :

GENERALS:

HAPPINESS

HEALTH

LIFE FOR LIFE'S SAKE

OLD DOG NEW TRICKS

REVELATION

RESTORATION

TEAM

TIME RECAPTURE

OVERS:

DEED OVER WORD

INACTION OVER IMPULSE

INSTINCT OVER INTELLECT

ORDER OVER CHAOS

SELF:

SELF AUDIT

SELF SUFFICIENCY

SELF STARTER

SELFLESSNESS

(No PNE Necessary)

IN ADDITION, CREDITS MAY BE AWARDED AT THE SOLE DISCRETION OF THE BOARD OF REVIEW FOR ANY ACT OR EFFECT, NOT LISTED, WHICH THE BOARD DEEMS CREDITWORTHY.

ANY ACT PERFORMED WHICH MERITS AWARD OF EITHER TIME ADDED, CREDIT, OR BOTH MAY, AT THE SOLE DISCRETION OF THE BOARD OF REVIEW, BE ENHANCED FOR THE FOLLOWING UNIVERSALLY CONSTRUCTIVE RESULT:

POSTIVE NET EFFECT: ADDITIONAL CREDIT WHEN ANY ENTITY OTHER THAN ONE'S SELF

DEMONSTRATES A REASONABLE PROBABILITY OF PRODUCING A POSITIVE NET EFFECT FOR ONE OR MORE FUTURE ENTITIES AS A RESULT OF ONE'S ACTION.

CORRECTIVE EFFECT: ADDITIONAL CREDITS FOR EACH ACT WHICH HAS THE EFFECT OF CORRECTING, CLARIFYING AND/OR RIGHTING A MISCONCEPTION HELD BY SOMEONE AND/OR SOMETHING FROM THE PAST AND WHICH CAUSES A POSITIVE NET EFFECT FOR ANYONE OTHER THAN YOURSELF.

LOSS OF CREDITS: IF YOU ARE A SUBSTANTIAL FACTOR IN CAUSING A NEGATIVE NET EFFECT WHICH AFFECTS ANY OTHER ENTITY OR BEING, YOU WILL LOSE ONE CREDIT OR PORTION THEREOF FOR ANY CREDIT THAT ENTITY OR BEING WOULD HAVE EARNED HAD YOUR NEGATIVE NET EFFECT NOT BEEN PRESENT.

MEMORY RULES: FULL CREDIT FOR MEMORY UNLESS IT IS YOUR ORIGINAL MEMORY. YOU WILL BE CREDITED FOR ONE-HALF THE PRESENT TENSE CREDIT FOR MEMORY-EARNED CREDIT IF YOU SHARE THE MEMORY WITH OTHERS. ALL MEMORIES MAY BE BOUGHT, SOLD, GIVEN OR SHARED, BUT THEY WILL BE WITHOUT WARRANTY AS TO UNIVERSAL CONSTRUCTIVENESS.

BOARD OF REVIEW/B.E.A.M.: IN THE EVENT YOU RUN OUT OF TIME, OR HAVE ANY DISPUTE WITH CHRONOLOGICAL AWARDS, OR ANY OTHER MATTER RELATING DIRECTLY AND/OR INDIRECTLY TO ANY OF THE ABOVE, YOU MAY APPEAL TO REVIEW/APPEAL FOR ADDITIONAL TIME OR RELIEF. CHRONOLOGICAL UNDERTAKINGS OR BONDS MUST

BE POSTED. IN THE EVENT THE APPEAL IS DENIED, AND YOU ARE OUT OF TIME, AND YOU CANNOT BORROW ANY TIME, YOU MUST PERFORM TASKS IN B.E.A.M. (BEING-ENTITY ALTERATION MANAGEMENT) UNTIL YOU HAVE EARNED ENOUGH TIME TO PROCEED WITH SUSPENSION REVERSAL.

THIS CONCLUDES THE INSTRUCTIONS I AM REQUIRED TO GIVE. YOUR FINAL SIX SECONDS TO OBJECT BEGIN NOW. (ONE, TWO, THREE, FOUR, FIVE, SIX) THANK YOU VERY MUCH.

"Voos ih doos?" Pearl was stretching her lower lip out again, but this time, the sponge cake had wiped all the lipstick away except the ghost of it, which uncovered her true lip line, no less than one and one half miles below where the lipstick once dwelt. Out came the compact, the whoopie red lipstick, and the retouch began.

Jake spake. "Well, I think it's pretty clear." Jake's logic and science classes from UCLA were coming back to him. "We've fallen into a crack in time. Wherever we are, we have to buy or earn all the time we get. It's definitely not free. Otherwise, we have to work in the equivalent of Civil Service until we earn enough time to continue on with the suspension process. I think we should talk about each one of these rules until we understand them."

Pearl was sitting next to Jake. He still smelled, but she wasn't repulsed by it, like she had been in the subway car. But she knew it was a bad smell. "Can we clean up?" Pearl asked, as she held the breathmints right in front of Jake's mouth.

"Thanks" said Jake.

"I would love to take a shower," said Nardo.

"Yeah, with me," thought Jake. He couldn't stop the

homophobic thoughts, but he recognized them as old tapes from his fraternity days. But, once again, more pressing issues masked the habitual hatespeak, and instead he said, "Let's go find a place, if we can."

"Look at our R.O.'s" said Norma. They're different now. And so they were. Jake's and Makeba's R.O. read "10:28:54". Norma's read "11:28:54." Under Norma's numerals was the phrase "PNE - STENO - 1C + 1C PNE BONUS." Also, where the R.O. formerly read "C0", Norma's now read "C2." Pearl's read "11:02:54" PNE-CAKE-SELFLESSNESS C1" and "C1" in the upper left corner as did Nardo's except instead of "CAKE", Nardo's said "COKE".

Jake said "PNE. That must be 'Positive Net Effect'. Norma must have gotten time and credit for using her steno power along with some extra bonus credit, and you guys must have gotten some for sharing." And so they had.

"Maybe 'R.O.' stands for 'readout'?" piped Nardo. And so it did.

3 - MEMORABILIA

"IT'S ONLY A MATTER OF TIME" read the giant sign in the square they had just come upon. It looked so out of place, surrounded with what towered like old Gothic buildings, with highly ornate facades and sandcastle spires. The main building had all kinds of figures carved into what looked like white stone, tarnished by years of lack of care and soot. Above three keyhole-arched doors, there was a parade of golden figures, a mixture of humanoid and others. A shiny moebus strip encircled the figures, and a silver orb rolled slowly around the strip, with no apparent connection to it. Everytime the ball reached the same position, lights would flash, and the figures would move one position.

Jake had seen something similar on a postcard when his father was in Munich, stationed there after the end of the Viet Nam war. Although he had never made it into combat, Dad's birthday was February 1, number 89 in the draft lottery of the USA, Earth circa 1970. Therefore, he was drafted, having lost his student deferment since he was into his fifth year at UCLA, attempting to finish his double science/engineering major. With the war winding down, Dad fortunately got sent to Germany, and was able to last two years there, unharmed.

On the postcard of Munich, there was a square very much like the one Jake was in now, with a Gothic building, and large gold figures on it. "A clock. A clock," Jake thought to himself as the insular Earthling crowd made a paraplus of the square. Jake looked again at the out-of-place building. The moebus strip, representing a circle with only one plane, provided an infinite road for the silver ball, and the figures moved with each denomination of time. He could not figure out the time units, however. In fact, time was very strange since he had gotten here. He knew it was moving. He could see and sense change from one moment to another. But it wasn't like on Earth. There, time sped up and slowed down, depending on what you were doing. There, you could lose time, daydream, or minutes seemed an eternity but you couldn't sometimes tell where weeks, months and even years had gone, seemingly whisking by even though the moments themselves seemed endless.

But here, it was different. Each moment seemed the same, of equal value. Time didn't slow down or speed up depending upon what you were doing. Time was consistent and constant. You felt each moment move by. You felt its loss. And yet, like when Norma, Pearl and Nardo had gotten the extra time on their R.O.'s, it felt like a reward or a pardon or a reprieve of some kind. Certainly the entire group was starting to feel very differently about time.

"Oysh." Pearl rubbed her calves out of habit. "I could stand to find a place to sit for a minute." People or whatever they were were walking in and out of the three-arch building. "Maybe they got a ladies room ova deah?" Even though her calves didn't hurt, and she certainly didn't have to go to the bathroom, Pearl was bent on doing something familiar. And it didn't seem like such a bad idea.

"Yeah. Let's do it." Makeba decided that at least this would give them a goal. Plus they would have to start earning some time. The R.O.'s relentlessly ticked away. 9:59:06 was the reading on Makeba's. She was having trouble reading it upside down, and her chin was thrust into her chest, while her eyes strained to de-dyslexize the numerals.

"Oysh! Watch out ova deah!" Pearl grabbed Makeba by the elbow and pulled her out of the way as a group of pinkish men with dark hair jogged by, dead set on the pathway in front of them.

"Thanks," said Makeba, internally chastising herself for not watching where she was going. Why did she wear these stupid spiked heels with those leopard spandex pants? The outfit certainly was not having the effect Makeba fancied it had downtown L.A. or the Beverly Center. There, she would be immediately recognized as an African American woman, on a mission, and don' shit around wit' her. But here, nobody was even looking. Even the people she was with now had lost interest in her persona. Luxuries like personas had evaporated with the new goals the group had before them.

Makeba noticed now that everyone in the group seemed equal. Each person was important, and no one could be spared. Clothes, backgrounds, dress, wealth, not to mention race, creed, gender, color, religion and sexual orientation, all dropped away as meaningless with the new tasks. "It's only a matter of time and circumstances," Makeba philosophized. "A different time, changed circumstances, a serious challenge, and all the old priorities melt away." Makeba looked up and read the great sign once more as she passed through the center arch with the rest of the gang. "IT'S ONLY A MATTER OF TIME."

The inside of the building resembled a chaotic Grand Central Station. There were high marble ceilings, very echoey, with the roar of voices creating a drone to the staccato loudspeaker. "CENTRAL LIBRARY STREAK, DEPARTING THIRTY SECONDS." The speaker sounded much like the response one receives at a drive-in burger window.

Flash. The flash bulb went off again, but this time much brighter. Our crowd turned toward the light, but no others did so, as if this were a common occurrence.

"Explanations! Slow and cheap!" The gang turned and saw another man dressed like the Cardinal. "Are you going to Memorabilia?"

"What's Memorabilia?" asked Norma, but not to the Holy One fearful she might be charged.

"You can only receive your Memory Credits on Memorabilia. I'll give you an explanation for forty-three minutes."

Now Makeba was in his face. "Listen, you used-car salesman. Don't f*%k with us." The color, so to speak, had come back to Makeba's oration. "We've already been had by your kind before."

"Okay. Fifteen minutes." The guy was evidently used to negotiating for explanations, in a heavy way.

"Fifteen minutes?!" Pearl practically spit it back in his face. "Too much." And to the crowd, "I know a place we can do bettah."

"All right! All right." The Holy One recoiled. "Things are a little slow. Six minutes. Each!" A small smile cracked on Makeba's face, although Pearl's remained poker.

"How do we know we're gonna understand him," Nardo added.

"Norma, get out your steno pad." Jake was once again in charge. "How fast can you take it?"

"Not more than two hundred," Norma responded, already digging in her bag for the steno pad and pencil.

"Very good. Very good," said the holy man. I won't go over two hundred words per minute."

"Six minutes at a hundred and eighty five or no deal," Pearl let it slip out as if she couldn't stop it. Face it, she even bargained with the grocer. He knew it and she knew it and, even though they both knew exactly what the final deal would be, they succumbed to the ritual, and both felt better for it. The Holy One agreed.

"That's my lady," said Makeba. "Are you ready Norma?" Norma nodded, and once again, in the middle of Grand Central, the harangue began, with the diminution in time from the R.O.'s. But this time everyone was contentedly smiling at the Holy One, knowing that they got a good deal on the explanation and that Norma would get it all down.

The Holy One's words trailed off, and Norma had to run after him to catch the last of them, but she did get them all. They all retired to a small alcove and the busy traffic passed them by as they gathered closely to hear Norma's translation.

"MEMORABILIA IS ONE OF THE THREE ISLES OF TIME. IT IS THE MOST TRAVELED OF THE TIME ISLES SINCE EARNING TIME AND CREDIT IS EASIEST BY MEMORY, EVEN THOUGH IT IS ONLY WORTH ONE-HALF OF ACTUAL EXPERIENCE CREDIT. IT COSTS TEN MINUTES ONE WAY FOR A STREAK TO MEMORABILIA. R.O.'S WILL CONTINUE DEDUCTION MOMENT BY MOMENT ON MEMORABILIA. IN OTHER WORDS, EACH REMEMBERED MOMENT COSTS ONE MOMENT FOR BOTH THE REMEMBEROR AND THE REMEMBEREE."

"A member-wha . . . ?" said Pearl.

"Shhh." said Makeba gently, holding her arm in front of Pearl as if she were keeping her from stepping into traffic. "Go on, Norma."

MEMORIES MAY BE BOUGHT, SOLD OR SHARED. THOSE SHARING MEMORIES BECOME ENTERED IN THE GIFT LOTTERY. HINT: USE ONLY MEMORIES WHICH WILL EARN CREDITS AND HAVE PNE. THOSE SHARING MEMORIES WILL RECEIVE CREDIT FOR THE PNE THE

MEMORY EARNS FOR EACH RECIPIENT, BUT NO CREDIT FOR THE MEMORY ITSELF UNLESS THE SHARING ENTITY GAINS CHARACTER BUILDING ABOVE AND BEYOND THAT GAINED IN THE ORIGINAL EXPERIENCE. TO ATTEND, YOU MUST FIRST STREAK TO CENTRAL LIBRARY AND CHOOSE TO GO TO MEMORABILIA."

"Whoa!" said Jake. What does this mean?"

"Well, I guess we can earn credits for sharing experiences with each other on Memorabilia." Norma was explaining her own translation. "TO ATTEND, YOU MUST STREAK TO CENTRAL LIBRARY AND CHOOSE TO GO TO MEMORABILIA." Norma read the last line again.

"Well," Nardo was interested in getting on with it. "I think we should go. After all, all of us have memories and we all need credits."

"And, we don't got no other plans," laughed Makeba. "I vote we go too." And there was unanimous agreement amongst the lot.

"CENTRAL LIBRARY STREAK, DEPARTING THIRTY SECONDS."

"Wheah do we catch the bus?" mused Pearl, envisioning a bus stop with torn Bruce Springsteen posters and graffiti.

Jake, looking around, opened his mouth to speak. "I don't . . ." FLASH. All were suddenly caught up in a bright light. No one could tell how long it lasted, but looking around they saw spots of people being transported in the light with them. So that's what it meant "you must decide to go to Memorabilia." Once you decided to go, you were whisked to the Central Library with no further adieu, and your R.O.'s were adjusted accordingly.

Momentarily, they found themselves in a great library, with bright lights, and three stories of what looked like books of all different colors, shapes, sizes. Jake glanced at his R.O. 9:40:23. He noticed Makeba's read the same. That was the six minutes for the spiel, the ten minutes for the streak, and the time it took to do it all. He was getting the hang of it, but was becoming concerned that he had not gained any time since they got there.

"Looks like the library at Berkeley," bellowed Makeba, not aware that the line pierced the silence.

Nardo winced. "Just my favorite kind of light," he thought. "Fluorescent. It makes me look green," noticing that Makeba also looked a sickly green, but that Pearl and Jake looked kind of purple, except for Pearl's lips which were now rocket blast red.

"Where can we get some help around here?" Makeba continued without a bullhorn, unimpressed by the quietude.

"Please, puhleeeease!" An extremely predictable Mr. Peeper's type androgynous being came up to them, his hands out in supplication. "Beings are attempting to study. Your loud conversation is interrupting their concentration, and wasting time."

"Whaa . . . " Makeba spun around toward the mincey voice behind her. I took her a minute to locate the source, since she was a good foot taller. "Shiiii . . . " Makeba looked for reactions from the rest of the gang, but found only disapproving stares, with Pearl's lip stretched full tilt once again. Makeba continued, turning the volume down to "1" and donning her most articulate Berkeley banter. "Yes, we would be interested in earning some time and credits for memories."

The Androgen smiled, having prevailed over the noisy one. "Would you be using stock memories, or sharing one from your group? Or perhaps you have a particular memory in mind."

Now Pearl's face looked like she had just popped a Kosher Dill into her mouth. "Voos ih doos?" She didn't know from the memory stuff, but Jake was eager to jump in and get going. He needed those points and credits, and the R.O.'s were relentless, and you never forgot about them, since everyone's was staring you right in the face.

"What's the difference?" Jake began. It was certainly nice that they were receiving explanations in real time, rather than the chipmunk treatment they were used to.

"Well, if you use a stock memory, you get half credit for the experience, and half credit for any time earned during the memory. But if you share a memory, the rememberor receives credit only for PNE earned by the rememberees, and no credit for the actual experience, since the rememberor has already experienced it." The explanation was rather myopic, but the Androgen said it like it made perfect sense.

"You mean that if one of us has a memory to share, we will get credit only if others receive a positive experience from it?" Nardo was catching on.

"Precisely. Plus, if the sharing entity extracts something new and positive out of reliving the experience, he or she may receive time and/or credit for it. And, if you don't charge for the memory, you'll get an automatic entry into the gift lottery." The Librarian seemed excited about that.

"What's the gift lottery?" Pearl asked since this was the only phrase she remotely comprehended, and it sounded like something she would want to do.

"Every time you share a memory for free, or give time or credits to another, you will be entered in a lottery, and if you win, you will receive the full twelve credits for your visit, with choice of credit categories. For example, if you won, you would have all the credits you needed to return to Plane of Origin, but you could choose Health and Happiness, or whatever category you wished to carry back to Plane of Origin. But the odds are really high, and not many win. Just like real gift giving. You have to give with no expectation of reward." The Androgen made sense.

This sounded complicated to Pearl, but she was beginning to defer to the wisdom of those a little hipper in the group, like everybody. But Pearl was a giving person and took great delight in seeing others enjoy her gifts, like the sponge cake. That was reward enough for Pearl.

"Well, what kind of memories can we share?" asked Norma. The steno pad was out by now and she was taking notes.

"Any memory which, hopefully, will create a PNE for the rememberees," offered the Androgen.

"You mean like winning homecoming queen or being elected cheerleader?"

"Y-yess," the Librarian said tentatively. "But normally those experiences don't create the most credits. It's the experiences of overcoming, challenge, and that sort of thing. The learning and character building experiences are high in memory credit content."

"What are the 'stock memories'?" Makeba was into it now, and, like Jake, wanted to get on with the show.

"The stock memories are contained in the volumes you see before you." Norma was busily notating. "These memories are free to the users, but you should study them first by looking in the computer card catalogues and the comments left by former users. Mostly, rememberees will get more credit for new experiences than they would for old experiences. For example, if you played sports or something like that, and you checked out a sports memory, you probably would not receive as much time and credit as you would from a totally new experience."

"How do we get started?" Makeba pushed further.

"Well, when you retrieve the stock memory you want, you just decide to live it and it will be done. If you are sharing a memory, you just decide to live it and it will be done, although I would suggest taking a short time to discuss the memory before you share it to decide if it's worth re-living. After all, only one visit to Memorabilia is permitted and only one trip down the path can be accomplished with that visit here. So choose carefully. And start there at the Memory Commencement Corridor." He pointed to an arch that was labeled "MEMORABILIA". The gang noticed that there were at least three major arches leading out of the great hall of the Central Library on that wall, and beings of all types were entering and emerging, each group accompanied by a blinding flash. Two of the other arches were mystically labeled "MYSTERY OF HISTORY" and "WISHES, DREAMS AND NIGHTMARES." So the Central Library was where all the tasks would begin.

"Vats to become of us?" feared Pearl to herself, but she popped a breath mint, snapped up her large purse, hung it in the crook of her elbow and waited for someone else in the group to take action.

"Puh-leeeese! Beings are attempting to study. Your loud conversation is interrupting their concentration, and wasting time." The Androgen was walking away and happily assailing a new clump of beings that had just arrived in the hallowed halls.

"So who has a memory?" Pearl said, wanting to get on with whatever it was. "Maury and I took I a nice vacation to Martinique once."

"Shouldn't we think of something with a little more content, or depth? Something with a little accomplishment in it. What was it he said? 'Character Building'?" Norma was trying hard to think of something in her past that would make a good memory, but something blocked her from remembering too much. "I guess I just have too much on my mind," she thought to herself, and immediately took more interest in what the others were thinking.

"Well. When I was in the band in high school, we worked real hard and won this big parade once." Nardo was trying to be helpful.

"Ha!" Makeba couldn't hold it back, scoffing at the idea that winning a band contest could possibly rise to the level of her background. After all, she had been expelled from one of the great Universities of the world. "We should share my memory of getting kicked out of Berkeley. I was protesting and exercising my right of free speech when I got kicked out." But we know she secretly hated herself for this.

"Really?!" Jake was impressed. "What did you do?"

"Well, I was in one of the first black militant groups. We set the administration building on fire, and held some professors hostage by tying them up." Makeba summoned up all the pride she could, but looking back on the incident, she wasn't very happy with it.

"Isn't that arson and kidnapping?" Norma offered.

"Civil disobedience for THE CAUSE is never a crime." Makeba tried to convince herself with her own words, but was wholly unsuccessful.

"Tell us about the band thing," Norma said changing the direction to Nardo.

"Really?" Nardo was surprised. He didn't think anything in his past amounted to much. And the feeling seemed generally to be shared by acquaintances. "Well. First, we had this real lousy marching band in high school." Makeba was rolling her eyes. "Anyway, I was real small and kind of feminine . . . well, small; and even the band kids picked on me, 'cause I played the flute and I couldn't speak very good English." Makeba raised an eyebrow. Something had struck a chord.

"I just came from Manila in my country to the United States. We went to a competition and screwed it up so much, we came in

45

dead last, and they never wanted to invite us again. Anyway, I was so miserable, I dreamed of running away to another high school with a good band, where people would treat me better and the band would be great. I just wanted that feeling of winning and feeling better about myself. Anyway, then just like magic, a new band director came to the school. He was from a school with a great band. He was like a god. Suddenly, we all started working together, and the band turned out great. We won the top prize at the biggest parade and people started treating me better, too."

"That sounds really good, Nardo," said Norma softly, and she meant it.

Jake was thinking about it, seriously. "Is this the memory we want to live?" he thought. "Oh hells, bells, what've we got to lose? We've got to do something." Jake spoke aloud.

"I can relate to the discrimination thing," said Makeba, secretly gratified that the arson and kidnapping experience had been so easily rejected and forgotten.

"Izzit walking? Dat marching band ting?" Pearl longed for her sensible shoes, not knowing what the future held. But she knew she kept a spare pair of walking shoes in the great carpetbag she schlepped.

"Come on, you guys. Let's get going or we'll never get out of here. And I'm not up for civil service." Jake began gently herding the gang toward the "MEMORABILIA" Memory Commencement Corridor sign.

The R.O.'s were still clicking. Makeba's read 9:04:23. She was pissed off that she hadn't yet earned even a nanosecond. "Yeh right. It figures. Black woman, she canno earn de time."

4 - UNDERDOGS

"But only the scags are left!" asided Sally Haynes, referring to the fact that Mr. Considine, the band director, had suggested that "Banner Girl" tryouts be held. Her hand shot up like a surprise erection. Mr. Considine kept talking very slowly and deliberately as Sally's butt rose from her first chair E-flat clarinet position while she ever-so-wider waved her arm for recognition. Mr. Considine talked.

The combination of Pearl's hair and Makeba's turban was doing an excellent job of completely blocking Nardo's view. Not wanting to chance a revolution, he opted to meekly tap Pearl on the shoulder and squeaked, "Could you please move your chair a little?"

"Shuah," said Pearl, and with as much friction as she could possibly put on it, she farted the rubber-tipped chair legs across the floor so Nardo could see. Her hand grabbed the clarinet in her lap, which she, for the first time, noticed. Nardo had his flute, of course, and Makeba had a huge baritone saxophone, which she had not yet noticed.

Finally, Sally's hand was recognized. You see, Sally was an all-too-eager Bulldog Band member who learned her part meticulously and made sure everyone knew that fact.

Unfortunately, she played the soprano clarinet which even the best players could only get to sound like a speeded up and reversed tape of someone playing the saw. It was, very unfortunately, audible above all other instruments in the band. Worse yet, since she was a senior, Mr. Considine placed her smack dab front rank, center. Clarinets in the front rank are usually a no-no for any high school band worth its salt.

"They've already had song girl tryouts, cheerleader tryouts, and drill team tryouts. That takes the prettiest one hundred and ten girls out of the running! All we're left with is the uglies." Sally was relentless. Nardo thought, this, of course, coming from Sally whose bottom took up two spaces in the front rank, was the height of ludicrity.

"Well, now," smoothed Mr. Considine, "when these young ladies are dressed up in their new, tight, red and white outfits, I'm sure they will look sharp, crisp and smashing."

"What are we gonna do for letters?" said Candy Brillo, first flute by default, with an IQ which hovered around room temperature. Candy also had the obligatory flautist braces on already perfectly straight teeth, and true to her name, her hair was a wire terrier. But Nardo liked her a lot because she never seemed to judge him, and she always helped him learn the eighth-note passages in the competition march.

Mr. Considine smiled broadly and said, "We're gonna use the traditional ALTADENA spellout letters sewed on the girl's chests. One letter for each girl, with an exclamation point at the end. That's nine girls."

"Mr. Considine! Mr. Considine!" Sally's hand was a blur. "That's geeky! Nobody does that anymore! Sheesh! We'll be laughed off the street," as if that wasn't going to happen anyway.

"Ms. Haynes. Tradition is never out of style." Considine loved to pontificate. And so it would be. Although Sally was eventually successful in getting rid of the exclamation point (Thank God!), eight of Altadena's most Medusan beauties would march in front of the band, each bending a letter over various sized adolescent chests.

But that wasn't all. Sally got the idea to have a "changing banner" like they did at Mt. Miguel. "They've got fans that change from 'Mt. Miguel' to 'Matadors' so ours should change from 'Altadena' to 'Bulldogs'. EIGHT LETTERS EACH!!"

"Hmmm." This idea was just cheesy enough to tantalize Mr. Considine. "A changing banner. How would we do it?"

"Well," Sally snapped, "I've thought it all out." This was not going to be good. "First, the girls, with ALTADENA on the front march sixteen steps forward. Then, they turn around and, bam, they're marching backward eight steps with BULLDOGS on their backs. It's cool!"

Makeba's mouth was too far agog to get any sound out. Pearl was still strangely fascinated with the clarinet. Nardo was absolutely peaked. Jake, who was standing behind a bass drum couldn't believe it.

Norma, poked her head around a lyre-shaped glockenspiel. She wondered if she should be taking notes on this. At this time, Norma was happy to remember that she could read music, and had studied home course singing and piano lessons, using the piano at the senior center to practice. Any keyboard-based instrument was basically the same, and so the glock parts were easy to her. "This is nothing like the 'Tejana' and 'Mariachi' music I learned from my family," she thought, "but at least it's music." Above all, she still would rather be singing the music of her ancestry, which she did prodigiously, especially for a girl so young. But that phenomenon was also prevalent among Latina girls her age, and was worn as a status symbol in her culture.

"When do we eat?" thought Pearl, even though she was not

hungry. "Rap, rap, rap." The sound of Mr. Considine's white baton struck the bottom of the director's music stand. He raised his arms up. Two big wet spots appeared under them on his shirt.

"We will now play the competition march, 'Americans We'." Down came the baton. The space troupe was completely bamboozled, except of course for Nardo, who remembered his part perfectly. He was better than Candy Brillo because there weren't too many eighth notes. Pearl stuck the clarinet in her mouth and began to blow. You know, it didn't sound half bad. The other half, however, stunk. Makeba managed to honk out a few gandersprachs on the baritone sax. Norma tried desperately to read the music. She found she could, a little, and now and then, even struck a right note. Jake found the beat and pounded the bass drum in time with Considine's baton. Considine nodded approvingly toward Jake, as if only they understood the true universal meaning of the word "march." Fortunately for the space tribe, the band sucked, and no one could tell how miserably they were actually playing.

CUT TO:

It was already dark the night of the parade. The band milled outside the band bus. Distant cadences lumbered through the ether. The smell of school bus exhaust abounded. Spare letter girls from other schools, one dressed in silver and blue carrying a "T" and one dressed in red and black carrying a shield with the head of an eagle on it nervously hurried to unknown places. It was the evening of the Huntington Beach night parade. Altadena used to get invited to the big Long Beach Parade, eighty bands, but ever since they stopped scoring above a "60," the invitational stopped inviting. So now, the Huntington Beach Night Parade, twenty bands, was the only invite beside the traditional Alhambra Hi-Neighbor Parade where Altadena last placed a lovely fourth out of four bands. Disgusting.

Pearl was spitting trying to get the feathers from her hat plume out of her mouth. Makeba's uniform looked like it was painted on, sausage style. Nardo's uniform looked like it belonged to his father, Norma looked snappy, with her hair neatly tucked into her shako. But the biggest change of all was Jake. Evidently between the first day of band and now, Jake had decided (or was told) to clean up. And this was the first time anyone could see his face.

He was gorgeous. Tall, sandy-haired, broad shouldered, with big ice blue eyes, a big white smile, dimples, and a huge cleft in his Dudley Do-right chin. Jake was a knockout. Norma was looking at him. Nardo was looking at him. Sally Haynes was hanging on him. Pearl and Makeba struck up a conversation. "What is going on heah?" Pearl's lower lip was getting quite a workout. "All of a sudden, we're in the band room. Then we're in the bus. I don't wanna know from this."

Makeba sucked on the reed of her saxophone, pulled the head off, and shook the spit on the ground. "You see. I don't even know why I did that. But it seems that we're in Nardo's band memory, and only living out the important parts. We skip the parts in between. I don't get hungry or thirsty. I never have to go to the bathroom."

"I do." Of course, Pearl did just out of habit. And she was totally lost without her own carpetbagger purse. Sure enough, she had a purse, but it was now buckskin with foot-long fringe, and she had been afraid to look in it. "Whaddya tinks gonna happen?" Pearl sounded very tentative.

"Well, I wouldn't worry about it. But I think we're gonna march in this parade now." Makeba put the head back on her sax and honked for assurance. Then she put her free arm around Pearl and gave her a squeeze. Both women looked at each other and smiled softly. A true connection had been made at long last, a friendship sprouted. Makeba's R.O. finally racked up some time, but she was too busy to notice.

"Tweet!" The drum major's whistle brought everyone to attention . . . eventually. "TWEEEEEET! TWEET, TWEET, TWEET." The cadence started. It was so surprising that, even with only a couple of lousy rattly snare drummers, two toms and a bass, the loud cadence instilled instant pride in the unit. Even though their ranks weren't straight, the files worse, and "diagonals? What's that?" They marched proudly, seriously and with determination. Even Candy Brillo's hair looked good under the hat, and at least they all knew that Sally Haynes' high clarinet part would be heard. Pearl was marching next to her. Left, right, left.

Makeba was in the second rank, next to Nardo, and Norma and Jake were in the percussion rank, number three. There were only six ranks of five. The thirty Bulldogs would have to play awfully loud in order to match the sound of Simi Valley High, with one hundred and ten in the band and eighty in the Pioneer drill team. Altadena already knew how to play awfully. Now they just needed to add loud.

Considine had been right. With a little makeup and the costumes, the eight Medusas had been transformed into passable letter girls. They had practiced the "ALTADENA/ BULLDOG" switch sixteen forward-turn-eight back step at least one trillion times, and had finally gotten it right. Patty Wagner was originally scheduled to be the exclamation point, but as the shortest, was now the first "A". Her bushy red hair had been coaxed gallantly into a French Twist, but the Coke bottles still remained her glasses. The girls high stepped, and actually looked pretty good.

A sign read "PRACTICE AREA" and the drum major tweeted for a roll-off. Norma quickly glanced at her R.O. and noticed that extra time had been added, even though it was clicking away. "It's working," she thought, but snapped to when the practice march started. 1,2,3,4,5,6,7,8,9,10,11,12,13,14,15,16, TURN!!! The banner girls all spun at exactly the same time, and the banner read "BULLDOGS" albeit with eight of the widest cabooses in high school history swinging below it. 1,2,3,4,5,6,7,8, TURN!!!

"ALTADENA!" The girls had correctly maneuvered again. Patty Wagner was ecstatic. Sally smiled around her clarinet reed as she proudly squeaked out the trio of "Americans We." Pearl knew something big happened. She even thought she hit a couple of notes right, or in harmony or something. Left, right, left.

The uniformed hosts held a sign reading "SILENT AREA" passing on the side of the road. The band stopped playing, the drums went to rims only. Marching, rack-a-tack, rack-a-tack, rickety, rickety, rickety, rack. The cadence lost something in the translation.

In the distance, the uniformed hosts held a sign "COMPETITION BEGINS." The band drew closer. In the distance, they could see the tail end of Simi Valley's Marching Two Hundred, silk flags waving. Nardo's throat began to tighten. He remembered. He remembered this moment. DE JA VU, and bigtime. The drum major pulled the band up to the competition line and halted. The banner girls all stopped simultaneously on cue. The silence was deafening.

Suddenly, Mr. Considine, dressed in his too-bright red band director's uniform, was running. Running towards the drum major. He whispered something in the drum major's ear. The drum major shook his head in understanding, and came back through the ranks saying "double roll-off! Double roll-off!" It seems that, at the last minute, Mr. Considine decided that the Judge's stand was too far away, and he wanted the band to be eight steps closer to the reviewing stand before they started playing.

Mr. Considine approached Patty Wagner, the first "A" and quickly explained the added eight count roll-off. Unfortunately, it was like a bad game of "Telephone". "A" tells "L", "L" tells "T", "T" tells "A". Uh oh. The head judge is waving for the band to start. Any extra time and the band gets penalized. Uh oh. The game of Telephone is thwarted in the middle. Half the banner girls still don't know about the double roll-off!

TWEEEEET! TWEET, TWEET, TWEET! 1,2,3,4,5,6,7,8 ba-bamm! The band steps off, sort of.

TWEET, TWEET, TWEET! 1,2,3,4,5,6,7,8 ba-bamm!

The music tentatively starts. The banner girls are intently counting and . . . TURN!

"ALTADOGS." A look of ghastly horror is creeping over Considine's face.

1,2,3,4,5,6,7,8 TURN!

"BULLDENA." The banner girls instinctively know something is amiss. Patty Wagner spins again, and the Coke bottles go flying.

"AULADOGA." The girls are spinning freely now and sobbing with reckless abandon. The drum major twirls for his salute and sends his mace flying directly towards the head judge. It misses her, fortunately, since she is bent over, urinating with glee.

"BUTADONA." No one is playing the march except Jake who is pounding the bass drum in rhythm and Sally who is squeaking out the last remnant of "American's We". The head judge is changing her pants. Considine is having a near-death experience. The ALTADOGS didn't win.

CUT TO:

"Ladies and gentlemen, please." Miss Gladys Whitebread (yes, that was really her name!), the principal, is speaking in front of the band room. Gladys or "Happy Bottom" (derived from Glad-Ass) as she is not-so-affectionately called has an announcement. She also has a very pink face and purple hair. "Pretty combo," opined Nardo to himself, referring to the colors only.

"As you know, Mr. Considine has taken his sabbatical this year. So I am pleased to introduce your new band director, from Mt. Miguel High School, Mr. Max Treadmore." Gladys flashed a row of false teeth, and began clapping loudly. A smattering of applause broke through the conversational drone that echoed throughout the band room.

Nardo thought to himself, "Mount Miguel? It can't be. Mt. Miguel won Sweepstakes at the huge Long Beach All Western Band Review last year. Mr. Treadmore? At Altadena." Nardo's senior year was going to be a trip.

"I know that we can do a great job," an unconvinced Treadmore boomed from the director's stand, as he looked out at the measly remnants of the ALTADOGS, now numbering twenty-five. Pearl didn't care if she ever did another parade. "OY, Gottinue." She winced as she remembered that fateful parade.

"That parade. That f*%king parade," smirked Makeba. And this is what we traded my 'fire in the administration building' for."

"The first thing I want all of you to do is to talk to all of your friends and if they play an instrument, any instrument at all, I want them in this class. Tomorrow. The competition march this year will be 'Benton's Red and White' and it will be memorized. By tomorrow. We need Ten Thousand Dollars for new uniforms before the first parade in six weeks. We will have our first student fundraiser. Tomorrow." Treadmore was not to be trifled with. He was an ex-Marine. He was an ex-football player. Nardo's heart quickened. But deep inside he knew Treadwell hated fairies. Flute-playing fairies. Nardo was reconsidering the merits of the BULLDENA band. Whatever, he would go through with it. After all, this was the band director of Mt. Miguel High School with the fan-banner, and he was an ex-Marine. This could be interesting.

The next day began a whirlwind that lasted throughout the

senior year. First, about twenty-five extra people showed up to class, making the total fifty in the band. By the end of the week, there were seventy-five, and one hundred by the month. Mr. Treadmore was pulling them in by the bucket loads. People were learning basic scales and basic marching techniques, never before attacked in this band. Sections had leaders, and even special rehearsals. Even the tiny Pep Band sounded better than last year's entire band.

Mr. Treadmore, aware that once again all the pretty girls had been taken for songleaders and drill team, simply asked the head songleader if they wanted to be banner girls also. They did. Nardo who, of course, was abundantly talented in costume and art design, having made all his own drag costumes, fully hand beaded and beautiful, designed the first in-line banner on a long pole, with separate letters. What do you know! Straight lines for the banner girls without even trying! This time it would be a "non-changing" banner to avoid an ALTADOGS reprise. Nardo and Norma also designed the new banner girl costumes, which were elegant military waistcoats with revealing French-cut shorts.

Makeba and Pearl decided that the first fundraiser would be a bake-off. Treadmore liked the idea and recruited parents for the task. But somehow Makeba's jalapeno cornbread and Pearl's strudel and chocolate-chip kugel were bound to be the best sellers. The bake-off was a complete success. $1750 was made toward new uniforms, including donations. The same was repeated two weeks later. Another $1500 was made.

Jake decided that he would take his "shoene punim" (beautiful face) and put it to work. Treadmore saw to it that Jake was now the drum major. After all, who could resist that six-foot two inch gorgeous hunk? This clearly helped with drum major scores. And, if he kept his baton work simple and precise, he looked great. Jake had a meeting with the "band Moms" and said it was time to go to the "band Dads" and get their businesses to loosen up their pockets. Remember, this was back in the days where

Moms generally did not own the businesses, except for a few. These Moms became the captains of the Booster Club. They managed to cajole over six thousand dollars out of the community, with a little help from the Chamber of Commerce, two local churches (one black, one white) and a temple. So far the total toward new band uniforms was over nine thousand five hundred dollars and in less than forty-five days from the beginning of school.

Everybody seemed to be learning their parts and the march, first considered to be out of reach for most of the musicians, was becoming easier. Nardo couldn't help but notice that many of the trumpet players had been moved to trombone or Sousaphone and the bottom section of the band was "booming." Pearl noticed that her clarinet wasn't sounding so much like a "shofar" on the Jewish high holidays, and Nardo's flute emerged from the "leaky steampipe" mode and began giving birth to quasi-lyrical tones. The band was playing in tune!

Mr. Treadmore looked at Nardo's sketch for a banner. He liked it, but eyed the little Manilan with suspicion. Nardo felt like he was naked in front of Mr. Treadmore, and was completely intimidated. Notwithstanding, Mr. Treadmore asked Nardo to "build it" and with the help of Makeba and Pearl on material, Norma and Nardo on sequin sewing, and Jake and the band Dads building the frame, the beautiful, spangly, and modern, non-changing "ALTADENA" banner slowly came to life.

New uniforms arrived in pseudo-military style with tall shakos and plumes, and arm stripes which moved in perfect synchronization with the high arm swing that Mr. Treadmore added. Also a new first, and probably an unconscious rebellion against the horror of the "double roll-off" of last year, Mr. Treadmore commanded a "silent" roll-off, leaving eight beats of silence whilst the band simultaneously marched and snapped their instruments into position before the "Red and White" began.

During a street rehearsal, excitedly running toward the band, arms waving, Mr. Treadmore bellowed, "It's coming . . . it's finally coming." He was hearing the sound from the band that he was used to at last, and wouldn't tolerate being without. The band was up to one hundred twenty members not including attached units.

CUT TO:

It was very brisk that late November morning of the Long Beach All Western Band Review. Nardo called it a "parade day." It had rained heavily the night before, and the air was still damp and crisp. The sky was bright blue and blotched with electric white cotton billows. Early mornings in Southern California winters brought steam from the mouths of that little-known troupe from the Foothills. Mr. Treadmore had managed to talk the head officials of the parade into reinviting Altadena, based on the fact that his former band had won Sweepstakes at the parade not less than ten out of the last ten years. This was definitely Mr. Treadmore's parade. Over eighty bands from the eleven Western United States would participate in the longest band review in history, lasting from early in the morning to midnight, when the Sweepstakes award would finally be awarded. All Mr. Treadmore's rival bands were also there: Grossmont, El Cajon, Arcadia, Anaheim, Azusa, Montebello, Antelope Valley and, of course, Mt. Miguel. . . all believing that Treadmore couldn't possibly win this year with any brand new band let alone the ALTADOGS, whose reputation preceded them.

Band Moms and Dads were running through the ranks, polishing instruments, shoes, noses and anything else that needed shining. Not a hair was amiss, not a shoelace, not a valve. The banner girls looked fabulous, the banner was stunning in scarlet and silver as it caught the morning light bouncing off the blue Pacific Ocean.

Nardo blew through his flute several times to warm it up. He remembered those freezing nights in the Rose Bowl when his lip stuck to the silver mouthpiece, it was so cold. Makeba's new uniform fit much better, and even Pearl looked good, although she still refused to tuck her hair in the shako, not when she had worked so hard to produce the Hadassah Wing that was hang gliding off the right side of her head.

Norma looked beautiful in her uniform, her great dark eyes winning her a spot on the judge's side of the band, with the long white plumes of horsehair swaying from her glockenspiel, glistening in the "parade day" sun. Jake was outstanding, all in white, with a gold "A" emblazoned on his chest, and his skyscraping white shako making him one of the tallest of all the drum majors at the parade.

Nardo smiled. This was his memory, and it was catching on. The excitement was raising blood pressure. The band stepped off and turned the corner onto the main parade drag. Band Moms and Dads scurried out of the ranks, and fell to the sides of the parade route, following the Bulldogs toward eternity, the Judge's Stand awaiting them only a Practice Area and a Silent Area away.

Early reports from the Moms were that Grossmont and Azusa had been superlative, and looked unbeatable. But the unassuming Bulldogs pushed on. They stood straighter. They played the practice march only through the first two strains. Mr. Treadmore cut them off. He wanted them to save their lips.

SILENT AREA, and the drums went to the rims. No full cadence this time, however. Only rat, tat, rat, tat, as the band absolutely synchronized each quarter of each step, moving as one, not a rank out, not a file out, not a diagonal out.

Nardo looked ahead. He saw the Long Beach band volunteers standing in the middle of the street holding a "COMPETITION BEGINS" banner. His throat tightened. The bathroom idea glanced over Pearl's brain, but by this time she was into it, and it fleeted away. Makeba was wetting her lips, and Norma dared to wipe a sweaty palm off on the side of her uniform when nobody was looking. Jake looked amazingly tall and handsome as he swung his baton to and fro, too elegant for a real cakewalk. Jake turned and snapped his baton up, bringing the band to a highstep halt.

You must know how the crowd quiets down when something is about to happen. People in front of the banner were wide-eyed looking at the great red and white machine looming before them, shielding their eyes from the sparkle of the brilliant ALTADENA. "How do they keep it so straight?" they thought collectively. Nardo's pole-banner worked like a charm. There was a moment of silence. The head judge waved his clipboard, Jake turned around. He breathed in deeply and the long sharp whistle sounded. He snapped around on his heel as the cadence reported. The band stepped off as one. Then came the infamous silent eight counts. The instruments whooshed through the blank sound as they snapped into place in unison.

Heads in the crowd jerked back when the first note shot through the air. Clearly this was no longer the ALTADOGS. What strange metamorphosis had taken place since the debacle at Huntington Beach a mere year before? The kids were basically the same. The parents were the same. What was it? Mr. Treadmore thought he would be satisfied with first or second in his division today. After all, winning this parade so many years in a row, it was only logical that he should step down, for a while at least. Treadmore was looking intently at his stopwatch. He thought the band was stepping out more than usual that day, pride and all. He didn't like it. One second too short in the competition area, and you are slapped with a penalty point. Out of a possible one-hundred points, you lose one. And in a parade that was lost or won by *hundredths* of a point, this was unacceptable. Mr. Treadmore had effectively given himself something to worry about.

Nardo's lump left his throat. Although on other occasions he had probably played the march better individually, he concentrated on making each note strong, in tune, and round, and put his mind directly to guiding and staying in his rank, file and diagonal. Even Pearl and Makeba simply dropped out on the notes they weren't sure of, and with no Sally squeaking the E-flat clarinet, the woodwinds were beautifully balanced that performance. There were nine trombones across the front of the band, and seven Sousaphones glimmering. The brass ripped through the morning air, and the woodwinds shimmered. The quiet, determined group had, at minimum, successfully shocked the audience. Even the judges were writing well into the next band's timeslot. But Treadmore was still uneasy about that stopwatch.

CUT TO:

The arena was full, almost thirty five thousand. The Miss Drill-Baton California Pageant had just finished. The small awards had all been given out. Flags, majorettes, and drum majors. Jake managed to take First Place in the Military Drum Major category. His RO was racking up points, and the space troupe was delighted, jumping up and down like high school kids. The six smaller classes of bands had gotten their awards, from EE class ("First Place - Tranquillity High School!" a one hundred person school from the depths of the San Joaquin Valley, if you could pronounce it) to A class, schools of up to twenty five hundred, large high schools for Southern California, but not AA which were the behemoths, like Grossmont, Azusa and Altadena. Altadena had forty two hundred students in a three year school, so, like it or not, the ALTADOGS were placed in the super-heavyweight category. Considering that the four top scoring bands in the parade would come from that division, Treadmore thought once again that second in the division wouldn't be bad.

Sweepstakes, of course, was awarded to the school receiving the highest overall score in the parade. If you won a place in your division, you didn't win Sweepstakes. Two hundred possible points for showmanship, three hundred points for marching and maneuvering, and five hundred points for music. One could see where the emphasis was. Treadmore was acutely aware of this fact, and sharpened up the marching, simplified the showmanship, and concentrated one hundred and fifty percent on music. If any band sounded like a Marine Corps band, it was a Treadmore band. He was still very nervous about the stopwatch. His normal contact wasn't there this year, and he couldn't get any advance on how the penalty points were going as he had in the past.

This is the moment. "Class Double A! Fourth place with a score of 93.6 . . . Anaheim! " Nardo gulped. Anaheim only got 4th place? This was the stiffest division. There were still six bands left who could win, including Antelope Valley and Montebello! "Third place with a fine score of 94.0 . . . Arcadia!" Norma's heart was beating rapidly. She hadn't expected Arcadia to win Sweeps, but THIRD. She was sure the ALTADOGS hadn't even placed.

Jake was sitting on the arena level with the other drum majors in front of the huge trophy stand. He had his First Place Military Drum Major Trophy, and caressed it as if it were the only trophy he might see this night. "Second Place with an outstanding score of 94.25 . . . GROSSMONT!" An audible groan came from the three full Grossmont sections. This Treadmore rival was sure with Treadmore out of the way this year they would win, and normally with this score they would have a Sweepstakes here, but not today.

Makeba slumped in her stadium seat, which barely fit her big buns. After all that work, not even a trophy. There was still Montebello, a former Sweepstales winner; there was still Antelope Valley, a former Sweepstakes winner; and there was still Azusa, Mr. Treadmore's severest rival, scraping the tail of Treadmore's scores for the past five years. Azusa was out for blood, and the Aztecs had played the most difficult march in the book, "Joyce's 71st Regiment." Reports were favorable. In fact, Azusa was the all-out favorite for Sweepstakes this year, even garnering nods of approval from the judges' stand as they marched gilded in blue and gold through the Competition Area earlier that day.

Pearl's legs were crossed tightly. This would be the one occasion on which, under no circumstances would she allow her bladder to control her life. She should get some RO points for that, she analyzed. "FIRST PLACE." Pearl bit her lower lip. Makeba grabbed the arms to her chair. Jake clutched the little first place drum major trophy. Norma wiped her glowing palms on her evening outfit. Nardo's face was white, dry throat. "With a fine score of 94.7, AZUSA!!!"

Treadmore immediately thought that Montebello or Antelope Valley had pulled a coup. They were cross-land rivals in their own right, and owned at least two or three Sweepstakes trophies from this and other major Western United States parades in recent history. Treadmore thought more and more about the stopwatch. The space troupe was beyond deja-vu. None of them could contain themselves. All one hundred twenty members of the band, along with the Booster Moms and Dads and the Banner/Song Girls collectively held their breath. It couldn't happen. Not Treadmore's first year. Not when so many others were in line.

"SWEEPSTAKES . . ." Pure silence, thirty five thousand strong. With a SUPERIOR score of 94.95 . . . " (the silence was deadly) ". . . an obvious newcomer to this year's parade . . ." (more lethal silence):

ALTADENA!!!!

The resulting ejaculation was fitting. Nardo, who had been sitting next to Mr. Treadwell, threw his arms around him, not thinking, and the hug was heartily returned. Makeba and Pearl were down on the stadium floor, screaming in tears, and Norma jumped down two rows so the three could circle jump and dance. Jake was light-headed and almost forgot to go accept the trophy. When he did, his simple baton salute drew roars from the crowd.

The UNDERDOGS, the ALTADOGS had prevailed. Where multiple years of "Mt. Miguel" had appeared engraved on the trophy, "ALTADENA" would be the next entry in spot eleven. Mr. Treadmore asided on his way out that a Rose Parade Official said that, breaking a seventy-five year tradition, Altadena High School would have a spot in the Rose Parade this New Year, albeit at the end of the Parade behind myriad equestrian units. Oh, well. They'd deal with the street fertilizer problem when they got there.

5 - TICK TICK TICK

TICK TICK TICK went the RO's as the entire group suddenly found themselves back in the library. "Wha' hoppen'?" mimed Pearl, still whispering as she reminisced on the Androgen who had formerly shushed them prior to the memory.

"WOW!" heaved Jake. "That was really some trip!" Jake still looked great, as he retained the grooming from the trip to Memorabilia. No beard, and well clipped. Everyone was back in their own clothes, and Pearl was happy to have her own gigantic purse back, *sans* fringe.

"I felt nude wit' dat otheh tingda [that other thing there]!" she said, referring, of course, to the fringed "Daughter of Woodstock" thing she carried throughout the band memory.

Jake looked down at his RO, and made faces while he tried to read it upside down. "What does this say, now?" he queried to the general crowd.

Norma put her hand on Jake's chest as she read the alphanumeric messages. "12:34:23. C-1 LEADERSHIP. I guess Jake must have gotten some credit for being drum major or something."

"He also got a lot more time," grumped Makeba whose RO only read 10:45:10. "Hey, what does this C-1, PITCHING IN (Bake sale) mean?"

Pearl chimed in, "Hey, I got one o' dem, too!" but her RO stated 10:59:59, just above Makeba's. "What's going on heah?"

Finally, Nardo spoke hesitantly. "We all got credit for time earned and credits earned. I'm starting to get this now," he stated, crestfallen, as everyone noticed his RO only read 8:45:54, and had only half the number of credits as his compadres. "I guess I didn't get much time or credit. I wonder why!"

"Remember, they said that the person whose memory would only receive half credits for time and credits earned by other people during the memory," said Norma as she pulled out her notes. "So you got half credit for the credits we earned, and half the time since it was your memory."

"Good thing we didn't take over the Administration Building," sighed Makeba to herself, glad that she had racked up extra time and credits.

Nardo was still visibly upset over the fact that everybody's time was higher than his. "How can I get my time increased?" he asked Norma.

"Can we do another memory? Somebody else's this time?" offered Jake, still secretly glad that he was flush in the time department.

"No," said Norma, who was rustling through her notes again. "I remember the library guy said " and she quoted from her notes "only one trip to Memorabilia." Norma didn't have to worry, either. Her RO read 12:56:10, the highest of all, and she had received credit for the glockenspiel and the banner, as well as self-starter credits. These, of course, were in addition to those credits she already had.

"How many o' dese credits do we need to get outa here?" shouted Makeba, remembering what an inconvenience this whole life-tangent was.

"Well, the original notes said we needed a combination of twelve credits to 'RETURN TO THE PLANE OF ORIGIN'," Norma was reading again.

"That must be Earth!" Jake analyzed. So we need to collect twelve credits each!"

"And not run out of time" said Nardo, sensitive to the issue. "Or . . . "

"Or we go to the (Norma was reading again) 'B.E.A.M., Being/ Entity Alteration Management.' That's starting to sound like jail or something!"

"Or something!' The Androgen's high-pitched voice was upon them again. "Well, how did you all like the experience" he whispered.

"GREAT!" bellowed Jake.

"SHHHHH!!! Other beings are . . ."

" . . . attempting to study," came the choral whisper from the entire group, remembering their first trip there.

"I'm really upset about my time," Nardo quivered, almost in tears.

"Don't worry," soothed the Androgen. Somewhere there was a connection between this being and Nardo. "There'll be plenty of other opportunities. And remember, you were entered in the gift lottery for sharing your memory! So it really all evens out."

"Whadda we do now?" asked Pearl out loud. "I tink we gotta do sompim' quick, sose we can get credits, like Mah Jong." Ooh, she longed for a relaxing night at Stella Fishkin's yelling, "One bam, two crack, MAHHHJ!!!" while she downed a half-dozen or so of Stella's knishes and gallons of perked coffee, along with two other Hadassah members.

"Look over there." The Androgen pointed and was all business again. "See those portals. The crowd half-right faced in unison to see two other great marble arches in the library walls, one labeled "WISHES, DREAMS AND NIGHTMARES" and one labeled "MYSTERY OF HISTORY." Pass through either one for your next task. Chances are, you will all have to go to both places in order to get enough time and credits to return to the Plane of Origin. Puh-leeeeeese!" The Androgen was irritated with newcomers. "Beings are trying to study!! Silence! Silencio!!" He rolled away under his long robes.

"Well, we better get going now," aspirated Nardo, who was getting antsier and antsier and growing more concerned with the time and credits factor. TICK TICK TICK. The RO's reminded them that time was precious in these parts . . . you had to BUY it. You had to EARN it. Collectively, they all knew that it was the same as money, but more dear.

Makeba was visibly impatient. "Let's quickly decide where to go. That whatever-the-hell he is didn't even tell us about what happens in these other places. And I don't want to spend anymore money, I mean time, on those rip-off explanations!" Makeba was with Nardo. Let's get going.

Pearl could relate to the money thing. "It's like throwing it out the windah, sitting heah, talkin' for tree hours. We coulda' been deah and back five times already." Pearl was raring to go. However, nobody quite knew what to do or what to expect.

Norma, in her most computer-esque style, rationalized, "Well, let's choose one. Dios mio, if we stick together like we did in the band thing, we oughta do okay. After all, we all got more time and credits when we were through." She could feel Nardo's discomfort level rising as she finished her last sentence, and wished she had worded it more carefully. Everyone felt the same way.

"Let's just go to the closest place . . . MYSTERY OF HISTORY." It was Jake speaking, and they were standing closest to that portal at the time. The RO totals as the gang began a tentative walk toward the portals were as follows (in first-name alphabetical order):

JAKE TIME:	12:30:21	CREDITS 3
MAKEBA TIME:	10:41:08	CREDITS 2
NARDO TIME:	8:41:52	CREDITS 2
NORMA TIME:	12:52:08	CREDITS 4
PEARL TIME:	10:55:57	CREDITS 3

Jake was into this. A smattering of achievement had been salted into his life and it felt good. "Let's get going," he anticipated. Makeba was basically a warrior. No challenge was too great and any side she was on was absolutely, positively one hundred percent right, and "Don' screw wi' her." Pearl didn't know from what was happening, but she liked everybody, and it was different from the Maj Game. She'd go one more round, as if she had a choice. Norma attacked this as she would any new assignment or chore. "I will do it until I get it perfect." That was the only tolerable standard for her. Nardo had very mixed feelings about the whole affair. He thought his life on Earth was semi-happy, from time to time. He had friends, or did he? He had a job, or did he? By now he must be late, and the blow job manager had long since been fired, so he had no job insurance. And with no job insurance, no health insurance. What a disappointment. Back to the free clinic and the five-hour waits for Keflex or the latest antibiotic. And what if he got something terrible? He was certainly better off here now, despite the craziness of the rules and the uncertainty. He would have to deal with it.

The Subway Brigade inched toward the portal, not knowing what awaited them. As each group had passed into the portal, of course, a blinding white flashed, but they never saw anyone come out. Jake said soothingly, "Look, everybody's doing it. What choice do we have?" He put his arm around Norma on one side and Makeba on the other. "Pearl, you and Nardo grab on." Pearl and Nardo hooked up, and the quintet was again ready for step off. "TWEEEEET. TWEET TWEET TWEET." Jake actually shouted the words, throwing caution to the wind about "Mr. 'Silencio'" and his "quiet orders." The quintet stepped off lined up in rank. The light blinded white. No one noticed that the RO's had added a little time to each for the comradery.

6 - THE PUB CRAWL

"GODDAMMIT! GODDAMMIT!!! Fockie, shhhhhh.....!"
The first scream heard was Makeba as she stumbled, twisting her
ankles while her spiked heels slipped into the cracks of the
cobblestones. "Why the hell did I wear these shoes?" she agonized,
grabbing her turban with one hand and Pearl's arm with the other.

"Oy mein Gottinhimmel" Pearl sympathized, glad that she
had the nurse's shoes on. People laughed at her, but she was
always comfortable in them. "Ah dose de only shoes you got
wityuhs?"

"How the damn hell am I supposed to have other shoes!"
yelled Makeba, looking down at the broken spike on one of the
shoes. "Did I know we were going to be here? I didn't have time
to f*%king pack, you know." Pearl didn't take it personally. By
now she knew Makeba, and she definitely agreed that the
prevailing conditions called for strong language, even though the
precise choice of words would not have been hers. "Did I know
we were going to land in the middle of . . ." Makeba stopped mid-
sentence.

The entire troupe finally took in the new environment.
Cobblestones, narrow streets, night, thick fog, flickering fuzzy
streetlamps, cold, stinging ears, smell of the sea, gray two-story

Georgian buildings, slate roofs, barely discernable yellow moon. "Clippie Cloppie Clippie Cloppie" the sound of horses and a carriage drew near and then attenuated. "Hoarsis," said Pearl. The lip went immediately into "Yiecch" position. But the rest of the group had a much better understanding of the import of the sound. They were not in their time. They were not in their usual place. One thing was for certain. They were to get no answers here for free.

"MYSTERY OF HISTORY" repeated Nardo out loud, almost shivering at the foreboding phrase. Goosebumps were universal throughout the quintet. "Fasten your seatbelts. It was definitely going to be a 'goosebumpy' night," smiled Nardo to himself, not thinking anyone else would get the joke. Truth is, they all would have, and they needed the laugh right about now.

"Clippie Cloppie Clippie Cloppie." Horses again. This time a masculine voice echoed down the seemingly deserted foggy lane, "WHOA!"

"Se Habla Ingles!" Norma let out without thinking. But everyone understood Norma's drift. At least they didn't have to learn a new language.

"Let's move on," Jake said.

"The Hell we will," Makeba retorted. Everyone had momentarily forgotten the important issue of the moment, Makeba's screwed-up footwear situation. "I ain't walkin' around like Peg Leg Pete," she ruled, referring to the bi-level position she now occupied, minus one spiked-heel.

"Give me the good shoe" Jake said.

"What for?" Makeba questioned absolutely everything and everyone for every purpose.

"Just give it to me!" Jake could get forceful if he wanted to, and he was bigger than Makeba and maybe even slightly outweighed her. Frowning her worst possible frown, Makeba relinquished the good shoe reluctantly.

"CRACK" went the heel on that shoe as Jake stepped on it to pull it off. "What the godamhell are you doing?!!" Makeba stuck her chest out as if to fight.

"Now try walking on them," said Jake softly. He was right. The shoes were much better on the cobblestones without the heels. Makeba would still take about ten minutes to get over the audacity of the whole thing however, clinging to the idea that Queen Latifah would not wear spandex leopard pants and FLATS. Funny, Nardo thought the same thing, but then decided that the look wasn't bad.

Pearl hung her head a little lower. She had that extra pair of shoes in her bag, but she was afraid she might need them. Five thousand years of Jewish guilt wafted over her as she pursed her lips, knowing that her silence had most probably ruined a perfectly good half-pair of spiked heels.

"Where the heck am I going to put these?" brayed Makeba, but she was already cooling her language down.

"Heah. Put 'em in my poise." Pearl opened the yaw of a huge carpetbag. "Wha?? Whea did dis come from?" Pearl's new purse was a bargiello tapestry. Pearl didn't care, she was already getting used to the purses changing from time to time. At least this one was bigger, albeit not stylish.

"Thanks ," said Makeba, as the heels made a "click" dropping into Pearl's bag. "Whadowedonow?" she changed the issue.

This carriage had pulled up to a stop down the street and since the driver was the only person they were aware of, Norma suggested that they go up to him and ask where they were, for a start. All agreed this idea was a good place to begin, so they clattered off down the damp lane, Makeba keeping up admirably in her new footwear. As they approached the carriage, its corner lamps became evident. Rounding the big carriage, a swinging sign squeaked in the night wind over the door to the building. "Saint Sabydus Tavern Inn" [sounds like "Saints Abide Us"] was the tarnished marking, lit dimly by the light coming from the two long storefront French windows. The group slowly approached.

"Whea aaaah we?" said Pearl to no one in particular.

"Now ain't it the question?" came the answer. Around the top of the carriage leaned a gruff red-bearded man out of the mist with a very black top-hat, and a cloak.

"Goosebumpy night. Goose-bumpy," said Nardo, this time out loud. "Excuse me, sir. Could you please tell us where we are?" Nardo was getting more aggressive, sensing the TICK TICK TICK phenomenon was still occurring, and nothing had happened to alter it.

"Well, now, that's the question, I'm wantin' to tellya'. If ya' wanta know where ye are, ya gotta find out. No one's gonna tellye! The more important question is WHO are ye!" At that time, the door to the Tavern burst open revealing a cacophony of cackling women's laughter, manly shouts, concertina music, and what definitely sounded like leaky steampipe music to Nardo.

"Thank God my flute never sounded that shrill," he opined. Out of the door burst two men in long capes and black top hats, and two flowered-and-feathered women dressed in yards and yards of full dress satin taffeta, about four feet in diameter each and bustled on the butt. In the dim light, Nardo could tell the fabric by the rustling of it, one in periwinkle and one in cardinal.

"What's the next stop, mates?" shouted the driver to the gossipy foursome, who did not even notice the strange out-of-synch quintet who stood by, watching with mouths agape. "The LILYWHOYTE, 'ow 'bout it girls," one of the men bellowed. The variegated Cockney accents were unmistakable. They seemed to be in late Nineteenth Century England or some reasonable facsimile thereof.

"Ow yeah, the LILYWHOYTE, 'at's a good one." And Lady Periwinkle cackled her way into the waiting carriage that was still shaking from the occupants taking their seats as the "Clippie Cloppie Clippie Cloppie" followed the "CRACK" of the whip.

The five were again alone on the street in front of the Tavern, with only the muffled sounds of the inside chaos to remind them they weren't alone. All of them eyed each other with trepidation, knowing that they would now venture through those heavy wooden doors, into whatever awaited them in the bowels of the Saint Sabydus Tavern Inn.

7 - SAINT SABYDUS

The pipe was screaming above the clatter of the plates and the roar of the people. One could barely make out the instruments, as the rough English male voice chorus yelled out verse after verse of some beer-drinking song. "LIKE US FER WHO WE ARE, BOYS!" came the repeated phrase at the end of the verse.

"WHO'S IN CHARGE AROUND HERE!" Jake had to scream above the noise. He walked right up to the bartender (who closely resembled the carriage driver) "ARE YOU IN CHARGE?"

"I don't know who *I* am? Who are *you*?" grinned the bartender. Finally the song stopped and the noise was reduced to clatter and loud conversation. "Do you know who you are?"

"I'm Jake"

Laughing "That's just your name, that's not *who* you are?"

"Where are we?" demanded Jake, as the rest of the gang giraffed their necks to see the conversation over the patrons seated at the bar.

"Yer at the Saint Sabydus, oldest Tavern in the Village. How 'bout a stout, mate?" The bartender was already drawing some draft for Jake.

"Sure, thanks." Jake said, as he happily took the mug. "How 'bout some for my friends?"

The bartender counted. "A total of five, it is. Right." The bartender poured them all and they all bellied up, wherever they could get a space. "That'll be fifteen minutes, three apiece."

Pearl sputtered her ale, and some, unfortunately, came through her nose. "We hafta pay?" The Depression was not yet over for Pearl, and she hated parting with anything she felt was in excess, except of course if it was for a tchkake, which was priceless, or a bagel.

The RO's all lost three minutes each. Nardo looked disdainfully at the ale. "Damn. I really didn't need this ale," but it tasted good all the same.

"Well, let's enjoy it!" chimed Makeba, whose ale was short by now. A group of five left the barstools, and the gang grabbed them. The "steampipe" band had taken a break, and for now, they could hear one another, and the bartender.

"What are we doing here? I mean, what is our task? The guy at the library said we would have one." Norma was intent on getting on with things. Pearl wanted to get settled. Makeba wanted, first another ale, to hell with the three minutes, and then sensible shoes. Jake and Nardo wanted to move forward.

The bartender leaned over. "Have not ye guessed yet?" The group looked more perplexed than ever. "You've already been told twice."

"We have?" in unison.

"You've got to find out who ye are! That's the whole point. Not just your name. That's the MYSTERY OF HISTORY. Before ye run out of time, ye must find out who each of you is, that's the ticket here."

"Oy vey" kvetched Pearl aloud. "It sounds like more walking. I just got done marching. Why is everyting walking?"

"How do we find out?" inquired Norma, hoping for an easy analysis.

"Not so fast, lass. It's different for each one. Ye can help each other, but the quest is up to ye individually."

"We wanna stick together," said Makeba, making up everyone's mind for them. "When and where do we start?"

"The sooner the better, and ye might want to drop by the LILYWHITE INN, although looking at ye, it don't really seem a fittin' place. Well, go outside and wait fer a carriage." And with that the bartender, poured more ale for some new arrivals, who looked as stymied as the gang did.

"Let's go," said Jake, draining the last drop of ale, and he started wending his way through the crowd to the door. All followed. As they walked outside the heavy doors, and the slap of the cold night fog hit them again, a change had come over them.

Jake was now dressed in a long cape with a "Sherlock Holmes" hat on. Nardo was decked out in a tight fitting neat suit, bowtie, and bowler, like Hercule Poirot. Makeba looked like a black Miss Marple, with a cloak and, fortunately, sensible shoes. It felt good to get out of those spandex pants for a change.

Norma was dressed in a forest green taffeta satin hoop skirt, with a smart hat. Not as tarty as the ladies they had seen upon entering. Pearl's clothes hadn't changed, except for the carpetbag. Outwardly she said, "Wha' izzit deah?" Inside she was *glad*. She had her blousey blouse, her comfortable slacks, her nurses shoes. If she was going to walk, it might as well be in style and comfort, as she saw it. She longed for her warm wool coat.

"Look at that place right across the street!" Norma said. The gang looked at another Tavern, this one dark with warm, glowing candles in the windows. None of the craziness of the Saint Sabydus.

"Land's End Tavern." Jake read the sign to everyone. "Doesn't look like much is going on there."

Clippie Cloppie Clippie Cloppie. Out of the fog came the four lighted corners of the carriage, with horses and, you guessed it, the carriage driver. "So, where ye be off ta'?" He shouted, laughing.

"The Lilywhite," responded Makeba, although the name did not hold any particular fancy for her. At any rate, she knew she probably would not enjoy the music, but her feet were now feeling "groovy."

"Climb in, mates and wenches!" The carriage driver laughed at his own sentence. Jake opened the carriage door, Nardo took the other side, and Pearl, Makeba and Norma with the big dress piled into the carriage.

"After you mate," mused Jake to Nardo who smiled and climbed in. Jake swung the door shut behind him. The smell of damp leather permeated the dark carriage as the gang peered through the sheer coach curtains, watching the Saint Sabydus and the Land's End melt slowly into the fog.

8 – LILYWHITE

"How many would you be seating?" The impeccable maitre d' peered over a *pince nez* and scrutinized the odd group.

"Five, please," answered Norma.

"And don't seat us by the kitchen!" Pearl knew how to get a good seat in a restaurant. "Do we haveta buy dinnah?" This time it was to the group. "I ain't dat hungry."

"Follow me please" and the mustachioed maitre d' predictably swished forward while the gang toddled behind. They came to an extremely wide and lush stairway, bathed in red carpet. Looking around and down the sweeping stairs, they saw a mammoth, elegant dining room, with white-clothed tables on the floor, banquettes sloping up around the edges, and much-too-much silverware. Mr. Moustache led them to a large banquette. "This will be adequate, I presume?"

"He presumes," thought Makeba, who would have just as soon barbecued this guy as anything. "It'll be fine." She was already scooting toward the back of the nice round booth. Pearl slid in next to her. Then Norma, with Nardo and Jake bookending.

They had just adjusted themselves in the booth when they sensed that a noticeable hush had come upon the entire dining room and they were being scanned by everyone in the place, including the waiters. Especially one waiter, who was cutting huge slabs of red prime beef out of a big rolling silver cart. He was looking at them and laughing as if to say: "You're busted. You don't belong here!"

Makeba was fairly impervious to this treatment, as was Nardo. They were used to this "misfit" status, but it came as sort of a shock to Pearl, Jake and Norma, still in their misfit infancy. "Wow. I feel like a hunchback or something." They weren't dressed right for the room, they had diverse colorings and looks, and, what the hell, they just didn't fit.

The pall lifted from the room as a waiter sidled up stating impassively, "And what would you be having?"

"I would be having a coahned beef sandwich, if I wasn't in dis' vercochte place," thought Pearl to herself. This was a little too fancy shmancy for her.

"Can I see a menu, please," offered Nardo.

"We only have one thing here," stated the waiter, as if everyone already should have known this fact. "We have prime rib, Yorkshire pudding, mashed potatoes and creamed spinach, and that's all."

That would be okay if you liked prime rib, Yorkshire pudding, mashed potatoes and creamed spinach. But that wasn't what was happening here. Notwithstanding, everyone but Pearl seemed hungry in this place, unlike Memorabilia where they never ate, so they all ordered the menu. The waiter rang an obnoxious little bell and, lo and behold, the silver slab cart pulled up, with the carver eyeing the group with his wry "You Don't Fit" smile.

"What kind of cut are you having?" he snooted.

"Whaddya got?" said Makeba, her mouth watering for a piece of the beef. "We have the Lilywhite cut which is small, but we don' got no Lily*black* cuts." And he laughed.

"What did you say?" said Nardo, empathizing with Makeba.

"We don' got no Lily yellow cuts or Lilyjew cuts either!!"

In a flash, the carver had been thrown up against the cart by Jake, the carving knife went flying. Jake simply threw him on the meat, and the great silver cart and waiter went crashing to the plush carpet. Nardo and Makeba pulled Jake off the pile. Jake said, "Let's get the hell out of here." Jake and Nardo helped the rest out and they found their way through the disapproving dining room, back up the fancy-schmancy staircase, toward the entrance. "Good. Maybe I'll get my coahned beef anyhow," Pearl mused. She was glad to get out of there, fit or not.

"How the hell are we supposed to find out who we are if we can't even stay in a place for five minutes?" Jake was still adrenalized from the joust.

Norma spoke in a considered voice. "Well, we didn't fit in here. We know this is who we *aren't*. Maybe you start finding out who you *are* by finding out who you *aren't*."

"We ain't Lilywhite," laughed Makeba. She had been thrown out of places far superior to this. They looked at each other, a fine group, dressed up in comical costumes, looking more than a bit foolish. "We sure ain't Lilywhite." Makeba considered her words the second time. The carriage soon pulled up.

The RO's had registered a little time for everyone, and more for Norma. Jake had a credit added for leadership. They once again climbed into the carriage. "Trouble at the Lilywhite, eh? I thought as much. Where to now, mates?" The familiar voice boomed through the window.

"Take us somewhere where we all fit in" cut Nardo to the chase, tired of the rat race. "Right." And the carriage jolted off, leaving the Lilywhite far behind.

9 - THE BANYAN

The carriage jostled over the knobby cobblestones. The tribe was still fixed on the new surroundings, trying to figure out what, exactly, was going on. Jake had one up on the rest of the group, however. After college, he had taken a student trip to Europe with a youth hostel pass and a second class Eurailpass. He finally hitched from the British Isles to Ireland on a fishing boat that dumped him in Dublin. With his buddies, they began barhopping at night, drinking their way through the narrow streets and legendary pubs. "Aha," Jake thought to himself. "This is like a 'Pub Crawl', going from pub to pub, talking and soaking in the local atmosphere. I've done this before." But never in late-Nineteenth Century England.

"All out at Banyan Bar!" boomed the voice, and the carriage pulled to a stop. The horse whinnied, and this time the door was opened by a brightly feather-capped black man with white gloves.

Makeba looked at the young and handsome black man. "OOOOH Baby, am I gonna like this place," she secreted.

"Watch your step, please," said the doorman, and the five climbed out onto the cobblestones. The doorman stretched out his hand curiously as to receive a tip. "The usual gratuity is one minute each."

Too tired to argue, they all quickly agreed and the doorman led them to a stone wall with an opening in it. The view of what was inside was initially blocked by bushes. "Here you go, you asked fer it." The carriage driver guffawed heartily, and the Clippie Cloppie pulled away.

The warm, balmy air of a tropical island smacked them in the face, and the scent of plumeria wafted through their noses. As they glanced down, the constricting garb of the capes and the taffeta dress had melted away, and the boys, Nardo and Jake, were dressed in shorts, sandals and flowered silk shirts. The ladies were dressed in flowered muumuu's, except for Pearl, who stayed in her Fairfax garb. Makeba was not particularly happy with the look of the muumuu, since she was so fashion conscious. But the comfort of the gown overrode the look, and her sandals felt good. Of course, Norma looked like an island beauty, with her long black hair dancing down her olive back. As the quintet cleared the bushes they were presented with a wondrous sight.

"Oy mein Gottinue." Pearl had mixed her metaphor or something. The group looked up at what appeared to be the largest Banyan tree in the world with a gazillion tiny electric lights hanging down from it, and a band playing with electric and acoustic guitars, and everybody dancing. All were costumed differently, and all different colors, shapes and sizes of people were dancing together. This was more their style, this was the kind of place they would fit in.

A very Millenium (you could never tell *when* it was in this place) pretty girl, tight black slip dress and white blonde (Madonna-like) hair, complete with grape lips and beauty mark bounced up to them. She wore a small black cabbage rose in her hair. Nardo immediately identified. "How's it going for ya' tonight?" This sounded like L.A. present time, and all were happy that one event reminded them of home even though Pearl "didn't know from that dress."

"Great," answered Nardo. "Great look, too!"

86

"Thanks, guy!" The girl was obviously flattered. "Will that be five tonight?"

"Definitely." Jake was looking at this girl from a different perspective. She was looking at him, too. It had been so long since Jake had felt any physical attraction to anyone. What with the drugs and the streets, he had not had time to think about it. But being Drum Major on Memorabilia and having all those admiring high school cheerleaders drool and so forth had awakened this long-sleeping sensibility. She was attractive and he looked at the curve of her slender figure, her big eyes and bright, wide smile. She returned the favor, as she hooked his arm and led the group to their table. This place was great.

Pearl and Makeba smiled at each other, remembering their own bygone sensibilities. Survival in a white world had taken over Makeba's life. She had been a producer of black docudramas on a public television station in Los Angeles, and had little, if no time for romance let alone sex. Oh yes, from time to time, she eyed one of the beautiful boys who interned at the station, knowing that as men and despite being black, they would have a better chance in the entertainment business than she had in her generation. She had let herself go to seed, and only used the sausage pants as a reaffirmation of her denial.

Pearl recently lost her husband to [whispered] "cancer". But even in those last years, her relationship with Maury was much more about companionship, and less about sex as in all seasoned relationships. Maury was her best friend, and for the first year after his death she was totally lost, relying on various mood lifting capsules, which by the way didn't help. Fortunately, they had a little money set by, and with social security, Maury's retirement, and the little money she made from baking and decorating cakes, cleaning houses, and sewing those wedding dolls, she made do. Her daughters, Erica and Jill, had long since married and followed their husband's job. To them Fairfax became only a foreign country that they visited once a year with the young grandchildren.

Before they were seated, once again, Pearl claimed that she had to go to the bathroom. Makeba offered to accompany her, the etiquette being that no woman should have to go it alone.

Madonna finished seating the rest of the crowd at a nice round table with a big lazy Susan in the middle. She passed out the menus and put her hand softly on Jake's shoulder as she said, "Are there any drinks?" Jake ordered a beer, Nardo a Coke (easy ice), Norma ordered three iced teas, guessing what the two bathroom-bound ladies would want.

Pearl and Makeba passed under the Banyan tree, through the crowded dance floor on the way to the Ladies Lounge. Pearl used to call it a "powder room" until she discovered that to be a hold over from when they used to powder wigs, which she wore. She suffered severe hair loss resulting from the mood elevators and now wore a full brunette wig with just enough gray sprinkled amidst the dark brown to make it look real. Nobody would've guessed that previously, she had been a dyed blond since her engagement to Maury.

The Ladies Lounge was something to behold, all pink shell sinks and marble, and scrupulously clean. There was even an attendant, though not formal.

"It reminds me of the Eden-Roc in Miami," said Pearl making small talk with Makeba.

"I've never been to Miami but I have relatives in Florida." Makeba was happy for the small talk break. So much attention was being paid to the RO's. Back on Earth (or wherever) she never had time for small talk. It was all business. Pearl closed the door to the stall but went on talking.

"Oh, you'd love it. Every day yuhs get up and sit on the beach, yuhs play cards and talk wit friends, and it's just nice like dat."

Unfortunately, Makeba's idea of a good time was not sitting on the beach or playing cards. But somehow she knew that this was Pearl's thing, and she respected it. She was glad Pearl had a place to go and be happy. "Wheah do you like to go on vacation?" Pearl had no compunction about speaking in echoes from the potty.

"Oh, I like Vegas, but I really want to go back to Africa, if I can." Makeba couldn't go "back" to Africa since she had never been there, but she used the word in the ethno-historical sense.

"That sounds nice." Pearl had absolutely no urge to go to Africa, but she had gone to Israel once with Maury, and understood about going back to the land of one's people. "What makes you want to go there?" The john flushed.

"Well, I want to trace my ancestry back and see where my relatives came from." Actually, Makeba was hesitant about doing something like that. She might not like what she found, and she knew it. Somehow, as Pearl asked the question, Makeba began to re-evaluate what had seemed to be a driving force in her life. Maybe she'd like to go to Africa, but tracing her ancestry wasn't all that important. Seeing Africa was.

Pearl emerged from the john, and the door slammed behind her. She availed herself of some of the various nice soaps, noticing the variety of fragrance, jasmine, lilac, plumeria, gardenia and ocean lotion. The attendant wanted a one-minute tip, and Pearl conceded with no fight.

The two girlfriends noticed there was a nice comfortable pink velvet love seat in a dimly lit alcove in the Ladies Lounge, so they proceeded to sit down, Makeba rubbing her ankles from the cobblestone episode and Pearl on general principle.

"So, wheah are yuhs from?" Pearl started the small talk again, and by the end of the less-than-ten minute chat, both women had handily explained most of their lives to each other. Pearl offered

Makeba a piece of gum from the carpetbag, and the ladies were off again back to the table. Neither of them noticed that their RO's had racked up a little "Getting to Know You" time, despite Pearl's tip.

Back at the table, the drinks had arrived and had been placed according to order around the table as the duo returned. "Izzanybody hungry? Wheah's the chow?" Returning through the dance floor, Pearl and Makeba laughed soon followed by the others. The band was distant, and the general level of noise was low, so conversation was easily heard.

"Hey," said Nardo, who was hungry. "These menus say only 'HOUSE SPECIALS'." At that moment Madonna once again appeared with a small chalk board with the SPECIALS written out in hand. "Tonight we have New York Deli Corned Beef Sandwich, Southern Fried Chicken With Choice of Three Sides (Corn, Grits, Collard Greens, Black-Eyed Peas and Rice), Fast Food Hamburger and French Fries, Home-Made Fresh Tamales With Mole Sauce and Sides, and Rice Table which includes a tasting of Indonesian dishes."

"I wuz dyin' for a coaned beef sandwich." Pearl's dream had come true. Maybe there was something to this strange place after all.

"I haven't had rice table since I visited my folks back in Manila five years ago," said Nardo, surprised that it would be on the menu.

Norma was looking forward to the homemade tamales and Jake's mouth stopped watering for Madonna long enough to begin watering for the hamburger and fries.

Makeba wasn't sure about the soul food. Secretly, however, she really liked it, even though it was fattening, as were all the SPECIALS. But she had stopped eating it publicly, thinking it far too predictable, and being secretly afraid that someone (a black person) might think she was perpetuating a negative image of black people by eating it. On the other hand, Makeba used to "sneak" out to a local restaurant on Pico named "Jhamal's Snack 'n Chat" where the Southern cooking was delectable. She would disembowel herself from the African wear, put on a non-descript house dress, dark glasses and sit in a corner and eat the soul food. Tonight, however, on this planet or wherever she was, she was going to order it, and she was going to do it unabashedly and publicly.

Madonna took the orders, and as expected, Pearl had the corned beef, Jake the hamburger, Norma the Mexican combo, Makeba the soul food and Nardo, the rice table. Before they could adjust their chairs, five waiters had appeared, each placing their respective dish in front of the recipient, but on the large Lazy Susan. The portions were huge.

"I'll never be able to eat all of this," said Norma, who normally ate like a bird. "Would someone like to try it?"

No one spoke up immediately, intrinsically knowing the "proper" answer was "no thanks." However, Jake said "What the hell, I'll try some."

"Me, too." Nardo went on. "Would anyone like to taste the rice table?" The rice table took up most of the center of the lazy Susan and was in its own compartmentalized pottery. A waiter appeared with five extra plates.

"Are we sharing?" he beamed. "Good." But the five had gotten the idea by themselves before he showed up.

"I know," said Norma. "That's what the lazy Susan is for. Let's all taste each other's food," and as they did so, each explained what the food was about. Nardo's story was the best, because rice table was only for the rich in Indonesia and the Philippines. He explained how, in his family, they got much more "rice" than "table." The quintet laughed, ate and drank.

Pearl was tentative about most of the other foods, except Jake's Hamburger and French Fries, with which she was familiar. She also liked the Fried Chicken, which Makeba spotted with honey, a trick she learned growing up in South Central from her single mother.

Norma was delighted tasting it all, and took notes on the origins of each food group. All the RO's were accruing time above that which they had spent, but Norma's was markedly above the rest.

After dinner, Madonna brought the dessert tray and set it on the table. "Help yourselves." Pearl "couldn't look at it," she was "stuffed like a potato." Makeba feigned being too full, but settled on a Napoleon. Various other French Pastries delighted the taste buds as the group sipped coffee, and wrapped up their conversations about the various foods, their origins, and learned something about each other's lives. The purpose of this particular pub was becoming apparent to the group.

Madonna came back and, flashing her long dark lashes (yes, even with blonde hair) said shyly to Jake, "I'd love to dance with you."

The band was playing "New Kid In Town" by the Eagles. Even Pearl had heard it. Nardo looked at Norma. He was so used to being refused when he asked someone to dance, but summoning up all his courage he offered, "Norma, would you like to dance?"

Norma had already been singing the melody to the song, with her attractive accent, one octave higher than the singer. Expecting his overture, she rose with her arm outstretched toward him, never missing a note. Madonna, Jake, Nardo and Norma got up to dance. Makeba looked at Pearl, now both with sensible shoes.

"Shall we?" Pearl didn't want to be left alone at the table, and thought it was a pretty good idea, even though she didn't know how to do that "rocky dancing like my grandkids" as she called it but the mood was right, and the three couples got up and danced to the long version of the Eagles tune on the crowded dance floor beneath the sparkling Banyan, in the balmy and perfumed air.

Madonna's eyes sparkled as she looked longingly into Jake's big blues. The band segued directly into a Big Power Ballad version of "Desperado" sung by a fairly capable singer who executed country songs well. Anyway, it was very romantic and seizing upon the moment, Jake drew Madonna close to him and she rested her head upon his chest and smiled. He was a good head taller than she was.

"Are you getting any closer to finding out who you are?" she said softly.

"Well, we decided we didn't belong at the Lilywhite, or whatever it's called, and so we left."

"Most do leave that place. The people who stay usually get caught in the seams there, and stay for a long time . . . wasting time. A lot end up in the BEAM." Madonna was talking like the Androgen.

"Hey, what's this 'caught in the seams' anyway. And do you work here? How did you get here . . ." She cut Jake off by putting her finger tenderly to his lips.

"Not so many questions, not so many. I'm here because after a long drawn-out process, I chose to stay and not re-enter my Plane of Origin, and was granted leave to do that by the Oversight Committee. But that happens very rarely. It happens only in extreme circumstances and special cases. The chances are one in a million. All of you will probably have to return to your Plane of Origin and finish out your time there."

"But what's this 'caught in the seams' thing you said?" Jake was intrigued.

"Well, if you lose sight of your goals, some get caught here, and just stay at one pub, or wander aimlessly from pub to pub. They never finish the crawl. They never find out who they are." Madonna sounded cryptic. "Or they become 'longtimers' and get caught on some other island. It's complicated."

"So this *is* a pub-crawl! That's what I thought!" Jake was finally getting some information.

Madonna tightened her arms around his waist. "Yeah. 'MYSTERY OF HISTORY' takes you to different pubs, and other places, and you have to solve the mystery of who you are by figuring out the clues at each pub. You can't leave one pub until you figure out the clue."

"What is the clue here?"

Madonna threw back her platinum, shook it and laughed. The ballad played on. "You know I can't tell you. But I can give you a hint. What did you have for dinner?" The song suddenly ended. Madonna raised up on her tiptoes and kissed Jake on the cheek. He liked it. "I've gotta get back to work," and she streaked away.

Jake looked around for the others. Norma and Nardo had danced the "Desperado" while Norma sang it an octave higher. They, however, danced further apart than Jake and Madonna. Jake noticed that Makeba and Pearl had seated themselves on the round bench circling the Banyan trunk, and they were both chatting and rubbing their feet. "I wonder why Pearl's clothes never change like the rest of us," Jake thought out loud. He approached Pearl and Makeba, who were both smiling in an all-knowing fashion after witnessing the Madonna/Jake slow dance. Nardo and Norma approached, Nardo fanning himself with his hand.

"So, what did you guys talk about?" Makeba ventured.

Jake explained about being caught in the seams and as much as he understood about working at this place. He also tried to explain about the "Pub Crawl," going from pub to pub looking for clues. Then he said, "and when I asked her what the clue was here, she said 'what did you have for dinner?' What the heck does that mean?"

Norma analyzed. "Well, at the last place, we found out who we were by finding out who we weren't. What did we find out here?"

Pearl said, "well, I liked the coaned beef the best, but I liked the enchilada, the chicken, the fries, and especially doze noshes with d' rice table ting."

"Hey, maybe that's it!" Makeba's light bulb went on. "We all tasted each other's ethnic food, we talked about it with each other, and we learned something about each other's backgrounds!"

Norma completed the analysis. "Maybe another way of finding out who we are is finding out who everybody else is, too?"

"Izzat all dere iz to it?" Pearl said, with the lip stretch. And so it was.

10 - SHADOW MANOR

A cold wind quickly replaced the balmy tropical night. The light bulbs on the Banyan dimmed, and the crowd faded. They were once again on the cobblestone road, fuzzy lights in the oppressive fog. Clippie Cloppie Clippie Cloppie. Evidently they had finished their task at that pub. And evidently "dat's not all dere iz to it!" Pearl's words echoed in everyone's ears as Jake swung the carriage door back open. They were all back in London fog gear, capes and gowns, except, of course, Pearl.

They silently helped each other into the carriage, knowing the drill by this time. The driver cracked the whip without asking. Pearl again wished she had worn warmer clothing. Makeba took off her cape and they both snuggled under it like a blanket, keeping warm. Nothing was said in the carriage. Everyone was thinking about the last three pubs. Everyone was contemplating the experience. No one realized that the skinny cobblestone street had given way to a country dirt road. No one realized that the buildings were gone, and the lights. No one realized that they were about to embark upon a major task. The group seemed tentative about going further. It was going to be hard to top the Banyan Bar, the close feeling of friends, and for Jake, the sweet smell of Madonna's hair.

Only bright blue moonlight illuminated the creaking sign on

the gate house as the great iron gates swung open. Norma could barely make out the name "SHADOW MANOR" on the crusty bronze sign. The trees had overgrown the narrow dirt road and the weeds wanted mowing. The wind crooned a slow howl as a small animal shadow darted across in front of the carriage. The clippie cloppie had diminished to dull thuds, and the dust replaced the fog as the means fuzzying the moon.

The quintet was quiet, craning their necks around to see what the dusty moonlight would bring them. As they rounded a curve, a behemoth stone mansion shone blue against the fluorescent clouds with dimly flickering windows, and a trillion gables reflecting the eggshell moon. Norma thought to herself, "how is there a moon here? I thought there were just those planet-island things?" She wasn't speaking aloud. In fact, no one was speaking, in absolute awe of the great chateau they were pulling up to.

The driver jumped off and opened the carriage door. "This'll do ya' fine. Here's where they separate the men from de boys, ye should pardon the expression!" Then he laughed, and in the dim light Nardo could see his great shock of red hair and beard. The driver jumped back on the carriage and was off in a heartbeat.

The five stood at the foot of a great stone stairway leading up to the huge doors of the mansion. Jake figured this was at least six stories high and made from pure granite, in the French style. Nardo would have a heyday with curtains for this place. It had at least 1000 rooms, and 10,000 windows. It rivaled Versailles in its faded elegance.

"CREEEEE" and the big oak door slowly opened.

"I ain't goin' in there," said Makeba, not being one for haunted houses.

"Neitheh am I," echoed Pearl, but really she thought the steps to be a very bad omen, for her feet, that is. "God only hopes they gots elevatahs heah!"

"Come on," commanded Jake, once again the Drum Major.

"Yeah," said Nardo, eager to earn credits and get going. Nardo grabbed Pearl's waist. "C'mon Pearl. I'll help you." Jake, likewise offered Makeba his arm which she first refused and then took. They began ascending the stairs, and the faint strains of a lush Viennese Waltz from a string orchestra drifted toward them, growing stronger as they drew near.

As they cautiously crept inside, they were met by two tall butlers in waistcoats and white gloves who bowed to them. The floor was traditionally pearl and black marble checkerboard in the foyer. A great double-helix staircase wound in front of them, traversing all six stories, and brass-railed balconies glimmered in the candlelight of the mammoth crystal chandelier which hung above them, dripping down almost two stories in length.

"We've been expecting you," said one of the butlers as the other closed the great door behind them with a loud "thump." His voice was low and resonant, and his ample Adam's Apple lumbered up and down as he slowly pronounced each word in stuffy British Butlerian. He walked a few steps up, turned and beckoned them to follow him down a dimly lit marble hall. Ever so tentatively they followed.

They could catch ahead of them the glimpse of a great party, and could barely make out couples swishing past the opening in grand style. The butler turned to Jake, who was at the head of the pack. "What is your name?" he whispered as softly as he could. Jake watched the Adams Apple bounce, and knew this man was tall since that apple was at eye level for Jake.

"Jacob Silver".

"SIR JACOB SILVER!" The butler announced Jake over the full orchestra. As Jake passed into the huge ballroom, his Sherlock Holmes drag faded into a while coat and tails, white silk shirt and ascot, and gloves. He was also wearing the mask of a white wolf, although he could not see it.

Norma timidly stepped up and whispered her name to Lurch. "MISS NORMA JARDINES!" As Norma passed into the expansive ballroom, her gown turned from the forest green taffeta into a meringue-shaped Cinderella gown of pinkish white and translucent. Her hair was swept on top of her head, in great dark swirls, and a diamond studded comb crowned the back. She had long white gloves and a mask of an angel at the end of a long lorgnette.

After seeing this transformation, Makeba wanted to be next and she stated, with emphasis, "MAKEBA."

"HER MOST HIGH, QUEEN MONA LISA EDWARDS!" came the booming voice.

"GODAMMIT! Where you git dat name!" Makeba forgot she wasn't speaking ghetto English here anymore. She gave the butler a very dirty look as she attempted to knock him down while she passed him. She wondered if she could pull out his eyes with no one noticing. Her gown turned into a West African silk tiger print, long and flowing, wrapped like an Indian "sari", and on her head was a golden turban adorned with a large red ruby. Silk flowed in a train from the back of the turban to the floor. On her face was the mask of a tigress.

Pearl was next. She didn't want to go, but Nardo pushed her forward. He wasn't sure he was going to like this party. Pearl barely got her name out when she heard, "MRS. MAURICE PELZMAN!"

Pearl shuffled slowly in as her red and white giant houndstooth rayon gave way to a black beaded top with three-quarter sleeves and a long black crepe floor-length straight skirt, exposing toeless black patent leather pumps with small rhinestone buckles. Pearl wore no mask. She carried a small black rhinestone encrusted clutch purse. Pearl reacted to her own glamour. This was her idea of getting "dolled up" in a 40's New York way. She looked very good.

Nardo inched up to the butler and tapped his arm. "Leonardo de los Santos," he managed to croak.

Nardo jumped as the Adams Apple voice boomed "MR. LEONARDO DE LOS SANTOS."

Nardo fully expected white coat and tails like Jake, but was shocked to see that his drab English garb was fading into the most spectacular gold and royal blue silk gown. His slender neck was enshrined with twenty four karat gold jewelry, and he held the Egyptian scepters crossed on his chest. His beautiful face was made up to the nines, with his dark coloring highlighted by azure eye shadow, and heavy liners. Berry stained lips shone from under the solid gold headdress crowned with the golden serpent rising above his head. Nardo was Cleopatra, Queen of Egypt.

Of course Jake and Pearl didn't recognize him right away, until Nardo spoke. In fact, Jake, forgetting completely about Madonna, let the possibility of a date with the Queen of Egypt brush across his mind before he fully understood.

"We're at a f*$&% Halloween party," exclaimed Makeba, who was not altogether unhappy with the African Queen thing, but still hated the reference to Mona Lisa, her real name. "I'll wipe that SMILE off o' his face," she thought, remembering the shudder which dripped over her when the butler bellowed her name.

"VALSE MARDI GRAS" shouted the musical conductor, in black tails, as he turned around, tapped his lengthy white baton, and began pumping some more Viennese out of the orchestra. Jake asked Norma to dance. She accepted. A fine English gentlemen in tails and graying hair and beard came up to Pearl and said, "May I have the pleasure?"

"Dis is bettah dan the senior center," thought Pearl as she accepted the hand of her new suitor.

A tall dark-skinned gentleman with a healthy moustache and thickly cleft chin bowed slowly to Makeba, and without a word they were off. Somehow Makeba did fine with the steps. This wasn't like the Ghanaian High-Life dancing she taught at the South Central Occupational Center every other Saturday, but she could 'valse,' especially with such a fine looking gentleman.

Nardo stood alone. "Alone again, naturally," he echoed the words of his favorite song. And the large crowd danced and whirled as the orchestra reverberated in the three-story marble hall with six of the huge drip-castle chandeliers swaying to the trinity rhythm. Nardo had never seen such a room. Three story windows of mirror, crystal and stained glass transoms, blue velvet curtains, with gold leaf everything, and soaring columns lining the parquet dance floor. Just at that moment, the music stopped, and a low drum roll took its place.

Nardo was in awe as the crowd slowly parted to each side of where he stood. As they parted, he could see a handsome man, dressed in royal ball gear, wearing a crown and with crests, medals and banners strewn across his chest. He slowly came forward through the fifty foot span toward Nardo. The crowd began to applaud.

Nardo turned around and looked in back of him to see if anyone was there. No, the Prince was coming directly for him. "This is definitely not as bad as I thought," breathed Nardo, as his heart began racing.

Nearer and nearer drew the dashing figure, and a gloved hand reached out for Nardo's. The prince was a good deal taller than Nardo, and they made a handsome couple. Nardo lifted his Egyptian-bejeweled hand, and when it touched the Prince's, the drum roll and applause stopped.

"TA – TA –" the first two chords of VALSE MARDI GRAS strain rang out again, and Nardo and the Prince waltzed alone through the crowd in Grand Ballroom style to the sounds of the adoring comments. No one had noticed that the lights had begun to dim and flicker. The rumble of thunder and the strobe of lightning began to creep over the Viennese pastry being served up at the ball. Somehow the eggshell moon had turned into a blue crystal ball, and if the crowd had noticed, they wouldn't have liked what they saw.

Norma practically tripped on the crinoline which enveloped her, finally noticing that the lights were awfully dim. The orchestra had stopped playing, and the lightning and thunder were making themselves known. The sound of the audience clapping faded into the applause of a hard rain pelting on the mirrored windows. When the lightning blinked, the silhouette of the towering trees outside the windows became apparent.

"This is getting really scary," said Norma, grabbing Jake's arm. "Let's find everyone else to make sure everything is okay."

"Good idea," said Jake, craning to see if he could notice Makeba's or Nardo's headdresses above the crowd. Pearl had lost her handsome man, and as Makeba turned to Pearl, hers also faded. Jake spotted them, dimly lit, through the crowd. "There's Makeba and Pearl, let's go!" He took Norma by the hand and pulled her. She scooped up as much of her dress as she could carry in the other arm and followed.

Nardo's Prince flashed a big white smile at him. Nardo's heart was pounding. He never had someone like this interested in him. God only knows what the Prince would do if he were to find out Nardo was really a man. Nardo had been bashed for a lot less than this. You couldn't tell when he was in drag. Even Nardo's whispery high voice, an hereditary trait in his family, was loath to give away the secret. "I just better not say anything," agreed Nardo with himself. He was having the dream of his life and did not want it to end.

As the roar of the crowd dimmed into whispers, the Prince slowly leaned over to Nardo's ear. Nardo smelled the masculine perfume, and breathed deeply. "Come with me." Nardo's heart leapt. What could this mean? The Prince put him arm around Nardo's waist, and whisked him through the crowd.

"Wheah is he going?" queried Pearl, back into the swing of things now that she was single again. Nardo and the Prince brushed past the group, and Makeba, fearless as usual, spoke through her tiger mask.

"We're going, too, aren't we Pearl?" she commanded and she grabbed Pearl and began weaving through the crowd after Cleopatra and Prince Charming. Jake and Norma, sensing the party was moving elsewhere, followed suit. They all quickly filed out the long hall through which they came. The hall was no longer lit, but the lightning intermittently showed the way.

Back in the huge foyer, the Prince began running up the double-helix staircase. "Quickly,. We don't have much time to waste!" he warned. This was too much for Pearl.

"Can't I wait in the cah? Doesn't this place have a ladies lounge?"

"SHHHH." Makeba was yanking Pearl up the stairs. This time both of them were in heels. As they ascended, they heard the sound of footsteps quickly descending down the concurrent staircase. Obviously guests were leaving in a hurry. Jake and Norma were climbing directly behind. Makeba and Jake had lifted their masks to the top of their heads. They were definitely getting in the way.

The staircase was interminable. Pearl was gasping for breath. The great chandelier grew large as they ascended. Out the great transom which arched above the front doors, in the dim, soaked moonlight, the faint light of the carriage gave away the fact that other guests were moving on, and quickly.

"This way," stage whispered the Prince as he hurried Nardo and the rest of the crowd from the fifth story white marble landing, past the alabaster balustrades, into the long hall which traversed the oceanside wing of the Manor.

11 - THE STUDY

The quintet filed through a warm oak door into a tall room with a blazing fireplace, animal heads, horns and rugs, and great brown overstuffed leather sofas and chairs. A huge desk loomed in front of the window, with a winged back swivel chair. The Prince allowed all to pass, paused at the door and said, "You must find the Book, and it's not necessarily here." With that, he looked into Nardo's eyes as he lifted his hand and gently pressed his lips to it. He was gone, and the door creaked shut.

"Oy, mein Gott in Himmel." Pearl collapsed into one of the couches. "My girdle is cutting me in half!"

"I agree with Pearl," said Makeba, still a little miffed at losing her date and the "Mona Lisa Edwards" statement.

"What did he mean about the Book?" poked Norma. "I mean, look . . . there's a thousand books here."

The fifteen foot high walls were lined with thousands upon thousands of books, all leather bound gold leafed, some in scripts and fonts that they never saw before. A tall wooden rolling ladder climbed to the upper shelves.

Jake noticed, "Hey. These books are in alphabetical order, it seems like." And as the group looked closely, they found it to be so. The "A's" started on the fireplace side of the room, and ended up in "Z" on the other side. "They seem to be people's names! 'Aabel, Anthony, Aarons, Miriam,' Jake read the names.

"I never hoid of any o' those authors before." And that was Pearl's contribution. She was still resting. "Life is no damn good when yuh dogs are tired!" She curled her lower lip for the first time since they got to this land, and simultaneously rubbed her aching feet.

"Jake, see if our names are up there," said Nardo, curious to see if he was in print, but not so curious to find out what was written.

Jake was as anxious as the next one, so he began following the books with his finger. "Nardo, what's your last name again."

"De Los Santos . . . of the saints," Nardo translated and smiled as he remembered his Grandmother in the Philippines giving him the small cross he still wore around his neck.

"It's up here." The ladder needed greasing as Jake dragged it to the right location. "Dagget, Donavan, De La Falanga . . . I found it! Here it is: 'LEONARDO DE LOS SANTOS'

"Open it up!" screamed Makeba, now becoming interested in the happenings.

Jake slowly descended from the ladder, blowing a great cloud of dust off the small, dark brown leather book. Opening to the title page he read, "SECRETS."

"Let me see that," insisted Nardo. Jake came all the way down and handed the book to Nardo. Nardo looked at the title page and read aloud, "SECRETS." He slowly turned to the first page, second page, third page and his face turned ashen.

"What does it say?" soothed Norma as she swooshed her dress over to Nardo.

Reluctantly Nardo handed the book to Norma. She had a puzzled look on her face as she read out loud, "This page intentionally left blank." Turning the page she read, "This page intentionally left blank." And so on for every page in the book. "I wonder what it means."

Nardo's evening-at-the-ball balloon popped. "I know what it means. It means I'm nothing, I'm worthless."

"Uh uh," Norma vigorously shook her head, "no." You are not worthless. Just think, Nardo. You were the prettiest at the ball tonight, and think about the great band memory, and you designing the banner and all those costumes and helping us all get that extra time and credits." Norma was heaping it on, but telling the truth at the same time. "No, it can't mean that you're worthless. It has to mean something else." She handed the book on to Makeba who was very curious.

"Hey. There's an inscription in here. [Reading] 'I'll always remember our wondrous waltz. I'm waiting for you in the little chapel, down the side staircase, through the gilt door. P.'"

"P." Now Jake was curious. Who is that?"

"I wonder if it could be the Prince! The Prince you danced with!" Norma was fairly intuitive about these matters. Nardo's faith was restored.

"Hey, let's look for my book," offered Makeba, and she began dragging the ladder to the "M" section. "Hellfire and damnation, it isn't here! Just my damn luck." At that moment, a dull thud was heard, and a small cloud of dust rose from the floor, around the "E"s. Jake bent over and picked up the fallen book. "MONA LISA EDWARDS," Jake read aloud. "Mona Lisa?"

Makeba bounded off her ladder, arms akimbo and grabbed the book from Jake's hand, "GIMME DAT!" She couldn't tolerate much more of the name game.

"What's inside?" asked Nardo tentatively.

Makeba was much more possessive with her book than Nardo. But her curiosity was one of her more famous traits. Fearlessly, she pried the shiny black book with gold lettering open to the title page. "THE QUEEN OF DENIAL." Makeba was livid. That's what her shrink called her. And every time her shrink called her that, Makeba wanted to stop the check. "A hundred and fifty lousy dollars an hour to be chopped up by this woman," Makeba would think to herself, all the while mad because that hundred and fifty dollars per hour could've been hers IF she hadn't gotten kicked out of school. There it was again. That damn school thing. Tying up the dean. What the hell was she thinking? "LEMME AT HIM!" Makeba made a worthless gesture towards the door, but it was all hufty-magufty, as the rest knew her so well by now.

"Is there an inscription." Jake chuckled to himself. Seeing Makeba's face turn red was quite a feat in itself. Makeba rifled through the pages, and a slip fluttered down to the bearskin rug at the foot of the fireplace.

"Martinis, guitars, conversation . . .

In this very place, revelation."

Makeba was simply not in the mood for the haiku. But she noticed the R.O. pinned to her sari-wrap was forever ticking time away, and really what she wanted most was to get the hell out of this place. "I guess I stay here, then," she added, disappointed.

"Get the rest of our books, Jake." Norma was totally ready to get hers. Jake rolled the ladder to "J" and grabbed NORMA JARDINES. He rolled to "P" for Pearl Pelzman after she said "remember, it's with a 'z'," not wanting to forget about Israel. But the book was very close to the floor on a lower shelf. Jake found his own book at eye level.

"One bam, two crack

Down the hall and three doors back." Pearl read this as if it were the "Sh'ma" the great call to prayer of Judaism. It was very cryptic to her. But, since it sounded like Mah Jong, she could do with planting her butt down for a couple of hours with a cuppa "coaffee."

Norma's book was tarnished gold, and the pages were scalloped. On the title page was an etching of an ancient bread oven. She recognized this as the ovens the early Aztecs and Mayans used to bake their crude loaves. Under the picture was the caption, "Read the play, unlock the key, the road back to you eternally." Norma was not afraid of new adventure. She just hated to do it alone.

Jake Silver picked up his dusty blue book, which matched his eyes. After hearing the sentences of the others, he was apprehensive, but after some jibing by Makeba, opened his book. The book was hollow, and in it was a key with an elastic band, like a locker room key. "HEALTH CLUB (TRUTH SPA) - BASEMENT" was the inscription.

The lonely band stood there looking at each other. So far, they had been together practically every minute and could keep each other company. Now each had been charged with a separate quest, and they instinctively knew that they had to go it alone. Pearl did not want to put her shoes back on. She did not want to leave the couch, but they all began dusting themselves off, preparing for their mini-journeys.

"Whatever happens, let's all meet back here when we're done." Makeba was used to giving instructions in uncertain situations. Jake stalwartly walked to the door, still dressed in white. Norma followed, Nardo helped Pearl out of the couch (not without groans) and with Makeba, the quints opened the door and Norma, Jake, Nardo and Pearl crept into the long hall, now filled with foggy smoke. Makeba looked at the fire and the warm leather couches. She was glad she was staying here.

"Oy vey, enough with the effects oveh deah," wished Pearl. And in single file the Subway Brigade minus Makeba marched through that warm oak door to meet their immediate and respective destinies while Makeba stuck her head out the great oak door, watching them all disappear their separate ways into the mist.

12 - ALL TOGETHER, ALL ALONE

Makeba pulled the door shut. She turned and looked around her. The great study was cozy. If she had to be somewhere alone, it might as well be here. She sighed and dusted off her book, opening it up to the first page. "How about a drink?" read the first line. "How about a drink, sounds good," Makeba repeated the line out loud. Finding the spot where Pearl had warmed up the couch, she plunged her great rear into the soft, worn leather.

The sound of a gentle silk stringed Latin guitar began playing softly. The lights in the room dimmed, and the flickering fire became the main source of red and orange light. The slow bossa nova guitar's rich and comforting chords juxtaposed with linear jazz runs. This music continued as Makeba became aware of a subtle and slow "whoosh."

A section of books began to turn as if on a carousel. Makeba could see that it uncovered a false wall. The tinkling of ice and the flickering of the fire, reflecting very small in the martini glasses, came slowly into view. A dark burl bar was swinging out from the wall, and behind it, in a snappy white shirt and tie, with sleeves rolled up stood a beautiful bartender. Makeba became enraptured with the hypnotic strumming, and her eyes fixated on the handsome, graying-templed tall man behind the bar. A huge white smile broke from his ebony face, as Makeba's eyes met his. This guy wasn't afraid of her or confrontation.

As the guitar slowly wound its way through the break and came around to the verse again, the Bartender began to sing in a slow and meaningful rasp:

"It's Sunday
Thank God
the week starts tomorrow again,
Easier to forget where I haven't been
All together
All alone.

Ain't cryin'
Because I know it's a little unchic
Gimme your number, guess I'll
give you a ring next week
All together,
All alone

"Mr. D.J. turn the music up
And you won't hear me
Weeping inside
As if I had something terrible to hide
I wanna shout out
Let's stop tearing each others'
Heart out.

And maybe
Later on we will all have our thrill
But 'til then we're just headed
Over the hill

All together

All alone

So take it slow and easy baby

All together,

All alone.

Makeba was hypnotized by the Nat Cole sound-alike. Her eyes were fixated like a cobra on the flicker of the fire, now in Bartender's eyes.

"Hello Mona Lisa," smiled Bartender.

"Call me Betty," thought Makeba. This time she didn't care what she was called, as long as this was the "who" doing the calling.

"Hi," she said back, unusually soft for Makeba.

"Are you by yourself?" Bartender looked up from the two martinis he had just poured. The words shot through Makeba like a truth serum.

Not knowing whether or not he meant "tonight" or "in general," Makeba thought to herself, "By myself, that's it, isn't it."

"Yes." She said it aloud to Bartender, and also herself. "I am by myself."

"What's a fine woman like you doing by herself?" Bartender sounded like he was making small talk, but this talk wasn't small. For in this moment, looking into the almond eyes of this handsome gentlemen, she realized that much of her life had been marking time. When had she stopped moving forward? All the rallies, the documentaries, singing gospel, the African dance lessons and seminars, the Kwanzaa celebrations . . . they were all marking time. All filling in blanks. But they *must* have some meaning. This all can't be lost life.

"Marking time," was Makeba's out loud answer, though for her it did not come as a response to Bartender's last question. Here in the place where time was not free. Here where you had to earn every second and make progress as well. Makeba remembered the R.O. ticking away, but the thought was quickly subdued by the more important life thoughts she was finally allowing herself to think.

"Care to join me for a drink," Bartender motioned his head for Makeba to come and sit on one of the ornate brass barstools. She complied, leaving the comfort of the couch for the comfort of the Bartender's ear.

"Wanna talk about it?" Bartender seemed to know exactly what she was thinking. Remembering the words, "all together, all alone," Makeba began voicing her thoughts, as the guitar lightly strummed in the background.

"I don't know what I've been doing for the last twenty-five years. Ever since getting kicked out of college, I guess I've tried to impose meaning on my life, proving I was right. In doing that, I've succeeded in stopping my forward progress. I'm now looking at what I've accomplished, and it's things . . . just things. Things you can write down. Things you can put on a resume. Maybe I could teach at a black college or black studies or something with my "things." But I can't live life with them. I can't get a relationship with them. And I'm not even talking about a man."

"You know, for instance, my friend Pearl." Makeba let it slip out without even knowing it. She called Pearl her friend. Pearl from a different planet. But it was true. "My friend Pearl and I were just talking . . . sharing little things about our separate lives. But it made me feel connected, more connected than all that super-imposed African speak I spend my life spewing. Oh, not that that's not important. It's just not *all* important, as I'm realizing now. It should be just a piece of me. Instead I tried to make it my soul. Where did you come from?" Makeba unwittingly let that last thought slip out to Bartender.

"Oh, a place where I learned to drop building my life on unessential things. A place where you cut to the issue, and forget about the chaff. I guess it's not the things you do, but what you take away from them."

Makeba and the Bartender continued talking. This person seemed familiar, like someone she had known for years. But that could not be since she just met him. What was it about him? Why was this conversation diving so deeply? At times she felt faint or dizzy with the long lost thoughts and feelings running through her mind. The more they talked, the more incisive the discussion became. Makeba felt radical changes occurring in her mind as well as body.

Yes, Makeba knew she was experiencing a life changing revelation in a conversation lasting only minutes, but seemingly for eons. Bartender was telling her what she already instinctively knew, but refused to admit for twenty-five years. She had been interested in the *what* a lot more than the *why*. It wasn't singing Gospel: it was the way it made you *feel*. It wasn't the African culture: it was the way it made you *feel*. The things you walked away with. These were the real "things," not the thing itself.

"What do I do about all the wasted time? What do I do about all the lost life?" Makeba's eyes searched Bartender's as the guitar brushed on.

"That's the nice thing about memory. You know that. You learned that here. You can relive the memory, the "thing," and you can learn from it each time. And you can do it over and over."

And so it was true Now that she had matured, Makeba could reevaluate all the "moments" in her life, and assess what the lessons were. And as she matured more, she could reassess and reevaluate, and learn more, and from different perspectives. So this was the lesson of the past. Makeba had learned the Mystery of History, and in doing so, she learned how to learn who she was.

"Can I get you another drink, Betty?" The Bartender flashed a smile at Makeba.

"Call me Mona Lisa," said Makeba smiling enigmatically as she clinked her glass with Bartender's and the two slipped into an evening of meaningful and intimate discussion. Not like lovers. Like lovers of life.

13 - SUPER NOVA MAH JONG

Pearl was glad the schmootzy fog was clearing up. Oy, what it was probably doing to her sinuses, and none of the pills really worked here. She had written down the verse on a slip of paper from her purse. "One bam, two crack, down the hall and three doors back." At least she wouldn't have to schlep up the stairs. Pearl counted the doors as she slowly ambled down the hall. She didn't want to remember that this was the first time the group had split up since getting on the subway car. But she missed them. "Like Mishpookah, family" she said to herself, as she reached the second great oak door.

All of a sudden, she heard such a geschrei [scream] from behind the door, followed by the cacophony of multiple female laughter. Taken aback at first then she thought, "So, this might not be so bad," Pearl timidly knocked. "Hello! Is anybody deah?" Pearl knocked again.

GESCHREI!! And the great oak door creaked open to reveal a picture right out of the Fifties, with some obvious changes. It was a Southern California tract house living room filled with smoke, cigarette smoke. Danish modern furniture, all blonde wood. Pole lamps. And Pearl could faintly make out three figures sitting around a card table. This was a scene she was readily familiar with, although Bingo had long ago replaced Mah Jong

("Maj") as a pastime, and the Hadassah Senior Center had replaced the living room.

"Fuh Gads sakes! Shut the door. You're letting out all the heat!" Letting out the heat? The place was a stinking inferno and Pearl had long since lost her immunity to roomfuls of cigarette smoke. But it sounded like Maj with Evelyn Finkle, Stella Fishkin and the girls, so she was game. This couldn't be her test. It was so unlike everything else that had happened to the Subway Brigade so far. So, she figured, while everybody else plotzed with whatever, she'd play Maj. And she was finally glad she was back in her "Pearl" clothes and out of that constraining black dress she'd had to wear to the Mask Party.

"Sit down, sit down. We needed a fourth. Esther can't make it. How 'bout some coaffee?" The figure with her back to Pearl was speaking. Pearl walked around the card table, complete with quilted plastic cover, to the empty chair across from the speaker. As she slid into her chair, she looked up and the lower lip did a major stretch, you don't know what. She looked at the "girls." Evelyn Finkle it wasn't. The creature sitting on her right was like a big, huge lizard, with cat-eyes, and clawed hands. Pearl didn't want to know from the feet. Immediate revulsion came over her. She wasn't about to break blintzes with a lizard. However, saving the creature from complete damnation, were the cultured pearl drop earrings, and the shirt and pants outfit she was wearing. The hair was a little bouffanty, and the most shocking shade of green.

Pearl's lip was petrified. Looking away, trying not to let her shock show, she got a load of the thing on the other side of the table. This looked like something out of "The Fly" with Vincent Price (ooh, but he was so good-looking). The head was large with antennae, black with strange thick black hair combed straight down the sides, large eyes and a strange tube for a mouth.

"The coaffee, the coaffee!" Pearl was searching for an antidote to the horror show she was witnessing.

"Right heah, doll!" A hand which was, at the same time see-through, but like you could see the atoms or molecules or something very strange held out the cup across the table. "Black oah yuhs want something in it? And take a kugel. Take!" The "hand" stretched out to Pearl.

Pearl didn't know what to say. What if the coffee was bug juice or something, and God knows what was in the kugel? "G'head, I just made it, fresh right now." The see-through pushed the kugel dish towards Pearl, and she was a little hungry, not remembering having eaten since the Banyan Bar. Pearl relented.

"Thanks." She still remembered her manners, that was something she brought with her. She took a kugel. It wasn't bad. It wasn't Aunt Matilda's kugel, but it was good and fresh, and the coffee was old-time perked to mud, just the way she liked it.

"Let's go, girls. Play MAJ!" For the first time Pearl looked up at what was sitting across from her. This "thing" you could see right through. Lights orbiting around other lights were whizzing where the head should be. However, solid rock Fifties Jewish-English was spewing forth, and it was a language Pearl understood.

The lizard spoke first. "I'm Lilah, honey. Glad you could join us. Have you ever played Nova Maj before?"

"SUPER Nova Maj," said the fly, then turning to Pearl. "Bat Zion, bubbie. [Pronounced 'Bot Zee-own'.] But call me ZeeZee. That's what my niece calls me. Aunt ZeeZee, 'cause she can't say 'Bat Zion'. And this is new, improved SUPER Nova Maj, all new tiles, Lilah. Get it right!"

"Big deal," responded Lilah, then to Pearl. "She's always right, this one" nodding that big lizard head toward the fly.

"Let's get going girls, so we can play again! Besides, I've got the whole house to clean when we're through. It's a disaster area, like a hurricane!" This from the whizzing atom lady.

"I'm Pearl," she offered timidly.

"I'm sorry, sweetie. I'm Eve. You know, like Adam and Eve. Have you ever played Maj before, like this I mean?"

Everything sounded so normal to Pearl. Most things looked normal. It was just that the people . . . no that's not right . . . the players were so weird. "Have yuh?" Eve was insistent.

"Well I played Mah Jong with the girls quite a while ago, but I remember . . ."

Pearl was cut off by the fly. "Don't worry, you'll catch on. It's real easy. Divee up the tiles girls!"

Pearl picked up her first tile. It was strange. Cool black stone, hexagon shaped, but flat on both sides. She turned over the tile and looked at it.

"Don't show it, honey! Put yuhs tiles on the tile bridge!" The lizard put a scaly hand on Pearl's and Pearl instinctively drew back. She wondered if anyone else from the subway was playing Mah Jong with lizards, flies and whatevers. The Maj Group divided up the strange tiles and placed them on their tile bridges so only they could see them.

"I'm the North Star, I go first," said ZeeZee the fly. "One Bang!" And she slapped onto the table her tile with a little exploding hologram on it. The fly picked up a tile from the stack.

"What's a Bang?" Pearl never heard that term in Maj before. It was always Bam, Crack, Seasons, Dragons, Winds.

"Bang. Like Big Bang!" Eve went next. "I'm East Rising. Nova." Eve slapped the tile on the table, this one had a definite spark above it. Eve picked up a tile from the stack. Pearl was beginning to recognize the game, but had trouble with the names.

"Two Warp" said Lilah the lizard, slamming her tile down on

the table. "And I'll take that Nova."

"Oh, she's up to something again, you're a lucky stiff Lilah," buzzed ZeeZee. "G'head, bubbie," to Pearl, "it's your turn."

Pearl picked up any tile and slammed it on the table.

"CALL YOUR TILE! This is Jewish Maj, honey, you gotta call your tile." Eve was giving the hints.

Pearl saw that there were two sparks coming from the tile so she said, "Nova."

"No, SUPER NOVA, sweetie." This was the lizard. "One Nova is NOVA, two Novae is SUPER NOVA."

"Oh, sorry," placated Pearl, being happy she was together enough in this zoo to muster up the hoich (strength) to say anything.

"Why did you throw the Nova, honey?" ZeeZee was talking. "You see she's collecting them!" ZeeZee nodded towards Lilah.

"Oh, sorry," said Pearl, resolved to do better next time, but Pearl could see that the "girls" were being incredibly patient with her.

ZeeZee said, "Don't worry. The game is young. And so are we! Three Bang."

And GESCHREI and cackles of laughter came from Lilah, Eve and ZeeZee, like "The Best of Milton Berle" was on.

"So how was the operation, Lilah? Did you feel all right? Six Warp." Eve slammed down her tile. "I'll take that Super Nova."

"Just to louse me up, but good," scoffed Lilah. "Now what am I going to do? And it's a procedure, not an operation. Binary."

Slam, went another tile.

"Procedure, schmedure! They cut your throat, what else do you call it!" Eve wasn't taking anything from Lilah.

"You had a procedure?" said Pearl, all of a sudden becoming more interested. You see, Pearl had a lump removed, but it was benign. What she went through. "What was wrong? Four Bang." Pearl put her tile softly down as she picked up another one, and looked at the lizard with as great a concern as she could scrape together.

"I had a swollen gland on the back of my tongue, and they had to remove it. You don't know the trouble, the pain."

"On the back of your tongue?" pressed Pearl, this time genuinely curious.

"Yeah, right heah!" And the lizard spewed forth a huge black slimy forked tongue and pointed to the back of it on Pearl's side of the table. Pearl almost fainted, but she saw the stitches.

"F'Gad's sakes," buzzed ZeeZee . "Keep that awful ting in your mouth! Are yuh tryin' to make us sick?"

"So she asked. So I showed. So what's wrong wit dat? And anyway, it's better than that big twirly tube you call a tongue." Lilah was not amused.

"Girls! Girls, please stop. You're both pretty." Eve calmed them down. "Pretty awful."

GESCHREI!! And more cackles of laughter. Pearl could not help laughing, that deep smoker's cough-laugh that she never got rid of, with lots of phlegm. She was starting to loosen up now.

"You need a tissue?" said Lilah, reaching for her purse.

"Tanks." Pearl gladly accepted the tissue.

"Neutron" buzzed ZeeZee, and the tile slammed onto the table. "It's so fragile, the body. When we were young, so there. You could do anyting. Dancing. Drinking. Whatever you wanted, you could do."

"Yeah, dose were the days." Eve continued the thought. "Seven Warp. So we get older and we start to fall apart. Last week, my doctah (I had him for thirty years) put me on a new energy source, which I have to expose myself to gamma radiation four times a day. You don't think that takes time?"

Pearl thought 'radiation'. That's what you have when you have cancer. But this woman (yes, Pearl finally had to concede she was a woman) took it for the good of her. What do you know? What's bad for the goose is finally good for the gander.

Lilah spoke. "Well I can hardly talk with my tongue. Trinary. The stitches come out next week. I'm choking every time I try to talk."

"Sounds like yuhs are doin' okay to me!" ZeeZee told the joke this time.

GESCHREI!!

"Moah coaffee, Pearl?" Eve was pouring, and Pearl was taking. She was feeling much more comfortable now. Whaddya know! Everyone in the universe has the same problems. Health, sickness, medicine, getting well. Whaddya know. This revelation led Pearl to relax. The barriers were breaking down. In fact, if Lilah kept that tongue in the mouth and ZeeZee kept hers in, they were pretty good company. Pearl thought of how she used to hate sitting near Makeba on the subway. Now Makeba would be the closest thing to home for her. "I don't tink she'd like the Maj," thought Pearl. "What's this?" Pearl held out a strange tile with tube holograms coming out of the top.

"A Worm Hole. It's like a joker. Keep it honey." Eve was coaching. "Throw something else."

"Pearl had been saving 'Bangs'. She only had one something else left, so she threw it and picked up another bang from the pile. Suddenly her tile bridge started to glow brightly, and send a web of light out onto the table.

"MAAAHHHHJJJ!!!" ZeeZee buzzed it for Pearl. "You been sittin' heah wit Maj fuh ten minutes and you didn't let out a peep!"

"Beginnuz luck" said Lilah, as she tipped her tiles back onto the table.

"I won," offered Pearl.

"You won, honey," said Eve. "Are we goin' fur anotheh? After all, we got all the time in the world!!"

GESCHREI!!

And so, as the evening of Maj, Kugel, Coffee, and the "girls" wore on, Pearl became more and more comfortable and less repulsed at the company. In fact, she felt at home, laughing and joking. At one point, she sneaked a peek at Lilah. Fully expecting to get nauseous again, she surprised herself by focusing on Lilah's neat bouffant hairdo. Obviously the woman (there's that word again) went to the beauty parlor. She was impeccably dressed, and the earrings kind of set off the translucence of the scales. ZeeZee was cute, with her "oriental" bowl cut, and though she still could make out no features on Eve, she was a very gracious hostess, and kept the coffee and kugel flowing. The girls called tiles and chatted. Same old stuff. "Isn't that something?" Pearl mused to herself. "A million miles away and it's the same old stuff." She was glad. She was very glad that everything was like everything else, but different. Now what did that mean? Pearl didn't care. She instinctively knew.

14 - TO THINE OWN SELF

The soft sounds of a slush-pumpy diapason organ-stop echoed as Nardo pushed open the doors to what seemed to be the Chapel of the mansion. The ceiling was three stories high, with white marble floors, but that was where the church-similarity stopped. The pews were not wood, as one would expect. These were plush white-on-white damask overstuffed couches, one in front of the other. Small tufted choir stalls on the walls were white. The flowers were white. In fact, the only color in the room was cast by the light through the great cut crystal window that rose above the altar bouncing off what seemed to be great eight-foot high apothecary jars, tall and narrow. They were filled with brightly colored liquids of green, yellow, blue and red. The chroma effect was a giant rainbow cast throughout the chapel. The light show was dazzling.

Nardo timidly crept forth, down the center aisle. The room was empty except for the great pipe organ which filled the entire room, under the stained glass window. Instead of metal pipes, however, the green, yellow, red liquid motif was bubbled up through glass pipes, creating a reflective rainbow above the organ. Strange how the organist was actually on the altar. That wasn't usual in the Catholic churches Nardo had been in. Of course, Nardo long since stopped going to church. He had learned of the Church's outward disdain for homosexuality. This, even though, as an altar-boy when the family first arrived in the United States, Nardo had been sexually entangled with several priests and altar boys. They just didn't talk about it. And the Lesbianism with the nuns. He just didn't get it. The hypocrisy was flamboyant in its idiocy. How could he reconcile a high concept such as a loving God with this conduct?

Nardo crept timidly toward the altar. He did not notice that anyone was sitting in the plush white couch pews. He heard a soft voice whisper. "Leni, Leni come over here." The voice was familiar. The smell of clove cigarettes brushed against Nardo's nose. He recognized the language as his native Tagalog from the Philippines. Only one person in the world called him Leni. Only one person he knew smoked clove cigarettes - his paternal grandmother, Rosalinda.

Nardo whipped around quickly. Sure enough, Rosalinda, his deceased grandmother, was sitting casually in one of the couches, with a cigarette hanging out of her mouth. Rosalinda was a stocky Philippino woman, mostly Indonesian look, flat nose, jet black straight hair, and large lips and teeth. Nardo had only fond memories of Rosa, as she was called. She had been the kindest to him, and had urged him to seek a career in the United States. She helped him pay for his nursing training in the Philippines, and he graduated with honors. She bought half of his plane ticket to the United States, and she talked friends of hers into letting him stay until he found a job. Unfortunately, there were no nursing positions available for a non-English speaking fairy from the Philippines. By the time he realized it, he was working the drag clubs, making enough money to squeak by. He lied to Rosa in his letters, telling her that he was fulfilling his nursing career. He never had the heart to tell her otherwise. Five years after he came over, Rosa died of cancer (probably the clove cigarettes). He had wanted to go back and take care of her, nurse her, give her some of her own back. But Rosa would have none of that. She decided that it was time to go, and said exactly that in the last letter she wrote to Nardo. He barely made it back to Manila for her funeral.

Continuing in Tagalog, Nardo spoke. "Grandma Rosa? Grandma Rosa, what are you doing here?"

"Oh, I'm about, Leni. I'm everywhere and everywhen these days," she said, chortling a low cigarette laugh. The ash on the clove cigarette dangling from her lips was growing longer.

Nardo could not keep the lie up. "Grandma Rosa, I have something to tell you . . . about the nursing, I mean."

"If you mean you never got a nursing job, I knew. I know and I knew. You think I'm stupid? They told me. They told me about the *maricon* clubs." Rosa was on top of things.

"You *knew* about the drag shows?" Grandma's vast intuition never stopped amazing Nardo, even though her formal education had been seriously lacking.

"Of course. I'm not blind. I just wanted you to be happy. I thought you would be happier in America!"

"I was," responded Nardo tentatively. "It's hard, but I'm doing fine." The ash on Rosa's cigarette was becoming excessively long.

Suddenly the organ music stopped. "Hey, get your grandmother an ashtray, sissy-boy!" The all-in-white organist turned around to face Nardo. Nardo froze as he remembered the cruel voice of his father. His father who used to beat him to try and get him to be more masculine. His father who put boxing gloves on him to fight his older brothers, twice his age and size. "GET YOUR GRANDMOTHER AN ASHTRAY!"

"Leave him alone," said Rosa, used to handling her son's demeanor.

Nardo took a deep breath. It had been a long time since he had faced the abuse of his father. Since he came to America, he had not seen his father, except for Rosalinda's funeral, and did not speak to him there. Nardo made himself a little life in America. He had not needed his family, and his father had long since not been able to affect Nardo's life in any meaningful way, save the cruel memories dragged up from time to time on lonely nights when even the liquor would not wipe them out.

And this troubled Nardo greatly. One thing he got from being both Catholic and Philippine was a strong sense of family. So the fact that he was estranged from his father ripped at his heart twenty-four hours a day. Although he rarely allowed himself to speak of it, he wished he wasn't gay so he wouldn't have had to run away. And that's why he did it. He never realized that his sexuality was simply his father's *excuse* for treating him badly. Even without it, his father would have found a reason to put him down. That was the only way Nardo's father could raise himself up . . . to put others down. Other's failures became his father's successes. Nardo couldn't keep that in his life.

Nardo had put up with his father's crap for years and years. But now he had his own life, something that was proprietarily his. And he wasn't going to let his father get away with it. Not now. He would not allow his father to tear down the tiny little reality Nardo had created. Not this time.

The words spilled out of Nardo's mouth, and he could do nothing to stop it. "Don't tell me what to do, you stupid failure," Nardo screamed to his father. All your children left you. You killed your wife and your mother with your selfish and abusive ways. Do you think you have any control over me? Not as long as there is a breath left in this body. I don't know what you're doing here and I don't care. But you're not going to tell me what to do. If you want to get her an ashtray, do it yourself, Failure!" Of course, Nardo was aching to get Rosa an ashtray, for HER. But because his father wanted him to do it, he refused. He turned and faced his grandmother.

The long glowing ash from the clove cigarette had fallen onto the white couch. She tried to brush it off, but in vain. A small flame had appeared.

"See what you did?!" The gruff sound of Nardo's father howled through the chapel. "Now you started a fire. It's your fault!"

Not wanting to feel guilty, but being at once consumed by guilt, Nardo thought quickly. Water, he needed water to put the fire out. But the only available liquid seemed to be that in the great red apothecary towering near his grandmother's couch pew. Thinking fast, he pushed the apothecary over, spilling the blood red over Rosalinda, the white couch and alabaster marble floors.

"You have killed your grandmother!" shouted Nardo's father.

But Rosalinda was brushing the red liquid off her white robe, and she said softly, "You didn't hurt me, Leni."

Nardo was panicked, and rushed away towards an arched door to the left of the altar. He pushed the white door open and found himself in a long, narrow dark room, with counters along the sides, and cabinets above. Nardo immediately recognized this as the poor kitchen of his Philippino home. Only a dim light shone at the end. It was the refrigerator cracked open. Nardo went quickly toward the light, and turned. Back at the door where he had run in, a dark figure loomed in the doorway. It was his father.

"Leonardo. Leonardo, come here. I want to make it up with you! I want to tell you that I'm sorry, so sorry for what I put you through," Nardo recognized his father's voice, but it had altered. His father's voice was soft, but to Nardo it was too little, much too late. Why was his father changing toward Nardo? What was behind the about-face? Nardo was more than skeptical.

"Keep away from me! Don't you touch me."

Nardo's father kept up the soothing talk as he slowly inched his way toward Nardo. But there was no place for Nardo to go. He was trapped by that refrigerator, and the dim light cast a cruel shadow on his father's face as he approached. "Nardo. Forgive me. I want to love you now. Touch me, Nardo. Be tender with me."

Nardo's father was within reach, and Nardo's heart was racing. He did not want his father to touch him. He did not want to be affectionate toward his father. He did not want his father's love, nor was he willing to give his to his father. "STAY AWAY, I'M WARNING YOU." The hair was up on Nardo's neck like a trapped leopard. Father crept closer and reached out his hand for Nardo.

In anguish, Nardo pulled open one of the kitchen drawers. Out of it he drew a very large, long screwdriver, thick, and at least a foot long. "STAY AWAY, STAY AWAY!!" He could stand it no longer. And Nardo stabbed the approaching man hard in the stomach with the deadly implement.

Again, the red-and-white of the blood stained theme *da capoed* as scarlet liquid spurted from the wound. Immediately, Nardo was overcome with tremendous and substantial guilt. "What have I done? What have I done?" Against expectation, the look on his father's face was strangely peaceful.

Nardo instinctively placed his hand over the wound in his father's abdomen to stop the bleeding as a nurse would have. Against his feelings, he touched his father. At the door was the outline of Rosalinda, haloed in the light of the chapel behind. "Grandmother. I have killed my father! I have killed my father!" Nardo was screaming in agony.

"No you haven't, Leni. You didn't kill him. He's fine. He is okay. Everything will be fine now. My son and your father is still well." Rosalinda was reassuring.

Slowly, Nardo drew his hand away from the wound, expecting to see the blood-red stain on his hand. But, lo, his hand was clean and the wound was healed as if it had never been. Nardo looked up into the smiling eyes of his father, and wept softly. He had rejected his father in the worst possible way. He had worked hard throughout his life to "kill" all parts and memories of his father; yet as a Phoenix, a new image of his father arose, strong and smiling. Inside, Nardo felt a strangely quiet peace pour over him, unlike any he had ever experienced. The image of the angel, Rosalinda, reassured him. In this strange and faraway place, he had reconciled with his father through a catharsis. He finally had separated the man from the masculinity. He now accepted those parts of his father that were himself, and knew the rest had been only human frailty. Yes, a strange, warm peace drained over Nardo and he knew he would take this feeling with him to his grave.

15 - SCHWITZING LIKE A PIG

Jake wandered down the gigantic hallway pondering on what fate awaited him. Having been so used to being alone as a homeless person, or "habitat-challenged" as the politically correct called him, the idea of being alone again after having served on the Subway Brigade since arriving at the floating islands was unsettling to say the least. "Oh, well, I've been here before, and in much less hospitable surroundings," Jake reassured himself. His "pat-on-the-back" mentality, however, was not as reassuring as he would have liked. What room was it again that he was looking for? He tried to remember the words inscribed in his book back in the study. He still had the white towel clutched in his hands, and looked at each door as he passed it to grab a hint as to where he should go. He saw a sign on the wall which had several listings, ostensibly different rooms, with arrows pointing the way and floor numbers. He found what he was looking for. "HEALTH CLUB (TRUTH SPA) - BASEMENT" with an arrow pointing down. Looking up, Jake saw the double helix staircase in front of him in the grand entrance. There was no one there, so he took off down the stairs, towel in hand.

Jake began his trek down the large marble staircase, noticing the weather outside had completely turned to rain with lightning and thunder. At least he was inside in a warm place. Again, memories ran through his head of spending cold nights in Pershing

Square, or finding urine-stinking tunnels to sleep in back in LA. Why couldn't he forget about that? "Damn that stupid agent bitch" was the relentless refrain that ran through his mind again and again. SHE got him on drugs. SHE made him spend all his money. SHE got his hopes up. And then SHE dumped him. "Hope you're enjoying that Jaguar you bought with the money I made you," Jake seethed to himself. Truth is, he would choke her if he had the opportunity. The hate blinded him. It had stopped him from doing anything. It had sabotaged his life. The only thing that blocked it out was the drugs. The drugs he had become hooked on. Fortunately, here in this place, he hadn't thought about drugs, hadn't had the need for them. But what if he had to go back? Wouldn't it be the same again?

Jake thought of his parents and family. His brother was a successful attorney. He felt his mother's tears every time he got enough money to call her. Jake was supposed to be the one who succeeded. Jake was supposed to have the charmed life. And the only "charming" he had managed to do was to charm that snake of an agent, who did him in. He would *love* to choke her, yes he would.

Jake's little dream sequence was interrupted as he came abruptly to the bottom of the staircase. It was steamy and damp, down here, like all the health clubs he had once been able to afford. Turning down the hall marked "HEALTH CLUB - TRUTH SPA," he opened the glass doors to find himself in a small lobby area. There was no one behind the desk, but on the counter was a sign that said, "Take your key, find your locker, and dress down to your towel. Keep your valuables with you. Thank you. The Management."

"What the hell is this?" Jake thought, as he relocated the single key strung on a loop of elastic that had been provided with his book. He knew this drill. Looping the elastic around his wrist, he pushed open the swing door to find rows and rows of lockers. Locating his number, he opened up the locker and saw further instructions. "Leave your clothes here, dress down to your towel, and proceed to the hot tub. Please shower first. Take your valuables with you."

"My valuables? That's a f*%king laugh. Ha!" thought Jake, remembering his only valuables were hung between his legs, as the bitch whore agent had so many times reminded him. Undressing, Jake wrapped the towel around himself. He still had the remains of his gym body, and a faint reminder of a washboard stomach, although not clean shaven like when he was doing underwear print ads.

"The public don't like no fuzz," the agent used to tell him, so he scraped his naturally furry chest with a razor until it was raw. At least he didn't have to do that anymore. Whoever heard of a man shaving the hair off his chest, unless you were a competition bodybuilder? Jake could not stop thinking about the agent. That was the one thing the Subway Brigade had done for him. All their adventures had finally relieved him of the constant harangue of the past. Now, alone again, the nasty spirits once again reared their ugly heads.

Fortunately, Jake located the showers. He washed with the scented soaps, shampoos and conditioners, reminiscent of the great hotels he used to be able to afford. The warm water beat against his body, and reminded him of the realities of having a body, being touched, caressed. These things he sorely missed since his floating address escapade began.

Out of the shower, Jake followed the signs to the HOT TUB. The entire place was shrouded in a hot-steam mist, and the gurgling sound of the tub was the only hint he had that he had finally found his destination. As he approached, the air cleared a little and he beheld a large spa, with several over-the-hill men in various reposes.

With nimble steps, Jake tested the water. It was scalding. "OOOO" and he quickly pulled his foot back out.

"So come in, so you'll get used to it!" Jake saw a mouth moving on one of the men, but no other movement. However, the accent was definitely New York Jewish. Jake recognized these accents from his dialect classes, and also his family members who had decided to remain in New York when Jake's folks came out to California.

"California, the land of opportunity," Jake mused to himself, thinking of the cardboard boxes he used to steal to provide some shelter for himself on damp LA nights. Dialect classes. Another one of the lousy extravagances the bitch had talked him into. Now, when was he going to play an old Jewish man? Not until he was one himself, he analyzed, and even then, not with that stupid accent.

"Mind your own business. He'll come in when he wants." A black man with salt and pepper graying hair mouthed the words. Then he opened his eyes and looked at Jake. "Hey, guys, this is a young one."

The Jewish man cracked his eyes open and said, "Tch. Tch. Tch. So young to be here."

"Callase! I'm trying to get some sleep. I gotta get outa here soon, comprende?" These words came from an old Hispanic man, and the accent was distinctly Mexican-American. "We all have to end up here sooner or later."

"Sooner, later, who the hell knows," added the Jewish man. "Is it hot enough in here? I'm schwitzing like a pig!"

"Zo, like a schwein das schwitzing. Zo gehen Sie aus! Stop complainink and get out! We're tired of hearing it." This outburst came from a stout man with many chins. The German accent made Jake shiver. It was something he never got used to. Germans.

"Mind your bizness! Noone asked you! If it wasn't for yous murdering Nazis, I could've had my father's clothing business in Berlin! But you stinking Nazis took it away from me. Killed my whole family, that's what you did! Go to hell. I watched my mother, father, aunts, uncles and sisters die. But what did you do? You stood by while the Gestapo shoved us in the ovens. Go to hell. You're the cause of my life, sheisskopf! Go to hell. I would only hope the same thing would happen to you. You'd like it if someone stole your bizness, everyting you had? You'd like it if your whole family was killed? I couldn't do nothing with my life because of what you did to me. Shut up and Go To Hell!"

"It's ganz hundert years ago this happened. You tink I did it? I did nothing. What was my father going to do? You tell me. If he said anything, my whole family would die too. Is that what you want?"

"It vouldn't be so bad." Obviously something had struck a chord with the Jewish man. These hates, these hates that never go away, Jake thought to himself. Look at them still arguing after all these years. But the fact was that Jake had the same feelings. His parents would never buy a German car. They had skipped Germany on their all-around Europe tour. And that took some doing. Jake recalled them trying to find a tour group that was *not* going to stop in Germany.

"Shut up. Shut up. *Ganze zeit!* All the time you sit in the tub and tell me vats happened to you is my fault. I vasn't even there. I had nothink to do with it. Don't blame me for your problems. My father told me vat was happening. You forget that, no. You conveniently forget that Germany vas in the worst depression possible because of vat the Jews did. You controlled the money. You were responsible for the downfall of the economy. Dat's vat Hitler promised, to save the economy!"

"So, by stealing from the Jews he saved the economy? So it wasn't so bad burning six million in the ovens, as long as the economic policy was good? Are you crazy? What do you want me to believe? Go to hell. You're a murdering Nazi. That's why my life is shit. You think it vas only the Jews, you Kraut bastard? Wake up! It vasn't only the Jews, it was the blacks, the schwartzes.

The lazy bums didn't do a damn thing to help. They should never have let them in the first place. A whole continent those schwartzes had to themselves. Why did they have to come to Europe and screw everything up?"

Jake was becoming rapidly nauseated by the conversation. The black man finally spoke up. "How would you like me to push your head down under the water for twenty minutes, man? Shut that Kraut mouth. Shut that Jew mouth! In fact, both of you shut up. Six million? Ha! That's a laugh. Ten million slaves died . . . died on the way over to the United States so we could make your goddam economic policy work. I never hear either one of you talk about that. At least when you burned in Auschwitz, it was over. You weren't slaves for two or three hundred years. They didn't lynch you, and rape your women. They gave you an education. That's why we can't get anywhere. You keep us down on the floor here! You wanna know who's to blame for MY life. You stupid Krauts and Sheenys — Whitey, that's who. You stood by and watched us treated like animals. Serves you right, the ovens. You Whiteys are all alike."

"Callase! Callase, I'm tryin' to get some esleep here. Talk, talk, talk, you all talk about what's going on? Did any one of you get your land ripped off. The land of my great ancestors was ripped and stripped by the European Spanish bastards. We had a simple life. We survived. You stupid European thieves came and stole our land, raped our women, brought disease and sickness to our land. Who's to blame? Callase, all of you! You are all to blame. Every place you touch turns to crap. You touched Africa, it turned to crap. You touched Hawaii. It turned to crap. You touched America, it turned to crap. Each one of you is to blame for why I can't get a job. That's why I'm stuck here. It's so stinking hot. Is it too hot? I gotta get out soon. I can't estand it anymore." The man closed his eyes again.

Jake was dumfounded. This must be hell. Gurgling hot water filled with the most cynical, bitter, abusive men possible. What could be worse than this? He ventured a thought. "Do any of you have jobs?"

"Jobs? It's jobs you want to talk about, Mr. Neophyte! We can't get a job. The illegals take all the jobs. There are no more jobs! God only help me, I should have a job. My whole garment business they shipped down to Mexico. You see that? I can't even afford to put food on the table. Jobs."

"Calm down, man." The black man addressed the Jewish Man. "You don't want those jobs anyway. You want to work in a fast food dive, sling hash, do gardening? You pussy-whipped Sheeny! You can't get a job? You don't want a job!"

"I vouldn't have to get a job if your people weren't stealing the State blind on food stamps and welfare. Don't tell me to get a job, Mr. Shoepolish. What do you do for a living? Are you running for President? You're a lazy bum, like the Kraut said."

"Stop blamink me for dat whole ting." The German man was turning beet red, and Jake couldn't tell if it was from the hot tub or his temper. "I vasn't here ven you had dat schlavery, vas I? How can you blame me for dat? Dat's it. Blame the Kraut for everyting! Did somebody turn up the heat. It's too hot, in two minutes I'm getting out!"

Jake ventured another thought directed to the German man. "Well, if you live in the United States now, you accept all the benefits, right? You use the roads, you use the schools, you use the hospitals, you vote, right?"

"So vat. I pay my taxes, too."

Jake summed up. "Well if you accept all the benefits of a place, shouldn't you accept its burdens too? I mean, that 'I wasn't there' attitude really doesn't fly. Whatever's wrong, isn't it up to all of us to fix it?"

"And what do you do for a living, Mr. No-Good on the Street?

You live off charity? You get health care from the State? Who are you to talk, Mr. Big Man? Mr. Welfare, like all those schwartzes."

"Hey man. I gotta job, no thanks to you." Then the black man turned towards Jake. "And you. Practice what you preach. What did you do for the black man? Attend a couple of Apartheid rallies at college while I was being denied admission? What kind of crap is that? You Whiteys are all alike. All bullshit, no action. It's getting hot as hell in this place. I gotta get out soon."

Jake wanted to say something but he thought better of it. Besides, he didn't have a chance. The Mexican guy started talking. "Hey, what are you guys talking about. You mad because we take jobs you say belong to you, si? You live on MY land. You stole this land from us. Give me my land back and you can have your job at McDonalds. You're all a bunch of lying hypocrites!"

"At least your people weren't slaves, Beano." The Black man, shifted his position in the gurgling of the tub. "They stole us from our land. You think we can get it back?"

"Señor ghetto! You think I can get my land back? We owned it all, North America, South America, Mexico, Central America. The Aztecs, Incas, Mayans and the Great tribes. Now we live in shacks in Tijuana, with cholera and tetanus for neighbors. You don't got it bad. At least I got an excuse."

"Scuse, schmoos. All of yuhs are stoopid joiks. Okay? Attitudes like Mr. 'Sheeny-every-other-word' over here. That's what keeps us down. There will always be anti-Semitism. None of yuhs will ever let it go. That's why we have to be on our guard every day. Why did they let the Krauts in? We won the war, didn't we, fuh Godsakes! Oy, I'm schwitzing like a pig here. I'm getting out in two seconds."

"Forty acres and a mule, and that's supposed to make everything all right. You think you got it bad, Jew-Boy! At least your skin's the right color. Try walking down the street with black skin. Hell, I can't even get a taxi if I want it. You can't undo two or three hundred years of oppression with a few stinkin' laws on the books. We can't even get a decent education."

"Zo schtop zelling drucks to dose kits. Mit the druks, mit the crack, mit the guns. You tink dats goink to get you places? No vonder it's schtill the same after tree hundert years. You tink dis is our fault? Did someone turn up dis heat? It's chokink me!"

"You should talk, Mr. Hitler. Don't listen to him. You'll end up in the ovens, that's his solution for everyting. You got no place to talk. *Six million! Six million! Murderer!* It's a thousand degrees in here, I'm gonna get out right now."

Jake closed his eyes and leaned back his head as the bubbling and the Blame Game litany melded into one. It seemed like it went on for hours. But there was something about the too hot water which paralyzed him from moving, Instead, he just sat there and listened.

"So, man. Why don't you have a job." The black man turned directly towards Jake, and soon only gurgling was heard and steam was seen.

Jake thrust his eyes open with a start. "Well . . ." and Jake commenced on his well worn story about the bitch agent, and the sparkling career cut short.

"She must have been Jewish," said the black man. "All those Jewish agents take everything you have, and leave you with nothing." Jake was not going to offer that he, too, was Jewish. He soon realized that his story had added absolutely nothing to the conversation.

"She was probably black," said the Jewish man. "The schwartzes are all the same. They fill you with drugs, and take your money."

"Vas are you sayink here? She was Jewish, she vas black. So

she made his life miserable. Dats vat dey do, dem Jews and schwartzes!"

"Shut up, you filthy Nazi! She probably drove a goddam Kraut car like a Mercedes or a BMW. You know they used slave labor from the concentration camps during the war to build those cars! Are you happy you got such cheap labor? I hope you choke. God, it's getting hot in here. I'll get out in two minutes."

"Well, amigo, she's driving around on my land, no matter what kind of car she has, comprende? Every step you take, compadre, it's on *my* land. Dios mio! It's muy caliente. I gotta get out soon."

And the harangue went on and on. And as the drone of the tired old men continued, it slowly dawned on Jake that, no matter how hot or uncomfortable this stinking, over-chlorinated, hell-fire pool got, these men were not moving – *ever!* Each blamed the other for his inaction, and one-hundred percent of their time was taken up with excuse after excuse for why they weren't doing anything with their own lives and who *else* was to blame. But they all had one thing in common: none took any personal responsibility for their own situations . . . it was always somebody else's fault.

Jake flashed on all his self auditing sessions at his "Know Yourself" seminar where he rationalized that it was his dysfunctional family to blame for where he was. His mother and father fighting, his father's failures in business, his mother's failure at marriage, his brother's successes becoming his own failures, and most of all, his latest rationale: THE AGENT DID IT. Jake was now truly nauseous. It WAS too hot in the tub, damnit! It was disgusting, it was the pinnacle of do-nothingness, of words instead of deeds. It was paralysis, it was boredom and it was the height of not taking responsibility for your own life.

Finally able to stand it no more, Jake opened his eyes and bounded up. He was alert, as it a great veil had been lifted from his eyes. The steam cleared, and the colors became vibrant. He scanned panoramically the sad story in the Hot Tub. The Jewish man who couldn't relinquish his terrible past; the Mexican man who blamed everything on the involuntary cessation of his ancestral lands; the black man who blamed everything on the Jews and Whiteys; and the German man who blamed everyone else, and took no responsibility for the occurrences in his homeland. Jake spat as he announced, "Good-bye, Gentlemen. I'm getting out."

"And where are you going, Mr. Big Shot? To find a job?" All the tub echoed in gurgles and laughter.

"To find my life again," muttered Jake, not wanting to waste one more breath on the quarantined quartet. Jake bent over to pick up his towel as he left. He smiled to himself as he stooped that the sight of his "smiling" toochas facing toward the tub crowd was about as good as any exit line he possibly could have rehearsed.

16 - COMING OF AGE IN EAST L.A.

Norma was afraid of being alone in this place. It was a new feeling. She didn't exactly know why, she was so used to being alone, having to do everything herself. From the beginning she always felt alone. Not learning English from her Spanish-speaking family right away was one reason. Going to school where everything sounded like gobbledygook for the first couple of years was another. Gracias a Dios that she had a head on her shoulders.

She was brought up in the barrio in East Los Angeles and barely made it to school and back safely. Of course, two other brothers hadn't been so lucky. Her oldest brother had been caught in crossfire from rival gangs in the area, and just when she and her family were recovering that tragedy, her youngest brother overdosed on crack cocaine. Fortunately, her other brothers and Norma seemed to get through the chaos unscathed. However, her parents were permanently scarred from the deaths. Her mother always cried, thinking that things would have been better had they stayed in Mexico.

Norma's parents eeked out a living, her mom cleaning houses and her father doing odd jobs . . . even joining the illegals on the streets. Thank God for the amnesty. Mr. and Mrs. Jardines stood in line at the Federal Building for six days when that occurred and finally got their green cards. Three years later, when Norma was fourteen, all of them received citizenship.

All these thoughts raced through Norma's head as she went down the hall. "What did my book say?" she said to herself, confused at the big mansion and the lack of comrades. Opening her steno pad she read the words aloud, "READ THE SCRIPT. In search of the Niñita." She wondered what that meant. The literal translation was "In search of the little girl." She slipped the steno pad back into her bag, now redressed in the old English dress she had originally worn, and continued down the hall quickly. "Curiouser and curiouser," she said, feeling like Alice about to eat the mushroom.

She turned the corner and saw a red light blinking over a door. Approaching cautiously, she read the sign under the light. "QUIET PLEASE. VIDEOTAPING."

"Where am I?" was just about to come out of her mouth when a buzzer went off, the light stopped blinking and the metal door swung open. Tentatively, Norma ventured through the door.

She had seen a Television studio before. At KMEX in Los Angeles, she had done a Spanish version of the Story of Thanksgiving, so she knew a little about what she saw. There was a gallery of risers where the audience sat, but no audience. There were two cameras on the floor with cameramen, and various other tekkies busying themselves around the studio. In the center of the studio floor was a cast, teleprompters, and a director . . . all the necessary accoutrements for a TV studio. Most of the cast was older than Norma, and evidently they had known each other for some time. The taping was obviously between takes.

"Niñita! There you are! We've been waiting for you! Didn't your agent tell you to be here at . . . oh, well, never mind, you're here now. SHE'S HERE, TIM!" A woman with very short white hair, dressed smartly came over to Norma and took her gently by the arm. "You're perfect! SHE'S PERFECT, TIM!" Norma was being ushered quickly somewhere.

"EVERYONE! QUIET EVERYONE! This is our Niñita!" Norma was being introduced to the cast. A friendly cacophony of "Hi's" and "Hellos" burst out of the cast, but they soon turned back to whatever they were doing.

"I'm Sheelah, S-H-E-E-L-A-H, the Assistant Producer of this soap. Whoops, excuse me. *Daytime drama.* We're not supposed to call them Soaps anymore, the non-detergent sponsors get their panties in a wad. We've got to get you to wardrobe and makeup. Did you get your changes?"

"Changes?" This was Norma's first word. Although she was flabbergasted, she tried to play along. Changes to what? One thing. Norma could fit in anywhere. It was one of the tools she had to develop in her situation.

"Never mind. Here's the new script with the changes, on the blue pages. Now, you'll be able to read off the teleprompter, but you'd better go over your lines while you're in wardrobe and makeup. I'M COMING, leave me alone!" Sheelah was distracted as she pointed Norma to the door marked "WARDROBE". "Listen for your call. You'll be in scenes 20, 21 and 22 today. You're PERFECT!" And patting Norma on the shoulder, Sheelah was off.

Norma walked through the wardrobe door in a daze. "Oh there you are! I'm Ricky, actually Ricardo." A slight, very good looking, obviously gay wardrobe man was standing in front of her. He reminded Norma very much of someone, but she couldn't put her finger on who. She just knew she liked him.

"Isn't that funny? You meet someone who reminds you of someone you like and you automatically like them." Norma made this observation to herself, and allowed Ricky to take her hand to the wardrobe racks.

"Say, you *are* perfect for this part. Who's your agent?" Ricky didn't care. He was already dressing Norma in his mind for this part. "Now, you're a fifteen year old Hispanic girl who lives in the barrio in Los Angeles."

"Good," thought Norma, smiling to herself. "At least I have *something* to draw on." But it sounded like her real life.

Ricky pulled a Catholic school girl's uniform out of the rack and held it up to Norma. "That's perfect. You're supposed to be going to Our Lady of Precious Blood Middle School and I think this will do just fine."

Norma had never worn a real school uniform. In reality she had been forced to go to public school because Catholic school cost so much money and her parents could not afford it. But she knew plenty of girls from the neighborhood who had attended Ramona Convent when she was a small girl in East L.A. so at least she knew something about it.

"Put down that script, and try these on," Ricky gushed. He knew that he'd have a perfect match for Niñita with Norma in these clothes. Norma obeyed and went behind the drape. Mysteriously her Old English dress had again disappeared, and she hadn't noticed. She was back in her subway clothes again.

"Curiouser and curiouser," again thought Norma, as she donned the "Our Lady" duds. She emerged and Ricky stood her in front of the three-way mirror, where three beautiful fifteen year-old Catholic School girls stared back at Norma.

"PERF, HONEY, PERF!" Ricky was pleased with his work. Don't forget your Script!" Ricky brought Norma out to the door again and told her, "Go into makeup. You'll love Alana, she's great!"

"NARDO!" The revelation shot across Norma's mind. Ricky reminded her of Nardo. That's why she liked him so much. All that creative talent and that great eye for fashion and design. Norma quickly went back out into the studio and located the room labeled "MAKEUP". More sure of herself, she pushed in. A short-haired woman on a cellular phone turned around and waved her to sit in the chair. The woman was obviously busy on the cell phone, which she crooked in her neck, and continued waving Norma in. "Alana?" Norma ventured. The woman smiled broadly and vigorously shook her head "yes." She never stopped her phone conversation. She placed Norma in the makeup chair in front of the bulb-studded mirrors. Norma was temporarily blinded.

Alana pulled back Norma's hair. "But do you think that we should have men at this thing, too?" Alana was on the phone, and she wasn't going to let anything interrupt that conversation. She gently brushed Norma's hair back, and stuck a couple of hot rollers in the bottom, just to give it some curl. "But I thought that this was a *women's* event." The hot curling iron was masterfully played through Norma's thick black hair, as soft ringlets were created around her face.

"Well, okay. Gay, Lesbian, Bisexual and Transgender, but I think it muddies up the works quite a bit." On cue Norma realized that Alana was a very masculine woman with a handsome face, wearing a smock, with telltale 501 Jeans sticking out the bottom. "I don't want this to turn into a drag show, if you know what I mean." Alana gently lifted Norma's face up into the lights. She began applying a matte finish pancake entitled "Aztec Gold" to the face. "Oh, I think we can get Holly Bonnefield to play. She always supports these events," as Alana leveled her face with Norma's to check for missed spots. "And she does a terrific job and brings a great crowd. So she's definitely in."

Alana applied only a hint of eye shadow, eyeliner and blush, remembering that Norma was supposed to be an innocent fifteen-year-old parochial school girl. "Yes, let's have Kitzie Blondell. He does a great show, he's not *over draggy*, and he'll bring all the guys in, anyway." Alana applied only a hint of mascara. Then Alan made a smiling face, emphasizing her cheeks like apples. Norma smiled, and Alana applied only a hint of blush. "No, you're right. We all have to stick together. We've got to have a diversity of the community represented, or we won't accomplish any of our goals." Alana pulled the hot curlers out of Norma's hair and did a quick brush. The hair was full and lovely.

Alana swung Norma's chair around and again leveled her face with Norma's. Still "crooking" the phone, she backed up and tilted her head from side to side, finally giving Norma the "perfection" sign by making a circle out of her thumb and forefinger. She removed the towel from Norma, patted her back, and walked her to the door. Norma heard the phone conversation trailing off. "Yeah, we'll just have to keep building it up. Somehow, we have to let the rest of the world know we're just like them, even though we're really *better!*" Alana laughed and waved. Norma reciprocated, picked up her still unread script and pushed out the door into the studio.

"There you are!" The man that Sheelah had called "Tim" was walking with a big smile across his face over to Norma. "We're just about ready for you, honey. Do you have any questions?" Norma, of course, had a trillion questions, but just decided to go with the flow. By now she had noticed that everyone was reading off the teleprompter anyway. "Good, no questions. You look fantastic, honey. Now, the setup is that you have been very upset at school, and the Head Priest is talking to you, trying to find out what's the matter. Here's your mark. When the Priest comes into the room, after he delivers his first line, I want you to turn away from him and face the camera and deliver your lines. We've already done scenes 21 and 22 with your stand-in so you won't have to do those. Don't worry. You still get paid." Tim laughed. "When you get to the last line, turn around to the Priest, but don't look at him before that."

Norma was placed next to a small chair in a very Spartan green room on the set. It looked like a private conference room in an old school, with a rickety old brown desk and not much else. "Ready on the set! And 5-4-3 (two silent beats)" and the director whispered "action."

Norma watched the doorknob turn, as the Priest entered the room. "Niñita. Niñita, my child. What is it that is bothering you? The sisters have told me that you have been so upset. Your grades have been dropping, you have become so quiet. You have dropped all your activities. Tell me, Niñita. What is it?"

Norma turned toward the camera and saw the teleprompter with "Niñita" on it. Taking a deep breath, and not moving a muscle in her face, she began reading. "I cannot tell you, Padre, I am too ashamed. I dare not tell you Padre, I will go to hell. Instead I have to keep this deep inside me and hide it until even I can no longer see it. But . . . but what of the confessional? What of holding this inside me when I have to go and tell my innermost thoughts, Padre. Will it be a sin also to hide it then?"

Norma was beginning to read the lines with deep conviction. Something inside her was awakening. A dark past life that only now fleeted through her mind. Little light flashes were beginning to shoot off in her brain.

"It is like I have no feeling left, Padre. When I think of this terrible thing, it is like I am frozen, and all the color has gone out of my life. If I thought I could get it back by telling you . . . someone. I cannot hold it inside much longer."

Padre: "Then you must tell me, Niñita. You must tell me in the confidence of the Priesthood what dark life haunts you so."

Norma had a knot in her stomach. Rationalizing, she immediately attributed it to stage fright, but knew in her heart that she long ago got over stage fright. As a matter of fact, she was fearless in front of any crowd, large or small. But something wasn't quite right. She knew it as she began reading further.

Niñita: "The music used to be great in my life, Padre. The songs used to excite me. And then one day they stopped . . . like a light was turned off. It was sunny that day, and my lungs hurt from playing outside so hard . . . softball I think it was. I had neglected to do my homework during lunch, which I normally did, so I went

153

to the library to finish it after school. I said good-bye to the girls who rode the bus with me, and told them I would walk home. It is not far, only a mile and a half or so."

Why was this script so familiar? Something about it. The knot in Norma's stomach grew and a lump began to form in her throat? What was the unknown fear? What vile beast was being scraped from her deepest soul? She did not know yet. She tried to swallow the lump, but it grew only larger. Catching her breath, she continued:

"The library is very quiet and lonely after school, Padre. Only the sisters are there and they are very quiet. When I had finished most of my homework, I did not want to take my books home on the walk home, so I decided to put them in my locker. To get to my locker from the library, I always take the South Stairwell, upstairs to the second floor."

"I gathered up my books and my back pack and went out the library door, smiling at Sister Theresa as I went. I went to the South Stairwell, and opened the door. It is very heavy, Padre. I barely got inside and began climbing the long wrap-around stairs."

As if on cue, tears began streaming from Norma's eyes. She knew this script. Was it from a book she'd read before, or a play, or a movie? What was this strange familiarity that scared her? Norma began to feel she had almost learned the script without reading it. Her eyes strayed momentarily from the teleprompter.

"I thought I heard something as I reached the first landing and said, 'Hello' but no one answered, so I kept climbing. When I reached the second floor landing, I tried to open the door but it was locked. All my books fell and made a crash on the floor."

"As I was on the floor, picking up my books, I heard something and looked up a little."

A stage direction on the teleprompter said, "Niñita begins to tear up" but by now Norma needed no prompting. The script was revisiting a dark moment of her own. A dark horror that she buried so deep, even she forgot it. Norma's own heart began to pound with fury. Her eyes were so blurred by tears, she couldn't read the teleprompter, but told the story, as if by some channeled memory.

"I saw . . . I saw a pair of big dirty black boots and jeans. When I looked up, it was the face of a man I had never seen. A cruel looking man with a beard who smiled at me and said, 'Are you locked in little girl?' I tried to run down the stairs, but he caught me by the hair, and I started screaming Padre."

Norma was sobbing uncontrollably by now. For by now, she realized that this was *her* story. The teleprompter held the precise script of the event she had hidden so deep, even from herself … so deep, it had stopped her from being a child. So deep, it made her into an adult in one instant. It had crushed her emotions, and made her want only outward perfection, with a complete abandonment of all inside. Norma was not reading anymore. She was overcome with terror, hate and fear. She looked no longer at the teleprompter. All the actors and the director stared at her, dumbstruck, believing this to be the greatest scene ever played on daytime drama.

"He pushed his hand over my mouth, and I felt something cold and hard pointed against my neck. 'Shut up, or I'll cut you, little girl. I'll cut that beautiful face.' And he pushed me down Padre. And . . . and he pushed me down on the stairs. He was too strong, Padre. I couldn't push him off. I tried. Oh, yes Padre, I tried so hard, but I could not breathe. I could not say 'no.' And then he pushed up my dress and it . . . hurt . . . hurt so much Padre, but I was numb. Why could I not scream? Why could I not help myself? Why was I not stronger? I tried to stop him, Padre! I tried so hard!"

Norma's head fell into her hands. Blurry-eyed, she looked back to the Padre, but was too guilty to keep her eyes fixed on him. She could hardly breathe the next lines.

"He stole from me Padre! He stole my childhood! He stole all my feeling! From then on, I could feel nothing, I could do nothing. I was too ashamed to tell my parents, too guilty that somehow I was to blame for not screaming louder. Guilty that I was too weak to overcome him." Norma broke down.

Padre: "Come, my child. And allow yourself to be a child once more. Only this way will you rediscover your feelings. You will overcome him, but not in the way you think. This is a terrible event that is over, and you must allow time to help you. It is hard for you to see now, but you must know this: God gives us our lives and it is not for any man or incident to take any part of that away; only God can take it away. What has happened to you is a horrible thing, but do not let it define your life. You have allowed this bad event to rob you of your childhood, your feelings and your insides and that cannot be. Now you must allow yourself to heal, and be whole again, to feel again; now you must succumb to God's wishes – that you live your whole life. He is holding it out for you and you must reach for it, and accept it.

Norma turned and embraced the Priest, sobbing. He put his hand on her head and said, "Now you will let the river flow again. Now you will let the feelings happen. Now you will live your complete life again. Only this way will you mature. Only this way will you travel the full extent of life's highways."

Norma heard the music swell up, and barely heard Tim yell, "CUT!" Tim came running over to Norma and hugged her. Norma could see that he also had tears in his eyes and the rest of the cast was whooping and hollering for Norma, applauding. "That was so real," cried Tim. And Norma couldn't figure out whether the cast was applauding the performance or the fact that she had finally come to terms with the ghost who stole her youth. A sense of warmth and freedom poured over her, as she rested her head on Tim's shoulder. The tears were real, and as each one fell, so did the dark shroud that had enveloped Norma's life to that time. She was alive again. She equaled one.

17 - LAND'S END

The quintet had made their way back to the study by now, one by one. But the group was extremely quiet, not as lively as they had previously been coming out of the masquerade ball. As they sat silently on the large leather couches, the main door creaked open, and a man came in wearing a pin on his lapel labeled "Librarian." In his hand he held a great book entitled, "Who's Who?"

Makeba spoke first. "What's that book you're carrying?"

"It's the book telling you who you are, but no one is permitted to see it. It is kept under seal and in a safe place. I didn't know you were here, so I'd better go and put it back."

The Librarian turned towards the door, but Jake got up and blocked his way. "I think we need to see that book, Sir."

Makeba jumped up. She had come this far. She wasn't going to leave without seeing what that Book had to say. The purpose of this trip is to find out who they were, and she wasn't about to give that up; for herself or any of her friends. The Librarian lunged for the old telephone on the desk, but Pearl grabbed onto it and held it. "Get it away from him!" yelled Makeba. "Grab that book!"

The Librarian began to yell, and Makeba and Jake put him in

the chair, while Nardo took Makeba's unraveled turban and tied his hands behind him, stuffing Pearl's handkerchief into his mouth. Makeba was shouting instructions. Norma grabbed the large gold leaf book and noticed that there was a book mark in it. The Librarian was putting up a noble struggle, but the quintet was intent on finding out what was written in that book about them. They had all come too far, worked too hard and waited too long for the quest to fail now.

"Are you comfortable at least?" asked Norma of the Librarian, and he grunted. Norma opened the book to the marked page, and on the top was written in gold "LOS ANGELES SUBWAY GROUP."

"Rip the page out and let's get out of here!" screamed Makeba. Norma carefully ripped the page out of the book, left it on the desk, and Jake held the great oak door open while Pearl, Norma, Nardo and Makeba streaked past and down the great hall to the double-helical staircase. They didn't see the Librarian easily pull himself out of his bindings, take the handkerchief out of his mouth and smile as he heard them run down the hall.

As they ran, they noticed in the lobby some newcomers who were first going to the masquerade ball. Norma remembered the group running out of the front door as they, themselves, had entered the mansion and experienced sort of a reverse déjà vu about the whole trip.

"So . . . Mizz big hero, Makeba," whispered Pearl to Makeba as the quintet clattered down the stairs and fumbled the front door open, noticing that the weather was extremely inclement, thunder, lightning and heavy rain. However, at the bottom of the stairs, in sort of an impressionistic blur stood their carriage with its corner lights blazing, and the driver holding open the door for them. Tearing down the stairs to the carriage, Jake and Nardo first helped the girls in, and no sooner had they landed on their seats, the carriage took off at a healthy gallop.

All sat and thought in silence and the carriage bumped furiously out toward the front gates. It was too dark in the carriage to read the page Norma had shoved into her bag. The group was once again in its Olde English garb, except, of course, for Pearl who was consistently the same. Norma felt like a great weight had been taken off her. She could feel deeply again. She could let all the emotions happen without stopping and not be so much a computer to help her hide her feelings. Jake felt that a new victimless life lay ahead of him and never again would he blame his troubles on third parties like those losers in the hot tub did. Nardo had resolved his very old fight with his father and realized that being a man had nothing to do with masculinity. Pearl sighed a sigh of relief in knowing that she could get along at a Maj game with anyone in the universe. It just took getting used to.

But it seemed that Makeba had undergone the most marked alteration. Makeba likened the just-past situation of tying up the Librarian to her fiasco at Berkeley. But now she was looking at it in a different way. Now she felt strangely comfortable with what she had done in her youth. She was the only one to cut the silence in the rattle and roll of the carriage. "You all know, at the time I did that, the Berkeley thing I mean, I felt it was the absolute right thing to do. We got kicked out, and I told myself I was proud, proud to fight for civil rights and my race. But I was only telling myself that. Inside, I was thinking 'I kidnapped a guy, tied him up, and set a state building on fire, and I'm a criminal.' But now, after this I know it's all a matter of perspective and context. Being a 'hero' only depends on who wins, and who writes the history books. I didn't write that book, so I guess I'm not a 'hero' in the eyes of most people."

"After this battle (after all we just tied someone up for the good of 'the cause'), I now know that, in context, what I did was right for me at the time. I know now that, given the same conditions, and given my same state of mind, and the times, I would do the same again because *it's part of who I am.* I thought I wouldn't do it now. I thought I wouldn't repeat it now with this maturity level, or these conditions. But, you see, I did repeat it for *our cause*. Because I *believe* in it. Therefore, it's all a matter of context and perspective. You call me a hero, Pearl, because of where we stand in relation to each other. Believe me, the authorities here wouldn't call me a hero. They'd turn me over to Scotland Yard, or whoever, as sure as I'm a strong Black American woman. I'm no longer embarrassed about getting kicked out of Berkeley. My statement is emblazoned as a part of my history, and I'm okay with the whole thing now." She stared out of the carriage. "Okay with it." Makeba could be eloquent if she wanted to.

The carriage had come out of the woods and was once again clattering over the water-glistening cobblestones. The rain had let up and the driver jumped out into the wet night street, opening the carriage door. "Land's End, mates," he said, pointing to a very compelling and warmly lit little Tavern, directly across the street from the noisy Saint Sabydus. The quintet shook hands with the driver. "Luck to ya!" he shouted and the carriage was off to pick up new voyagers. The quintet was glad to get into the warmth of the near-empty Land's End tavern. They all sat together on great couches in front of a cozy roaring fire, took off their outer cloaks and whatnot and drank warm spiced drinks.

Norma pulled the page from the gold book out of her bag and said, "Does anybody want to hear this?"

Of course, everybody was intent on hearing what the Book had to say. After all, that was the point of this whole fiasco: to find out who they were. "Read it, Norma." Nardo smiled at her. The group was fixated on her. She read:

NORMA IS NORMA AT LAST.

MAKEBA IS MAKEBA *AND* MONA LISA.

NARDO LOVES NARDO.

JAKE HAS RETURNED TO JAKE.

PEARL REACHES OUT.

"Cryptic messages," mused Makeba.

"But I think we all know what they mean," added Nardo. And so they did.

18 - NUMBERS

The loud bustle of the marble in the main library was echoing. "Quiet! Quiet please! Beings are attempting to study! Quiet!" The familiar ring of the Androgen was welcome fare to the group as they wended their way through the tables. Norma almost felt like Lot's wife as she turned to look at the great arch they had just emerged from. She shivered as she read "MYSTERY OF HISTORY" still emblazoned in large letters across the top.

Nardo looked at his R.O. He had earned a "Revelation" credit, as had each member of the group. Makeba had earned an additional credit for "Self Auditing" and Norma had earned an additional credit for "Recapturing Lost Time." Jake had earned a credit for "Self-Starting." Pearl had earned an "Old Dog New Tricks" credit. Each also had a new credit for "Team" ostensibly for the tying up the Librarian fiasco.

"Well, at least I finally got some credit for tying someone up," Makeba laughed at the irony of her situation. The R.O.s were still ticking away, and much time had been gained by the group for various earnings they had garnered during the Mystery of History Tour. The R.O.s read as follows:

| NORMA: | 12:30:22 | C8 |
| JAKE: | 10:22:01 | C7 |

PEARL:	10:45:56	C7
MAKEBA:	11:21:34	C7
NARDO:	9:54:04	C5

"What the hell is happening here," exclaimed Nardo. "I can't seem to get any credits or time! Why does everybody have more time and credits than I do?"

"You've got plenty of time," said Makeba, trying to appease him.

"Oh, yeah. You can say that because you have 11 hours and 7 credits. I only have 9 hours and 5 credits. I'll never get out of here. I'll end up at that work camp or whatever it is."

"Nardo, hush up. You will not." Norma put her hands on Nardo's shoulders and looked straight at him. "After all, we still aren't finished. We can't be. We all have to get twelve credits, or we can't go back to our Plane of Origin."

"Well, let's get going already." Pearl was ready to get this over with. "You wouldn't believe what happened to me in that last place!" Just at that moment, Pearl ran her tongue against the inside of her teeth and a delightfully sweet flavor filled her mouth. A little piece of Eve's kugel had stuck in her tooth, and she remembered how much she had enjoyed the Maj game.

"Last chance. Last chance." The voice of the Androgen popped through the drone.

"What do you mean, 'Last chance?'" said Jake.

"I mean that you only get three chances to do this, and this coming up is your last chance. So you'd better get going."

"And what happens if we don't make it?" ventured Nardo, still upset about his numbers.

"Well, you'll find out then." pontificated the Androgen. "Until then, stop wasting time, and get to your next task!" The Androgen turned. "Quiet! Puh-leese, quiet!"

"Well, where do we go this time?" asked Norma.

The Androgen turned back. "You can earn a lot of time and credits in 'WISHES, DREAMS, NIGHTMARES' but you also spend a lot of time on things there too, so you have to be careful. It's like your Plane of Origin. You eat and sleep there and, unlike the other two places so far, you live every minute each day. You spend more time, but you earn more time. As I say, it's more like your Plane of Origin. It's a big gamble, but judging from your R.O.'s, you'd better chance it. You don't have that much time left! Quiet!" The Androgen went back to his job.

"Oh great," said Nardo. "Just what I needed. To spend more time on things."

"Well, I for one think we should do it." Makeba was speaking now. "We've been fairly successful working together this far. And we can't fool around much more. Look at these things!" Makeba pointed to her R.O. still unsympathetically ticking away.

"I'm for it. Let's get going." Jake said. Everyone finally agreed, although Nardo agreed only grudgingly. He was still trying to figure out why his R.O. showed less time and credits than the others.

"There it is" said Norma, as she pointed to the great archway on the other side of the huge hall with the words, "WISHES, DREAMS, NIGHTMARES" arching over it. Judging by what the Androgen said, this was going to be the most difficult task, although each thought that the last one was pretty difficult.

"I'm ready for it, God only hopes it ain't walkin'!" shouted Pearl with verve, and the group began to file through the library tables toward the looming archway. When they reached the gaping hole, they all stared into the blackness. What the hell was out

165

there? Who knows? The quintet gave each other knowing looks and hooked elbows in one long line. Jake gave the high sign and with R.O.s ticking away, as a united front, they once again marched into the blinding white flash.

19 - PURPLE FARTS

The bus reminded Norma of those old Mexican buses she rode with her mother when she was a little girl in Mexico. Full of chickens and "purple farts" as her mother used to say, the bumpy bus was making her carsick. She looked outside as the rickety old vehicle barely chugged up the winding mountain road. "Where are we going?" she surprised herself out loud.

"God only knows. Thanks God we're not walking!" Pearl was used to these buses having ridden lousy, lousy buses for years in New York and prior to the subway being built in Los Angeles. As she looked around, she was gratified that the bus was full of humanoids and not flies and lizards. Pearl caught herself. "I liked ZeeZee and Lilah. I hope that tongue healed properly," she wished to herself. "She shouldn't have *anotheh* procedure!"

The bus was pulling into a wooded area, more on the flats now, and occasional wooden houses were popping up along side the road. Now and then there was a gas station or some kind of store. The bus stopped.

"This is where you get out!" he barked, looking in the rear view mirror towards the five.

"Us?" questioned Makeba, not wanting to move as she had finally acclimated her buns to the seat.

"Yeah, you. This is where your ticket takes you. If you wanna go further, you gotta spend more time." The driver was growing impatient. The group looked at each other and shrugging, reluctantly got up. Jake and Nardo helped the ladies again, and they piled off the bus. The bus flatulated, the gears ground, and off it went in a cloud of dust.

"Well." Nardo shook his head. "I guess it's not going to be first class this time!" Everyone agreed. As they turned they found themselves in front of a ramshackle old motel. The painted wooden sign was very cracked and peeled, but Nardo was able to make out the words, "The Launch Pad Motel." "I guess we're staying here."

The five then filed into what they thought was the office, a small room with a scratched-up counter, two wooden chairs, and some dried flowers on a little end table. Up on the wall was a sign that read "Room Rates, No Pets Allowed".

Daily Rates
Single: 45 minutes
Double: 60 minutes
Extra Bed: 10 minutes

Makeba boldly rang the bell on the counter. Nothing happened. She rang it again, this time repeatedly.

"Hold yur' damn horses, I'm comin', I'm comin' fer corns' sake!" A toothless wonder appeared from the door behind the counter. You couldn't tell whether it was male or female, but no one really wanted to find out.

Jake took the lead. "We're lookin' for some rooms."

"Well, lemme see yur' R.O.s Okay, yuh gots enough time. It'll be 45 minutes per person per night." The attendant was doing okay for not having any teeth to speak of .

"Wait a minute. You think I can't read?" Pearl's Judaism bolted out. "It says a double is 60 minutes – that's 30 minutes apiece . . . per night. Izzat right, or what?"

"I was thinkin' yud each have yur own room," said the scamming attendant. "Okay. How many do you want?"

"Two doubles and one extra bed." Norma was way ahead of the game. Turning toward the crowd she said, "That's all right, isn't it?"

"It's okay with me if it's okay with Jake," said Nardo, glad he could save a few minutes by doubling up.

"Fine," said Jake. "We'll double up and you ladies can triple up."

"I don't like no loud noises or music or nuthin'. No smokin' in the rooms, and keep yur TV's down. I don't want no trouble here!" She seemed to look straight at Makeba when she said that. Makeba, back in her turban and tight spandex pants didn't appreciate it, but Pearl headed her off at the pass.

"You don't ask for trouble, you won't get none," Pearl offered.

"Yuh gotta pay in advance for the first night, okay?" The group reluctantly agreed with the attendant, and the guys got 30 minutes deducted, while the girls got 23 minutes deducted each. "I'm giving yuh an extry minute, because yuh look so nice."

"Thank you, ma'am," said Norma, hoping she had gotten the gender correct.

"Well, now. Yur very welcome. Very welcome indeed. Now here's yur keys." She threw them on the counter. "You got the far cabins, numbers 4 and 5. Just call down here if yuh need anything." Before they could say anything else, the attendant smiled a very toothless smile and disappeared behind the swinging doors into a room where a T.V. was blaring.

The group was too tired to do anything. The bumpy trip and the whole ordeal at the Mansion was wearing on them. They actually felt tired and hungry, which was new to them. Since they had gotten to wherever they were, they hadn't felt the need to eat (except at the Banyan), and did so just when the occasion arose. Now they felt like sleeping and eating. Pearl's stomach was growling, and she kept envisioning the apotheosis of Eve's kugel in front of her.

"I'm famished. Where's the chow?" yelled Pearl.

"Well, I noticed a little market across the street. I guess we could go there and get something." Norma was trying to be helpful.

"Well, I'll go with you," Jake offered. "Why don't you others tell us what you want, and then go and check out the rooms . . . er cabins, I'm sorry," Jake corrected himself.

"What'll we use for money?" Nardo said.

"Looks like we'll have to spend our time here. Remember what the guy in the library said. We'd have to spend time and credits here. But we could make some back. Now what does everybody want?" Jake was getting very tired of buying time, and spending it.

The group finally decided on sandwich stuff, fruit and lemonades, if they had it. If not, do the best you can. As Norma stepped down from the office, she noticed a sign. "Mountain Ridge Talent Contest — Saturday Night — Grand Prize, 2 hours. All categories welcome."

"Hey. Look you guys. A talent contest. Why don't we enter

170

it?" Norma was fairly excited, especially since her triumph on the soap . . . daytime drama.

"Are yuhs kidding?" Pearl was not amused. "You think I'm going to play that clarinet again? Take a deep breath."

"I'm sorry. I guess it's a silly idea. Sorry I said anything." Norma recanted.

"Hey, but why not? We could sure use the time. I mean now that we have to buy everything. How good could the local talent be? I mean we *were* already in a band together." Nardo was anxious to earn some time and credits.

"Yeah," said Makeba. We *could* put something together. After all Norma sings, and I sang in a gospel choir and did African dancing. Nardo plays the flute, and sings in Spanish and we could fill in the rest. It's sure worth a try."

"I played the guitar a little in college. We really don't have many other choices," said Jake, who remembered that he was good on stage, and that he liked being drum major in Nardo's memory. "Why don't we do it?"

"I'll find out how to sign up," Norma offered. "Then we can have a meeting and see what we should do."

"CAN WE EAT FOIST?" Pearl was becoming insistent and the specter of the kugel was growing larger and larger. "Don't even think I'm gonna make with dat lousy clarinet again," commanded Pearl.

Laughing, Jake grabbed Norma's hand. "Let's go before they eat us." Jake and Norma took off across the narrow street, no sidewalks, just missing another "purple fart" bus roaring down the road.

"Well ladies . . . let's give this a try!" Nardo offered his elbows to Pearl and Makeba, which they gladly accepted. Unfortunately for Makeba, the spiked heels were back, fixed and in full force and they weren't doing too well on the gravel.

"Heah! I gotta pair o' walking shoes, very comfortable in my bag." Pearl reached in and brought out the shoes with the toes folded into the heels. The new Pearl had no problem sharing her last pair of shoes with Makeba who tried them on, holding onto Nardo for balance, and they worked. Good for Pearl. Her R.O. racked up another credit, this time for Selflessness, and some more time, but she didn't notice. Then the trio made off to Cabin 4 to see what they could see.

20 - MEDLEY IN BLACK AND WHITE AND BROWN

Actually, the sandwiches weren't too bad. What reeked was the combined smell of must, mildew and Pinefresh that permeated Cabin 4. The quintet was scarfing down the food, which was fresh.

"Ah yuhs sure about the talent tingdeah [thing there]?" Pearl was not happy, remembering the extensive marching in the band and that "hell hat no fury like a woman's corns!" or whatever that old saying was.

"Don't worry, Pearl. We'll be able to put something together. Besides, this town looks so small, there can't possibly be any good talent here." Nardo wasn't reassuring.

Pearl shuddered a little as she looked around Cabin 4 at the Launch Pad Motel. "OY VEY," she screamed inwardly. The bed was pure moosh, the pillows were damp from all the moisture in the air. "My hair must look like a cyclone," she feared, but turned just in time to see Makeba and her 'fro becoming more 'fro by the second. Now she had something to be happy about. Someone else was having hair trouble.

Pearl's eyes scanned over to the television set. "Toin it on?" she asked Norma who was sitting closest to the set. The set, very old, black and white, and with an almost oblong tube, had a bent wire coat hanger stuck in the top. Nardo recognized this as the antenna. They had used this method in the Philippines many times.

The TV whined as Nardo pulled the "ON" knob, and then he spent a couple of minutes trying to make a picture out of the snow. When something finally came into view, it was obviously a public access station or the equivalent, with a talent show. "Hey, now we can see what the competition's like," Nardo exclaimed. Pearl was very happy there were no clarinets on the show.

As the amateur hour plodded on, Jake said, "You know. We can do at least this well." Jake knew approximately ten chords on the guitar. If they could get a few more instruments, Norma and Nardo could sing, and maybe Makeba. "We could even find something for Pearl to do," Jake verbalized, after telling his idea to the rest of the crowd.

"Don't gimme no moah clarinet, oveh deah [over there]!" Pearl quickly added, "You know, I had a friend in the Salvation Army. A Shiksa of course, but they needed tambourine players for the band. So I learned."

Nardo was duly impressed. Pearl knew an additional instrument, although he couldn't imagine what could be made of a guitar, flute, tambourine, two Spanish voices and a Gospel singer. Oh, well. They'd just have to do the best they could.

"Well, we'd better get something going. We're gonna have to get instruments." Norma was still good at calculating what was next, in what order and the priority thereof.

"Let's ask the lady without the teet!" Pearl figured she would know. Finishing up their un-gourmet meals, they cleaned up, and made the trek back to the front office.

"Are ye performers? Well whaddya know? We had some

174

geetar players here before, and some o' them Mexican trumpet players yesterday. I think they're gonna be in that talent contest, too! Er mebbe they're jes checkin' out thee competition!" The toothless lady lisped her way through a short speech about the "famous" people who had stayed at the Launch Pad, and then, with a brand new respect for the quintet, told them how to get to the local music store.

Of course, they had to take the Purple Farts bus for about a mile, and there was actually a little town there. The music store was really a pawn shop, and the quintet was sad and happy. Sad that the selection of instruments was poor; happy that they wouldn't have to spend much time (from their RO's) on buying the stuff, it being used equipment and the like.

As they entered the little shop, they noticed that every single inch of space, from floor to ceiling was being occupied by some formerly pawned item. Fortunately for them, many of them were musical instruments. Jake happened to notice a stunning sunburst guitar in the window. He couldn't make out the identification markings (it wasn't a Martin!), but the fact that it had six strings, a neck, a body and a sound hole was awe-inspiring. It was almost impossible to get through the narrow aisles of the store without knocking something down.

Pearl quickly located a cardboard box full of tambourines. She looked for one that fit her hand easily, was worn on the sides, and that didn't have sharp edges on it. "Oy d'pain," she thought as she remembered the blisters. As she stood there, Makeba came over and picked up a tambourine and began beating out some African rhythms, and humming a West African chant that she had learned in her Music and Dance of Ghana class (extension) at UCLA. Of course, she got into UCLA Extension using the name Makeba because the black mark from the Sixties had been under the name "Mona Lisa Edwards."

"That sounds *great*, Makeba!" said Jake, very surprised.

"Yeah. Maybe you could teach me some a' dem riddems deah," Pearl said, also extremely impressed.

"Well, that would be good. Two tambourines is very original, as long as we have a rhythm instrument and melody instruments." Nardo was more musician than anyone except perhaps Norma who could also read music. But Nardo knew how to *interpret* music, having had to copy the styles of the many drag divas. Along with Melissa Etheridge, Diana Ross, Shirley Bassey, even Eydie Gorme were also among the strong impressions of Nardo. In addition to giving him a vibrant sense of stage presence, it also gave him a durable sense of musicality, a trait that the quintet would definitely need in the coming time. Finally, Nardo had a great flair for the dramatic, and having worked with decorators and costume designers, knew instinctively what looked good, although how he was going to dress the ample Makeba and Pearl for stage . . . he didn't know. "Oh, well. Fiddle dee dee. I'll think about that tomorrow," Nardo laughed to himself, confident in the knowledge that whatever happened, he could help this group look and sound much better than it really was.

Jake was at the guitars. He hadn't played in such a long time. Since fraternity days, anyway. And the last guitar he had was filled nicely to the brim with shaving cream by one of the pledges in ZBT, Zeta Beta Tau, or as it was commonly referred to, "Zion Banking and Trust." But he took the guitar down and was able to get through the nine or ten chords he knew well (G, A, C, D, E, sometimes F, A minor, D minor, E minor). He also remembered his "Puff the Magic Dragon Fingerpick" which was very impressive at Beer Busts when the Alpha Phi Gammas (best Jewish Sorority House on campus) were there. Anyway, with the good looks and the fingerpick, he usually scored. That conquest, however, was far from his mind now, concentrating mainly on what the heck this group was going to do for an act to win the "TIME PRIZE." He looked sullenly at Makeba and Pearl banging the hell out of their tambourines. Nardo had picked up a flute, but even that sounded better since he had brushed up in Memorabilia not too long ago.

"Norma should just sing, without an instrument," Nardo said, blowing warm air through his flute. She's the prettiest, and she should really *front* the group. And for the guys, we should let Jake sort of be the resident "hunk". We need some kind of sex appeal in the group. Makeba caught herself prior to extolling the virtues of the Black Miss South Los Angeles Pageant she had won at the age of sixteen. Fortunately, Mona Lisa came to her rescue, oxygen came to her brain, and she realized objectively what Nardo was saying. Put the ornaments in the front.

"All right. But then I get to sing some of my Gospel riffs," Makeba staked her claim. Then, looking at Pearl she said, "and I am going to teach Pearl a few interlocking African rhythms on the tambourine to give us some kind of soul and beat." Although she spoke with assurance, she didn't really know how Pearl's Mount Sinai rhythms would match the Ghanaian rhythms from her class. But, Lord love you, she was willing to try. Pearl's lower lip stretched.

The owner of the pawn shop was also missing a good portion of his teeth, and smiling seemed to be one of his favorite things. As he came over to Pearl and Makeba, he said, "Kin I help ye?"

"Whaddya want fur dis?" Pearl blurted out. Pearl held out the bashed-in tambourine.

"Oh that's at least forty-five minutes," slurped the pawnbroker.

Pearl grabbed Makeba's tambourine and unceremoniously tossed both hers and Makeba's back into the cardboard box. "Ah yuhs crazy? Do we look like Rockefelleh, heah? We wanna tambourine, not a Tiffany tiara!"

"Well, how much do ye' think it's worth?" The pawnbroker bit on Pearl's wisdom.

"Well, you can see the whole ting's worn down . . . it's very used." Pearl didn't let on that this *added* to the value of the instrument. Makeba turned away from the deal so she wouldn't laugh. "Ten minutes."

"Ten minutes? I lent more on it than that!" The pawnbroker was exasperated.

"Come on, Makeba." Pearl grabbed Makeba's hand and pulled her away.

"All right. Yer making me lose money on this deal! Ten minutes it is!" The pawnbroker relented.

"For both!" Pearl wasn't finished yet.

"BOTH! What are ye trying to do? Put me out of business?!"

"Look. Dis is used stuff over heah. You tink I'm made of money, I mean *time*?" Pearl was not about to let this deal go. "Besides we have other tings to buy heah."

"Are yuhs all together?"

"Dat's right. We got a lot of poichuses [purchases] to make heah?" Pearl was in the best form ever.

"All right. Ten minutes fer both, but yer robbin' me blind." The pawnbroker grabbed the tambourines and slammed them on the counter. Pearl squinted at Makeba with that "all knowing, stick with me kid" air.

The picky-strummy sounds of Jake's guitar wafted through the room as the now mellow tones of Nardo's flute and the pretty soprano of Norma's voice attempted "Blowin' in the Wind" with Norma's tiny little Mexican-American accent. Nardo was now playing an octave lower and the sound was a lot warmer than the steampipey march sound he was used to.

"Hey, that sounds pretty good," said Makeba who grabbed a tambourine and began humming some soulful harmony. Pearl just played one of her "Hadassah" tambourine rhythms and, lo and behold, it created a nice interlocking rhythm with Makeba's. It wasn't the New York philharmonic, not even Peter, Paul and Mary, or even close. But the quintet was once again making music together as they had in the Marching Band. And there was something about the music that pointed to that little history of teamwork . . . something.

21 - THE BLUE BARN

Nardo was fairly used to what he was seeing. It was a large old blue barn, with paint predictably cracking. The insides had been gutted and formed into the local recreation hall. This community was too small for Mooses or Elks or whatevers, so some old lady died and deeded the Blue Barn to the Township and it became their City Hall, Metropolitan Opera House and whatever else they could think of. In fact, two sides of the large barn had been recently painted, the other two still showing signs of fossil antiquity.

These were the types of halls that Nardo was used to doing his drag shows in. Sometimes, a shower curtain was the only excuse for a dressing room. Sometimes the microphone was old and dented from years of hand-me-down use. The sound systems were buzzy, farty and crackly. But they all had two things in common . . . a chintzy silver mylar curtain backdrop and a mirror ball. For these people this was glamour, and Nardo remembered many a night of silvery excitement when he would win a drag show. To him it was show business, and could have been La Scala for all he knew or cared.

It was clear that Nardo had the most experience in this type of live entertainment. After Pearl had worked her magic at the pawn shop, the troupe located a second hand store. This, of course, was a second home to Nardo who fashioned all of his costumes from second hand clothes, a little ric-rac, some sparkly lamay, and the like. So the entire troupe had a "look" created by the House of Nardo. He managed to get black pants for himself and Jake which fit okay, black skirts for Makeba and Pearl and white button shirts for the four of them. Fortunately, he had located a glittery tight dress which fit Norma handily. With a little stitch-witchery, Nardo dolled it up, and Norma made a formidable "front" for the group.

Norma had picked up the application for the talent contest. They would have one shot and one shot only. One song. Norma thought this to be a Godsend since the group only knew one song. Back at the Launch Pad Motel, in the Pinefresh cabin, the group had practiced "Blowin' in the Wind" *ad nauseum*. Makeba, Jake and Nardo managed some simple harmonies at several points. All in all, the group was basically in tune, having had the Marching Band experience to spruce them up. Nardo had coaxed Norma to sing a little louder and use more of her chest voice. It was far more ample than anyone had expected. Of course, at selected moments, and the right ones, Makeba threw in a "soulful" lick, and as a whole the quintet got the thing to sound not quite unprofessional.

Nardo borrowed Pearl and Makeba's makeup so they didn't have to waste any time credits on that. Fortunately, Jake was not adverse to makeup having been a veteran of several soap opera recurring roles. The makeup was a little heavy but interestingly enough, it looked professional and created a unique look for the group.

The Blue Barn was packed. The entire place probably held about a thousand people fully jammed, and you just had to know everybody was there, with cousins to the fourth degree (if that were possible in this small town!) Norma had handed in the application and there were at least twenty groups on the roster, which was a large blackboard with the names of all groups on it.

The group had decided for the time being that "The Subway Singers" was the best they could do on short notice, and so that's what their entry read. They were smack dab in between the "Sugar Twins" and the "Frying Pan Symphony Orchestra."

As a matter of fact, Pearl was already sick to death of The Sugar Twins. Everybody was talking about them. She heard about them from the lady at the Launch Pad front desk. She heard about them from the pawnbroker. She heard about them from the seamstress at the second-hand store. "Sugah Twins, Sugah Twins, Sugah Twins. It could give yuhs sugah low!" They obviously had won first place three years in a row, and were a clear favorite for tonight. "The whole ting is fixed over heah!" scowled Pearl to herself, and the lower lip stretched with complete abandon.

Cacophony, of course, reigned for the first hour they were in the Blue Barn. The "Frying Pan Symphony Orchestra" somehow thought that constantly running their piece ("The William Tell Overture!!") at this late time, and over and over, would increase their chances of winning. Jake had it on the best authority, however, from the toothless "concierge" at the Launch Pad who was also present at the Blue Barn, that the "Frying Pans" had never even placed.

Jake was also informed that the first two places at the local would advance to the Super Regionals. He looked around in disbelief. People were doing Hog Calling, Gurning (making faces) and various other and sundry crazinesses. He had absolutely no concept of whether or not a "regular" song like "Blowin' in the Wind" would even be received at all by the audience, who was obviously desensitized to any musical event whatsoever.

"BOOM BOOM BOOM. Whoooosshh!" Somebody was now beating on the microphone and blowing into it. "Test, one two, test!" Makeba looked up at the stage. There was one spotlight, full bore, and hot pink lighting up a woman in a house dress, ostensibly the Mayor. "Welcome! Welcome again to the twenty-third edition of our local 'Shooting Star' show. We have some great acts for you tonight, including our former winners who have gone onto Super Regionals for the last three years, THE SUGAR TWINS!"

ROAR!!!! The crowd was ecstatic. "You'da thunk it was Jimmy Hendrix, risen," thought Jake. What the hell were the Sugar Twins anyway? Nardo had a lump in his throat. Blue Barn or no, he always got stage fright, and his severe dry mouth would last until twenty-five seconds on stage. Then he would be fine. Makeba "knew" she was the best thing they'd ever seen, so wasn't worried.

Norma, of course, looked at the whole thing very analytically, and was able to objectify the situation. Although, after her revelation *de novo* at the Television studio, there was something less objective about her singing. She had developed a little cry in her voice, and now much more began to resemble the Tejana and Mariachi singers she so admired. "Why couldn't I do that before?" she wondered to herself, knowing inside that the catharsis had opened her soul, for better or worse. Jake was a rock solid anchor. He knew his guitar part. Luckily, another guitar player had a stick-on electronic pickup microphone and Jake made arrangements with him to borrow it for "Blowin'" so the guitar would be nice and loud. Nardo would have no problem with his flute being heard, but cautioned all the singers to "keep their heads close together by the mike" so the harmonies, such as they were, would be heard. Makeba's voice was loud enough without the mike. Pearl knew her job was to stick by Makeba in the tambourine section.

"Like glue I'll stick." Pearl was not about to let Makeba out of her sight. And the evening was off to a good start. The Hog Callers opened the show. Fortunately, Pearl noticed that the Frying Pans were saved until last. Nardo also knew this was good since everyone's ears, including the Judges', would never recover from this slam-bang raucous rendition of Rossini. On a sour note, however, the Subway Singers were smack dab right after the Sugar Twins, probably because they were the "newcomers" and had to have the worst spot on the "randomly-picked" roster.

Another unfortunate thing was that the Subways had no opportunity to run their song prior to the actual performance, or take a sound check. Actually "sound check" was probably not part of the local vocabulary, thought Nardo, since nothing was sounding very good. They would just have to pray for the best when they got up there. In the front hallway, while the show was progressing, Nardo "blocked" the number, showing everyone exactly where to stand, reminding Jake that he had to "stick" the guitar pickup on, and basically doing a "dry run" of the number. Things were a tad tentative, so they ran it a couple of times softly sans tambourines to "get the feel of it."

"Subway Singers. Subway Singers!" The Mayor's voice attracted the quintet's attention to the Mayor who was over by the side waving them to come. "You're on in two!" The lump in Nardo's throat grew. Why the hell was he so nervous? Why did he get butterflies and stagefright? He knew one thing. He'd never get used to it. It used to put him off performing, but he learned to conquer it, even though the feeling never went away. It was like roller coasters. You just get yourself on it, and then go for the ride. He looked forward to the twenty-five second marker when the dry throat would disappear.

The fivesome was standing in the "wings" which was simply a non-hidden, off-to-the-side area when the roar of the crowd again erupted. Rushing past them, Jake saw two very cutesy identical twins in short white jumpers with blue polka dots, and white short gloves climb up the steps onto the stage. The Mayor had just announced the "Sugar Twins" singing their "hit" (although it was only a "hit" in the small mountain town) "Sugartime!" This McGuire Sisters song was perfect for two part harmony, and the girls had professional sounding specially recorded karaoke type tracks to back them up. In fact, they sounded exactly like the McGuire Sisters, minus one, of course. And well they should, Norma found out, since this was the same song they had sung for the last three years, since they began winning this event. They had well put-together choreography and, like sisters, their voices blended impeccably. Makeba, looking at the wild crowd, instinctively knew that this was their competition, if any. She never considered the Hog Callers or the Frying Pans to be in the running.

After the short two-and-one-half minute "Sugartime," the girls bowed identically and skipped offstage. The crowd was on its feet. It *was* the best thing so far, and would probably save the tiny town from embarrassment at the Super Regionals. Aside, the Sugar Twins never even placed at the Super Regionals.

"And now, joining us for the first time at Shooting Star here at the Blue Barn, a great group doing their own unique version of that old time favorite, 'Glowing in a Wind'." The crowd clapped handily, as locals will do to encourage new talent. Nardo was not impressed, however, since the Hog Callers had gotten similar preferred treatment.

Nardo had the group lined up in order as they walked on stage. Jake helped Pearl up, and the other guitar player stuck the pickup mike on Jake's guitar. The group landed as they had rehearsed in front of the mikes with the voices placed close together for maximum one mike benefit. Jake gave a few strokes on his guitar, and to his surprise, he could hear it, it was in tune, and it didn't sound bad. Nardo had been blowing through his flute to warm it up from the cold mountain air that circulated readily throughout the Blue Barn.

"Picky Picky Strum Strum" and the four-bar vamp introduction to the song was off and running. Nardo picked up his long, low sweet flute backup notes during the intro, and the interlocking tambourine rhythms began. A sudden hush fell over the quieted crowd, and they stared. The Subways sounded good.

186

Norma's newly plaintive cry cut through the folk sound. "How many roads must a man walk down . . . Before you can call him a man?" The audience was strangely calm and listening. On the chorus, the three part harmony was soft, but strong. As the song progressed, Nardo filled with flute licks, tastefully of course, and toward the last verses, Makeba began tossing in the soulful cries.

Norma was disconcerted by the calm of the crowd. Didn't they like it? Were these people so tied to the Sugar Twins that the Subways had no chance? The feeling made her voice stronger and more convincing. She sang the song as it was meant to be sung, with conviction, and her backup group followed suit. Then came the half time repeat of the last line, with full harmonies, and tambourines blazing. "The answer is blowing . . . in the wind!"

A split second of silence deafened the Blue Barn. Without warning the crowd was fully on its feet, giving our quintet the greatest ovation of the evening. Pearl could "taste" those time credits being added to her R.O. Whatever the outcome, the group had achieved their goal. They had put a little "combo" together and it worked. In fact, no one noticed the R.O.'s all simultaneously racking up time and credits.

The top five were called to the stage in no particular order. An acrobat, two jugglers, a fiddle player, the Sugar Twins and the Subways. "Fifth place, Nadine, the Flying Sprite!" And the acrobat took home a tan ribbon. "Fourth place, Manny Nuperl, fiddler!" And the fiddle player took home a yellow ribbon. "Third place . . . The Bodie Boys" and the jugglers took home a green ribbon.

"Ladies and gents. For the first time in the history of our Shooting Star contest, there is a TIE for first! The first half of the tie is, of course, our favorite daughters, THE SUGAR TWINS!" After a major crowd eruption, the Sugar Twins accepted their blue ribbon with a synchronized bow. Nardo's throat developed a lump, shared by the other four. It was like the Long Beach Parade again. The same exhilarating feeling drained over the folk five.

"And the second half of the tie, joining the SUGAR TWINS at Super Regionals . . . THE SUBWAY SINGERS!"

Again the crowd rose to its feet, this time the roar was beyond decibels. The little mountain town had new heroes, or at least, new shared heroes. Norma, not quite as composed as usual, did the honors, accepting a red ribbon with customary beauty pageant tears. However, the Mayor whispered that it would be changed for a blue one as soon as Millie's Fabrics and Remnants opened the next morning, and Millie could "run up" another blue one.

The Subway Brigade took an extra curtain call, and then another, and finally ran off stage and back into the front hall of the big Blue Barn. Everybody was hugging each other. You would have thought they had just won an Oscar for their performance. And the foretelling of it was just that. Somehow, amidst all the brouhaha each and every one of them came to the same conclusion: it is these first and unexpected *little victories* that feel the very best, that mean the very most. Any others down the line will be expected and, if not won, will loom as chasms of disappointment. And others down the line, if won, won't taste so extremely sweet as this first unfettered surprise. Because there is no better win, no more unencumbered win, than that first unexpected one. This is the one everyone really wants. This is the one they would remember.

22 - NEW RIDERS OF THE PURPLE FARTS

They really couldn't afford much more. The mayor told them as the old "Purple Farts" bus pulled up in front of the Launch Pad that the town was sorry, but lack of funds would prevent the limousine company from picking them up this year to take them to Super Regionals for the competition. Of course, the Sugar Twins had gotten streak limos all three years prior and, this year somehow, there was enough money left in the "Sugar Twins Booster Fund" to rent them a streak limo to travel to Super Regionals. And another thing, the streak limo was a time-streak limo, which means instantaneous teleportation. Unfortunately, the Subway Singers were stuck with the Purple Farts bus. At least this one would be an "Express" which meant that it stopped in only half of the podunk towns that the Local did.

Nardo didn't care. He was still jazzed over the great night three weeks ago they had at the performance. In fact, the fact that *anything* was paid for was a perq for all of them. They had not expected anything. So just above anything was more star treatment than they had ever received.

The local paper had done a close-up on all of them. Of course, Norma being the front-man got the largest coverage, and Jake's looks got him a nice little write up. Makeba, Pearl and Nardo had to be satisfied with being tagged as the "back up" band. But that was okay. Nardo looked at the whole thing as a team. So did everyone else.

In the three weeks that followed, the group met and rehearsed diligently. "I think we should try something a little more difficult, and maybe up-tempo," Nardo kept insisting.

"Oy vey, I got to learn anotheh tambourine part!" Pearl was not ecstatic about the prospects. Makeba was all for it, since "Blowin' in the Wind" was a little too tame for her. Jake found out that the Pawn Shop owner was quite a guitarist, and so he availed himself of some free lessons.

Nardo and Norma had put their heads together, and decided that a Latino song would be the most effective. First, Norma could sing in Spanish and so could Nardo. Second, the Latin rhythms were related and suited to the West African interlocking rhythms of Nigeria and Ghana which Makeba was extremely well-versed in. Third, the up-tempo idea seemed great, since that was one of the things that the Sugar Twins had over them so far.

Nardo and Norma went over songs that they knew together. Norma was well rounded in Mariachi and Mexican folk music, and much of the Philippine music had the same type of feel. The problem would be putting it all together in some sort of cohesive symphony which would drive the rhythms, sound harmonious, and that the group could handle.

All of them were not really enchanted with their makeshift name, the "Subway Singers," so they began searching for a new one. However, the local committee told them that their names had already been submitted, so for the Super Regionals at least, they would be stuck with that handle.

Nardo was again racking his brain for costuming ideas. He had really drawn a blank until Pearl, of all people, gave him a great idea. "Look, honey. I used to sew in the sweatshops downtown. Fancy schmancy stuff, you know. Shirring, pleating, brocades. Goahgus tings [gorgeous things]." That's all Nardo had to hear. He and Pearl went down to the second hand store again and got some white collared dress shirts to fit everyone. Nardo got tight black pants for himself and Jake (he knew Jake would be a hit in these.) For the girls, Nardo was able to find three matching black full slips, Gaucho length. There were two XXLs, perfect for Pearl and Makeba who wore about the same size, and a Large, which Nardo knew he could help Pearl size down for Norma. Nardo could see the costumes coming together already.

Then, he took Pearl to the fabric shop where Pearl worked some of her magic. The result was phenomenal. Pearl managed to get a remnant bolt of bright pink brocade, and some cheap satin. Nardo happened to find some black appliqués which were going to be thrown out since the sequins were a little melted. "But they sparkle just the same." Nardo had worked under these conditions before.

Pearl once again worked magic with the lady who owned the fabric store, by giving her a few sewing lessons. By the way, this was the same lady who had transformed the second-place red gro-grain ribbons into blue ones for our gang. She was so pleased with Pearl's work, that she allowed Pearl to used her souped-up machine off hours to put together the costumes. In fact, the whole town was very much behind the Subways, especially since the Sugar Twins were already so well taken care of.

Nardo sketched out each costume in color, and assisted Pearl by ripping out stitches. Pearl enhanced the white collared shirts with some soft white tooling. She fashioned tight pink brocade vests with expertly sewn on black appliqués. She then sewed pink brocade stripes and black sequined appliqués down the seams of the men's trousers, and around the hems of the slips. Nardo didn't like the slips the way they were, so he added some major black shiny ruffles at the bottom, and Pearl shirred and pleated until the full Maria Clara skirts looked like ball gowns.

Jake rounded up some boots at the second hand store for Nardo and himself. The shoemaker in the Mountain Village dyed them black, shined them to a gloss, and they were worn *over* the tight pants, giving a very Latin, Gaucho feel. Makeba was in charge of boots for the women. Nardo's sketches had been based on the Gaucho look, so the high boots were necessary.

"Yiecchh" spake Pearl when she realized that she would be teetering around on those high-heeled boots. But Makeba made her go to the pawn shop with her, and the Pawn Shop Owner turned them on to a lady who sold cowboy boots. When she found out who wanted them, she was only too glad to help. Ta da! The girls had their boots.

As for the new song, Norma had chosen a Latin-Malagueña sounding song from Mexico that her father taught her. Jake was able to get a great-sounding strum together (the only one that sort of sounded 'Flamenco') and for a few minutes from each R.O., they were able to buy the electric guitar pick-up so they wouldn't have to worry about the guitar being heard above whatever din awaited them at Super Regionals.

After Jake had gotten the chords down with Norma and Nardo (Nardo adding some Latin flute licks to the mix), Makeba brought Pearl in for the interlocking tambourine rhythms. Soon, Makeba had a high-life rhythm going under the markedly Mexican song. It sounded delightful.

Norma's voice had been getting stronger by the day. She was singing more with the rounded chesty cry of a true Mariachi singer as time went by. Makeba got the idea to add a cabasa to her rhythms, and so the interlock took on a new dimension with the one tambourine and the one cabasa. A *cabasa* was originally shells around a gourd, but Makeba was lucky enough to find one with a gourd and metal beads in the Pawn Shop. Nobody had bought it before since nobody knew what it was, there being not too many Black people in the little Mountain Village. In fact,

Makeba was already being treated like a celebrity, half due to her bigger than life demeanor, and half due to the exoticness of her race.

"Well, what do you know about that?" Makeba mused. "Black is working for me here. Here in a lilywhite community." She compared how different she felt now than when they were in the LILYWHITE Tavern in Mystery of History. "It's all a matter of time and place!" Makeba's R.O. racked up another credit for Revelation, and more time. Another lesson learned.

By now the quintet had a ritual for rehearsal. They would each get their individual parts together before trying to put them together. Time was of the essence, so they couldn't waste a lot of it waiting for each other to learn parts. After the individuals, sections would rehearse together. Rhythm, vocals, backups. Makeba was naturally inserting her African riffs into the mix again, and the ensemble was taking shape nicely. The Mayor had allowed the group to practice at the Blue Barn, and someone was always providing them with food and drinks. They were sounding better and better. "Better than dose fattening ol' Sugar Twins," Makeba laughed as she used Pearl's phrase in Ghetto English to herself.

The town came out to wish them well as they piled onto the sputtering Purple Fart Express. Gifts were lavished upon them, and amidst the "Good Lucks" and the "Break a Legs" the quintet felt very good and very quiet, and very determined not to let these people down.

Nardo stood there while an old steamer trunk donated by the Fabric Lady filled with their costumes was loaded on top of the bus and tied there well. Suitcases had been provided courtesy of the townspeople, and each had donated a little time to the group's R.O.'s so they wouldn't starve along the way. Super-Regionals were to take place in the capital city of wherever they were, and the Mayor's brother-in-law knew somebody with a nice Motel where they could stay. A couple of rungs up from the Launch Pad they were told. However, they didn't complain about the Launch Pad, since the toothless concierge had seen fit to cancel their entire bill after they became local celebrities. Norma wrote a nice note to her, and with the left over pink brocade and black ruffles, Nardo had reupholstered the two nasty chairs in the registration office. Things were nice on this level.

The team climbed into the bus. The bus driver knew who they were. In fact, they met some other contestants, local winners from other poor communities. "It's nice to see that the Sugar Twins had some competition this year," said the bus driver. He was really ticked off because the Sugar Twins got to take a streak limo while the rest of the plebeians were relegated to the Purple Farts bus. Norma noticed however that, even though the bus was old and rickety, it was clean. Torn seats, and the like, but clean. Norma was used to that. The high upkeep, even of old things in disrepair. It was she had been brought up on. Nardo noticed it, too. And Makeba. Pearl and Jake noticed that the seats were a little uncomfortable, but Pearl passed out some cookies made by a townsperson (to the whole bus, of course) and soon the Subway Singers were on their way to Super Regionals and the unknown.

23 - FALLEN ANGEL

Abraxas was having trouble getting his hand out of his jeans pocket. Of course, they were much too tight for him, but he learned long ago to keep his R.O. in his front jeans pocket. It was the "thing to do" for all those who, like him, were seemingly permanent fixtures on Chronos, or "longtimers." He was delighted with the amount of time he had just received from one of his sources. This was the most lucrative of jobs, he thought to himself and as long-timers went, he was one of the most successful and, therefore, the most sought-after.

The Galactan had long since given up the idea of credits. Not for the likes of him. How long had it been since he left his Plane of Origin, unpronounceable in any language we knew anyway? For purposes here, Abraxas called it Galaxos, although it was really much less poetic sounding in its native language. It was as a young man going nowhere, he fell into the crack in time with several of his cohorts. They all fell off, one at a time, he knew not where. He assumed none of them made it back to the Plane of Origin and, like him, became Chronos long-timers. He hadn't seen them since. He was at B.E.A.M. countless times and spent countless time each visit there. So many times he had lost all his time and credits, if any, trying to scam this and wheedle that. These poor novices. They really didn't know what was in store for them, thinking it was so easy to earn the time and credits to go back to the Plane of Origin. In his case, he really didn't care anymore. He hadn't been doing that well on Galaxos anyway, although you wouldn't think so to hear him tell it.

"I don't know why I'm here in the first place," was the common refrain of the Chronos long-timers. These were beings who couldn't make the time and/or credits to return to the Plane of Origin, try though they might. After losing all time for the two or three thousandth time, they'd resigned themselves to never going back.

That's where Abraxas was. And why should he try to get back? It was just a waste to try and get the twelve credits anyway. Besides, with his scam-skills, he was making a pretty good living here. But he couldn't even tell himself that so convincingly. Resignation is death . . . death of hope, death of future, death of soul. And that's where he was, resigned to his timeless fate.

Not even the authorities on Chronos cared about the long-timers, it seemed. They knew him well at B.E.A.M. every time he ran completely out of time, and when he earned credits (or stole them) eventually they were lost, gambled away, or taken back by the authorities as not being honestly earned.

But why was he thinking about that now? He just made a killing. He just got a great assignment. Five know-nothing novices and all he had to do was tempt them. All he had to do was devise a way to make them lose all their time and credits, so other long timers could obtain the clean time and the clean credits. "Laundering" or "scouring" they called it, when long timers traded "dirty" and stolen time and credits for "clean" or "spotless" time and credits. Usually, the newcomers would fall into disrepair, end up at B.E.A.M. and/or maybe become long-timers themselves. Abraxas didn't care. He couldn't. That was actually how they set it up, he thought. They make it so you don't care about anyone or anything. They don't show you any light at the end of the tunnel, so the only way you can make it is to steal, scam, pilfer. Then you can live a decent life, make enough time to live comfortably. And Wishes, Dreams and Nightmares was the place to do it.

"I mean, if they don't know that bad things can happen, too bad. Let them go through what the rest of us had to go through." Abraxas was a master of rationalizing his flawed existence. He shoved his hand back into the jeans pocket and pulled out his R.O. He had at least three months of time. Three months. That's a billionaire in Chronos terms. Back slid the R.O. into the jeans. Abraxas had chosen a humanoid form because his natural form was not acceptable to most humanoids. Humanoids, in fact, made up the majority of the life forms from this quadrant of the universe, not counting the smaller life forms who were dealt with in varied ways at various other sites. Chronos just wasn't that bad, as places went.

Abraxas looked at the dirty crystal computer in the corner of his messy desk. He would dive into these five. He would do his usual research, he would pore over every detail. There would be nothing about the unsuspecting jerks that he wouldn't know. He would find every weakness, every button, every crack in their personalities. And when they were most unaware, he would push, shove and break them. This was his desire. He wanted to earn his money (time).

On the way over to the desk, he stopped and looked in the mirror. "Not bad," he said. He had jet black hair and a swarthy face, square jaw and shortly cropped facial hair. Although this was his normal appearance (it only cost minimal time to keep up this countenance), Abraxas could get good deals on morphing. Morphing was a large part of Abraxas' modus operandi. He would have to make himself as attractive, alluring, disarming and tempting as possible. That's how he would deal with these five. That's how he got his reputation. Three months in the bank. Life was good. Life was complete. Abraxas wasn't counting his lack of credits, or his utter lack of possibly returning to his Plane of Origin. Resignation.

24 - B.E.A.M.

The first time Abraxas had been banished to B.E.A.M. (Being and Entity Alteration Management in case you forgot) he had no idea what was happening to him. Oh, he had made the obligatory tries at getting time and credits. He even tried to work with the beings that had fallen with him from Galaxos, but he couldn't seem to make it. And every time he got close to twelve credits (not many times), the damn things would disappear for this reason or that. It was clear Abraxas had some serious soul searching to do. He remembered that drab day when he looked down and all his time and credits were gone. It took a long time 'cause he ended up "pawning" his credits for time, and then, of course, never had enough to buy them back out of hock.

The first hint of B.E.A.M. had been a streak. He remembered watching his R.O. tick away the last few seconds, almost curious as to what would happen. He wished his curiosity had been a little less rampant. Of course, he would be back and forth from B.E.A.M. many times, and was as used to it as a being could get, but that first time was certainly a shock.

B.E.A.M. was a graduated scale type of a setup. After the initial streak, Abraxas found himself on a deserted desert island, with no others around. This makes for a very lonely existence, but the policy behind the place was that you had to come to terms with yourself, self evaluation, self starting, self governance, and all those personal responsibility traits that he had lost somewhere along the way. On Island, there is no help from anyone and from the resources around you, one must eat, sleep, provide shelter and, above all, *learn*. That's the part he couldn't get, the learning part.

Every morning he would wake up and look for things to eat. There were certain trees, shrubs, berries, mushrooms. A couple of times he had poisoned himself on the food, so he learned how to eat just enough of any new food to find out whether or not it was healthy. There were some fish in the sea, and unlike on Galaxos, he was in a humanoid form, so he had to adhere to their rules and regulations. It seemed like weeks before his R.O. actually started adding up any time, but eventually he had learned how to live with himself.

He built a shelter out of sticks and twigs buried in the ground, and woven together with palm frons. The roof was layers and layers of woven palm frons, and he covered the layers with palm oil to waterproof. Although Abraxas ached terribly for companionship, it was not provided on Island for him. He had heard of other beings going to B.E.A.M. but they were not all in the same place. Some were with a few others, some were in more like a structured jail situation, some were working on a farm. It just depended on what the higher-ups thought you needed. And in this case, Abraxas needed to be alone to finally "get it" in the self-sufficiency department.

Funny thing about B.E.A.M., Abraxas thought. Although it helped you, you also became very bitter towards the whole system. Overcoming the loneliness was one thing Abraxas was almost loathe to do, it was so hard not to have anyone to talk to from day to day. Abraxas, however, was not strong enough to simply take the good of B.E.A.M. and leave the bitterness behind, which was one reason he had not been successful on Chronos so far. Instead of fully taking personal responsibility for the path of his existence, he would blame it on anything and everything else. B.E.A.M. simply became the next in line of things to blame.

It seemed like ages spent on the relentless beach, with the sun. (Now that's funny, since it was constantly dusk all over the rest of Chronos; why was the sun so bright here on the beach?) But that's as far as the questions went. The day to day drudgery of taking care of himself, collecting food, staying out of trouble, and keeping himself occupied, and not going completely berserk was certainly a full-time job. Abraxas had missed the point of Island. It wasn't just about survival. It was about self auditing and searching out weaknesses, and correcting them. Abraxas never considered himself weak, either on Galaxos or here in humanoid form. He was strong, physically. Unfortunately he mistook this as personal strength which it was not. Spiritual strength was what he lacked and, eventually, that is what would keep him coming back to B.E.A.M.

Subsequently, Abraxas had learned that many on Island were able to earn *all twelve credits* and return to Plane of Origin. But he was not yet ready to face himself to this degree. Oh, no. His salvation would still be a long time coming. He would see B.E.A.M. many times and in every conceivable format before any progress would be made.

Abraxas slowly came out of his reminiscence and looked at his R.O. "Dreaming again," and the R.O. had lost several minutes. He rebooted his computer which had frozen in the meantime. Now he began delving into the five victims, his next targets. He didn't have much time before Super Regionals.

25 - SUPER REGIONALS

The night of the Super Regionals was finally here. The Purple Farts bus was coming to pick up the quintet at their motel, which was actually heaps above the Launch Pad cabins they had recently gotten used to. This one had a coffee shop right on the premises, and here they really got hungry and had to spend time from their R.O.s on food, shelter and the like, unlike MEMORABILIA and MYSTERY OF HISTORY. Also, they never seemed to skip time as they had on MEMORABILIA, just as the Androgen had warned. So, once in the Coffee Shop, they all had the specials, still trying to conserve as much as possible.

In fact, Pearl was big on filling shopping bags from the store with day-old bread and fruit, and she could cook up a storm. So breakfast and lunch were usually Pearl concoctions, and they tasted pretty damn good. Pearl didn't notice she had actually received credit and time for these money/time saving efforts, but her particular R.O. was extremely sensitive to such issues and was enhanced each time such a contribution was made.

In fact, nobody looked at their R.O.s much anymore, having the much greater task of the Super Regionals in front of them. Norma's song, which she had taught to the group and which Nardo, Makeba and Jake arranged had a paso-doble feel to it. Jake was able to adapt another of his college guitar strums since

"Malagueña" was a staple of the college guitar playing set, and everybody who had a guitar, no matter how beat up or sandy from the beach, could strum the first four bars of "Malagueña" in what they considered a fairly convincing pseudo-Segovian manner, especially if one bit his or her lower lip and tossed their hair about a little. In any event, the strum was apropos to the song, and Norma's new-found voice accompanied by Makeba and Nardo's harmonies began to make for some pretty reasonable sounding music. Add to this the interlocking rhythms of the tambourine and cabasa, and Makeba's intermittent "soul screams" and a unique sound began occurring within the group. This was certainly a great leap from the "Blowin' in the Wind" folk five who had played at the Blue Barn.

"My God, how am I going to get all these appliqués on," Nardo spoke, as he and Pearl were last-minuting the bright pink vests for the evening's performance. Norma was warming up, Jake put new strings on his guitar and taped the pickup on so it would not pop off during the performance. The quintet rested during the day, as they had decided to do, and only a short warm up was held before they, once again, heard the honk of the Purple Farts bus.

"Oy vey, how ah we going to get all dis done befoah dis perfoamance!" Pearl was becoming a little rattled.

"Don't worry, we'll finish sewing the appliqués at the theater, or on the bus," Nardo assured. "We'll get it done."

"I can help," Norma offered, having had to sew, resew, repair, and remake most of her family's clothes. Nardo and Pearl were happy for any help they could get. Jake and Makeba helped the bus driver load all the costumes and instruments onto the bus. The group was becoming quite a little entourage what with all their trunks and instruments. Makeba liked it better when they were traveling lighter.

"Oh, well. De price o' de fame," Makeba mused in her pseudo-Jamaican dialect to herself. If Makeba only knew what she had said in that one little sentence.

"How far is the theater from here?" asked Jake to the driver.

"Only about twenty minutes." This, of course, meant not only twenty minutes of time, but twenty minutes lost from the R.O. The group was becoming much more sensitive to time issues, but realized that all their hard work was also earning them time (and hopefully credits).

As Jake was helping the driver close the understorage bins on the old bus, he noticed a sticky substance around his foot. "What the hell is this?" Jake lifted his shoe, rubbed his forefinger over it, and sniffed. "Brake fluid! The brake fluid is leaking!"

Without hesitation, the bus driver had backed under the car. "I've got a flashlight in the front. Get it for me please." Jake ran into the bus and to the driver's seat.

"What's going on?" Pearl wanted to know.

"Looks like we got a break fluid leak" Jake grabbed the flashlight and ran to the back of the bus, where the driver was still under the rear wheel.

"The brake lines have been cut! Dammit. Sabotage!" The driver spoke with authority.

"Sabotage?" Jake could hardly believe what he was hearing. "What do you mean?"

"I mean one of your sweet competitors, if you get my drift, doesn't want you to make it to the Super Regionals on time!" By this time the rest of the kids were out of the bus, incredulous at the revelation.

"You mean those Sugar Twins?" Makeba was planning their demise, complete with visuals. "I'll turn them into maple syrup, those sickly white . . ."

Norma butted in. "Stop, Makeba. This is *exactly* what they are counting on. Us losing our heads. We know better than this." Norma turned to the driver. "Can it be fixed in time to get us to the theater?" Norma clicked back into her computer mode.

"Probably not. We'll have to get other transportation. It's gonna take at least an hour to get another bus up here. And the Vehicle Club won't be able to fix this one. They'll have to send a tow truck, and that'll take days."

"Oy mein Gott in Himmel. So what are yuhs gonna do?" Pearl woe-is-me'd to the rest of the group.

"We have to get other transportation. I noticed a We-Haul-Um rental place across the street." Nardo was used to renting dilapidated vehicles, or borrowing them, as the case may be.

"I'll go along," said Norma. Nardo was glad for this. A pretty girl could go a long way in any business deal. They wouldn't know that Norma was probably the real brains behind the outfit.

Norma and Nardo darted across the boulevard. Unlike the mountain town they had come from, this was a mid-size city with traffic and the like, and the cars whooshed by without regard to pedestrians, to crosswalks, and barely to traffic lights.

"Tanks God somebody has a brain at a time like dis." Pearl would have probably crossed herself, if she'd only been Catholic. Instead, she let a stretch of the lower lip perform the same function as she watched Nardo and Norma dodge traffic over to the Gas Station with the We-Haul-Um trucks.

In short order, the entire group looked over and saw the most dilapidated of the trucks, a funky old flatbed stake truck with chains around the bed, start up with a plume of white smoke erupting from its over-the-cab tailpipe. Only one of the brake lights and backup lights came on, as the tin lizzie lumbered backwards, throwing up clouds of dust in its wake. The quintet could barely make out that Nardo was at the wheel and Norma was in the passenger seat.

When the truck finally negotiated its way over in front of the Motel, everyone was told that the Truck Rental story would have to wait until later if they wanted to make it on time.

"Shady Grove Theater, it's a theater in the round, is where the Super Regionals are held." The bus driver gave Makeba specific instructions, since she demanded that she drive the truck. She had actual experience driving an old school bus, getting ghetto kids back and forth from daycare, and was used to vehicles with grinding gears as their foundational sound. The three girls rode in front, Nardo and Jake hopped in back, tying down the instruments and trunks, and holding on to whatever they could.

"Reeeeeeeeeeeeee" ground the flatbed truck's gears, as Makeba grimaced and forced the transmission into first. With an amazing jolt, the five took off down the road, jerking their way down the street. Norma had written the directions on a pad. She was screaming them to Makeba over the truck's incessant grinding. Pearl wished for some kind of pill. Anything, even Tums, Maalox. Pearl's hand was over her eyes, leaving a crack through her finger that would allow her to close it at any time. She used this trick at the movies some times. "Now it's real life, or whateveh it is, oveh deah!"

The bus driver smiled and shook his head as he watched the quintet fade out in the broken down old truck spewing white exhaust clouds down the street. "Unity in the face of pure crap!" he thought to himself, turning to face the widening pool of sticky brake fluid, his more pressing problem.

26 - SHADY GROVE

It was later than they thought when Makeba finally got the truck into the parking lot at Shady Grove. Of course, they couldn't find the artist's entrance. Jake had to get out and go to the main entrance and ask the ticket window attendant who didn't know, but then Jake insisted he call his boss and then his boss's boss and then finally, some answers trickled.

Jake noticed for the first time the grand poster for the event, which he had not seen before. On it were around twenty names (none of them theirs). Of course the Sugar Twins were featured in bold print with a picture. "What a bunch of crap," thought Jake as he awaited instructions to the artist's entrance. He had gone through many credit fights before. "All the Sugar Twins give me is intergalactic sugar low," he thought harshly to himself, proud of his cosmic joke, but at the same time ashamed of his open jealousy. "Oh, well. I'm not perfect," he rationalized.

"Drive your car around the back to the stage entrance and ask the custodian where you're supposed to go. By the way, the show's started and you're late. Hope you didn't miss your spot!" The ticket attendant went back to reading his magazine. Jake couldn't raze him with a hot poker now, even if he had to.

Makeba saw Jake running from the front entrance and flailing his arms, motioning for them to drive around the back. After renegotiating the silly truck into position, Makeba "reeeeeeeeed" it back into first, spewed a cloud of white smoke which just caught Jake jumping onto the flatbed, and jerked away toward the back of the round theater maximus.

The custodian was waving his clipboard and yelling something, but nobody could hear it over the squeal of the truck. "Shut up!! Shut that thing off!!" The custodian finally got up to the window of the truck which was finally in neutral. Coughing from the cloud of white smoke he screamed, "the show's started! Don't you care? That thing's a rattletrap." Having been used to the major acts arriving by Streak Limo, he did not seem to be impressed with the Subway's mode of transportation. "Bring yer stuff backstage, set it up in section fifteen. Yer on right after the Sugar Twins."

Jake was disappointed that the truck noise hadn't ruined the Sugar Twin's act. He couldn't believe how petty he was becoming. He just kept thinking back to the cut brake lines on the Purple Farts Bus... "Cut brake lines!" That sounded like somebody wanted to hurt them. They hadn't had much time to think about it, but Jake's wheels were grinding. "Oh, well, no time to think about it now," thought Jake as he, Nardo and Makeba began unloading the costume trunk and the instruments, and began their caravan to section fifteen, backstage. Makeba offered to the custodian to move the truck, but he was horrified at the thought of starting it up again and so they were able to park right by the loading dock. Besides, they wouldn't be in the way of the Streak Limos who came straight to the VIP entrance, of which our quintet was not apprised.

Nardo's heart leapt as they entered the backstage and he heard the roar of the audience. "Thousands" he thought quietly, as he concentrated on the task of moving the heavy costume trunk with Jake. Nardo breathed in deeply to smell the musty smell of the old theater. The way to backstage was through an underground passage and a semi-circle of a stage was down while the other part of the stage was up in full view of lights and audience. The upper part of the stage revolved so it could be seen by all while the lower part continued the setup of the next act.

"Fockie dat shit!" yelled Makeba out loud as she happened to notice a lineup pinned up on the wall of the underground corridor on the way to section fifteen. "We're right after the whitebread Sugar Twins, damn!!" As we know, Makeba wasn't a big fan of the saccharin duo, either. But what was this, to have to go on right after them again?

Norma made sure everyone was getting things together properly. She wasn't paying much attention to the other acts which were milling about, but something very familiar caught her eye. The glint of a wide, sequined-trimmed sombrero, kelly green, lying on the side of the stage. As she looked up, she saw on the semi-circle stage, about to be raised after the current act was finished, a genuine, full-bore Mexican Mariachi band of about eight or nine, complete with Marimba, guitarron, guitars, trumpets and fiddles. She didn't have time to think about this now, but her gaze was transfixed on a sight which brought her back to the fiestas she attended with her parents as a little girl. This is where she got her hankering to be a singer. This is where she was introduced to music. This is where she learned the secrets of the Aztecs.

"They're supposed to win, you know. They came in second last year at Super Regionals." Norma whipped around and saw a pretty girl in a short outfit and tap shoes and realized she was from the act who had just received the thunderous applause while the five entered the building. "They're really great. Is this your first time?"

"Si, I mean yes," said Norma, surprised at the youth of the girl, almost as young as she was. "We tied for first at the local up in the mountains." Norma was still wondering how a Mariachi Band got into this place, wherever in the universe it was.

"Oh, that's good. That's where the Sugar Twins are from. That's a real hard local to win, I hear." The girl was extremely cordial.

Norma glanced anxiously at her four mates, remembering that after Mariachi and then Sugar Twins, they were next. The girl graciously let Norma go back to what she was doing. Norma couldn't help but take a quick glance at the Mariachi again. These were extremely expensive costumes, as she well knew. She thought back to the trips with Nardo to the second hand store, and sewing second hand sequins on second hand clothes. Although their pink brocade and black sequined outfits were sharp, they didn't have a chance. Not a glimmer. Not next to these professionally done costumes.

Without warning the audience erupted again, this time deafening as the group was now located right below the stage. The lights faded as the one semi-circle began to lower and the voice-over (this time much deeper and more professional than at the Blue Barn) announced, "And now Ladies and Gentlemen and Entities of all kinds, one of our perennial favorites from desert valley, Mariachi Verde!"

"The Green Mariachi," thought Norma to herself. She glanced over and saw that a young handsome Latino was fronting the Band, and the Mariachi began with verve playing an original tune in the quick "Mariachi gigue" style, 6/8 time. The trumpet triplets ripped throughout the massive theater, and the audience roared. These were the favorites. The Sugar Twins even paled in comparison. "Well," Norma thought, "that's a mercy anyhow."

Nardo could not help but be impressed. "Concentrate on us. Concentrate on us." This he kept saying to himself. This was a parameter he had learned at the drag shows. No matter how well the guy did before you, you had to go out there and give it to them, no matter what it took. The Mariachis simply strengthened Nardo's resolve. He went over to Pearl, who was duly glazed over with the magnitude of the whole thing.

"I don't wanna know from this," whispered Pearl in her stage whisper which could be heard above the roar of a roller coaster.

"Don't worry, Pearl. You know your part perfectly. Just pretend that it's you and us, stare at the back row, and you won't see a thing. Just shapes and shadows of an audience. You just pretend that they are enjoying the hell out of it, no matter what!" Nardo's drag background was divine, actually. Sometimes the club wouldn't even have two people in the audience, but you had to perform anyway. In one club, they had an applause machine to "fill in." It desensitized Nardo to the need for audience love and response, and therefore he learned how to concentrate on his performance. He always fantasized that he was at the Hollywood Bowl or the Greek Theater, and even with just a smattering of applause, bowed as if he had just finished singing "Un Bel Di." Nardo was a trooper.

As Nardo came out of his flashback, the group looked over just in time to see the Sugar Twins take their places on the stage, accompanied by a tall, dark and handsome man with a full, short dark beard. "Lookie, dem bitches got demselves a manager." Makeba was trying to be unimpressed, but the Sugar Twins had brand, spanking new costumes, and a full band behind them. The bearded man seemed to be listening to instructions from the Twins as they quietly prepared for their performance.

Above on stage, the Mariachi was performing flawlessly, with the sweet beautiful sound of the lead male singer echoing above the symphonic mariachi sound. "So unusual for a Mariachi," mused Norma who was used to the normalcy of sour tones from everyone but the marimbas and the percussion at the Puerto Vallarta airport. This sound was dulcet.

Instant roar. The Mariachi's had finished. To the obvious standing ovation of the crowd, the lead singer yelled, "Gracias! Gracias!" as the lights faded and the semi-circle once again began to descend.

The deep-voiced announcer once again took the microphone and announced, "Ladies, Gentlemen, Entities of all kinds. The darlings of the High Mountain Community of Rim-of-the-Stars . . . the fabulous . . . SUGAR TWINS!!!!"

The banjo began plunking the initial strains of "Sugartime" although it was phenomenally hard to hear over the deafening roar of the crowd, who was obviously on its feet. These were also favorites, worse luck.

Jake shook his head, sullenly. How do these people get there? He *hated* their song and hated everything about them. Although as a performer, he was told never to bad mouth any other act, it was all he could do to keep from gagging. But you can't argue with a standing ovation. "That's what makes the world go 'round," he laughed to himself, as he tickled his brain with the thought, "what the hell *world* was this anyway?"

Nardo and Norma would not let anyone sink into any feelings other than concentrating on their performance. Jake had spent time tuning his guitar, Nardo had blown warm air through his flute. The quintet was each duly cinched into his or her striking electric pink brocade and black sequined vests. Rag-tag though they were, they somehow made a striking appearance, defying all logic and norms of what a group was supposed to look like. They looked different, diverse. Other than the costumes, they didn't match. All their musical styles were different. They used only simple harmonies, and allowed only the strong points to shine.

All at once, Sugartime was over. The Subway Brigade was on the riser. It seemed awfully lonely there, the five of them about to face a Coliseum full of voracious onlookers. "Christians and lions," thought Pearl to herself, paralyzed with fear. Just before the announcement, Makeba put her arm around Pearl and kissed her on the cheek.

"You caught on to those African rhythms great, honey. You'll do fine. Just stay with me." That's all Pearl needed. Whatever, she knew she had a friend on stage. Maybe not a Mah Jong friend, but a very special friend, indeed. And when Pearl made a friend, it was usually for life. Yep, for life. That's how Pearl worked.

"LADIES, GENTLEMEN, and ENTITIES OF ALL KINDS. Again from the faraway community of Rim-of-the-Stars, a newcomer to our Super Regionals tonight. Let's give a warm Super Regional Welcome to La Quinta!

"La Quinta!" That was the name Nardo and Norma had come up with, and Makeba thought it was okay, although it really had no African ring to it. Oh well. It was better than the Subway Singers, or whatever they were called before. They would just do the best they could. Thank heaven they got a new name, anyway!

Jake's guitar sounded astoundingly good as the stage began to rise and he confidently strummed the four bar introduction of the Malagueña that Norma had taught them. Something about the sparseness of the sound caught the crowd. They were listening intently.

Out of the spotlight rose Norma's beautiful face, her hair pulled back in a traditional Latina bun, compliments of Nardo, with the pink light accentuating the bright fuchsia vests. Over the silence rose Norma's new voice, as strong as it had ever been with the first three words *a cappella*, without instruments. "Yo Soy Ma-la-gueña!" And then the interlocking African rhythms began accompanied by Latin-Blues licks of Nardo's flute, and the tight strum of the guitar. At selected points, on chorus, the three-part harmony kicked in. All the stops were in the right place, laying splotches of silence among the unique music. And to top it off, Makeba's constant rhythm and blues vocal wails reminded everyone of the diversity of the musical mix.

Now the half-time, double time ending, with three part harmony soaring and the five shout, "Malagueña!"

Like the Blue Barn, there seemed to be a moment of hesitation, silence. Norma stood there looking up at the lights with her hands outstretched. As if it were rehearsed, the audience was on its feet and the roar was beyond decibels. None of the five could tell if this applause was more or less than the others they had heard, but Nardo's heart was pounding furiously. This was not an applause track. There was no mylar curtain behind him. There were not two drunks in the front row. This was the sound of audience adoration, and somehow they all knew it. Again, they had a surprise attack of love from the audience, as they witnessed at the Blue Barn.

They should have been tipped off that at least something was happening when the announcer first called for an additional hand for "La Quinta" and then had to ask the audience at least three times to quiet down.

Backstage was a blur. People running toward them. Even the Sugar Twins came up to them to congratulate them, but Pearl smelled a phoney. It's one of the things that Jewish women are endowed with. The Phoney-Sniffer. It comes with the package.

During the onslaught, Jake learned that only the top winner from this show would go on to Inter-Galactics. This was the first they had heard of this further competition, but Jake was soon informed that these "famous" bands and groups he was seeing on television and hearing on the radio were all former winners of Inter-Galactics, and that this had been their springboard to stardom.

Pearl was agog with all the adulation she was receiving. "Where did you learn the tambourine like that? That is so cool. How did you guys ever get together?" Makeba overheard the tambourine line and smiled and winked at Pearl. Makeba had her own entourage, and was giving instant crash courses in Nigerian Percussion when the Director of Activities began placing all groups on the stage for the announcement of the awards. It was right after the last-year's Super Regional winners played.

216

Unfortunately, they were not able to place in Inter-Galactics. If it had been known, all eyes were on the Mariachi to become the first Inter-Galactic placers from this Super Region. Of course, the Subways knew nothing of this or any other politics. In fact, they were unaware of any of the underpinnings of such competitions, and the actual stakes. They pretty much stuck to their own performance, as they had nothing else to concentrate on.

Just before the stage rose, Nardo looked over at the Sugar Twin's "manager." The astoundingly handsome black-bearded face and cool blue eyes met Nardo's instantly. The seemingly ever-present lump in Nardo's throat got bigger. What was this suited hunk looking at? Nardo, not in drag, could not believe anybody would look at him in this way. Before Nardo had time to further contemplate the matter, the stage began to rise, with tympani roll and a fanfare from the resident orchestra.

Shades of the Blue Barn rose in Jake's mind, but this time it was different. Much bigger, much grander, much more Academy of Motion Picture Arts and Sciences.

"Third Place, with a score of 93.9. Our Mountain Favorites, the SUGAR TWINS!" The Sugar Twins had finally placed and, although disappointed that they did not win first, they were pleasantly exuberant. The crowd roared again. Obviously there were many fans from the Rim-of-the-Stars local, and they were absolutely ecstatic that the Twins had finally placed in the Super Regionals. Although Pearl smelled phoneys, the Twins acted properly surprised and humbled by the experience as they accepted their third place award. But you could tell they were really disgusted.

"And our Second Place winner . . . and remember Ladies, Gentlemen and Entities of all Kinds, that in the event the First Place winner is unable to perform at Inter-Galactics, the Second Place winner will go . . . our Second Place, again from Rim-of-the-Stars, LA QUINTA!!!"

A wave of dizziness passed over Pearl as she had never before experienced a feeling like this. How in the heck had they won second place? How did they beat the Sugar Twins? With their lousy second-hand store costumes, simple harmony . . . it just didn't make any sense. But the crowd was, once again, on their feet. The crowd had loved them, and so, obviously, had the judges. Norma smiled her very pretty smile and strode up proudly to pick up their trophy. Along with this trophy, they would find out, came a healthy portion of time which would be added to their R.O.s. In addition, they had earned a substantial amount of time on their own by their enduring teamwork, and many of the quintet had earned credits for the various types of individual achievements that this topsy-turvy world rewarded. They would not, however, be going to Inter-Galactics. That was saved for the First Place winners.

"And First Place, and to nobody's surprise, let's give a great hand to our representatives for Inter-Galactics this year . . . MARIACHI VERDE!!!!!!" And the crowd went wild for the expected winners.

"Well," thought Nardo. "At least we got Sweepstakes in my memory with the ALTADOGS." He wasn't the only one of the five who confided this thought to themselves.

27 – THE LAST TEMPTATION OF PEARL

"I'm dyin' fuh a coaned beef sanwich!" Pearl re-exclaimed as she combed the mid-size town for a Delicatessen. She was not afraid of walking on her own, although she really didn't know what was out there. "I'm from New Yoak!" she said to herself, convincing herself that if she could walk the streets of New York, she could walk anywhere herself. And on this particular floating island, for whatever reason, you got hungry and you had to spend R.O. time on buying food. So she would make the best of it.

Pearl stopped in every shop along the way, encountering "God Knows What" kinds of beings, and asking if there was a "Jewish" deli anywhere. "It has to be Jewish. Don't gimme none o' dat Italian traif. It goes right tru' me!"

Finally, Pearl had victory. Her persistence had paid off. She located the "Hello Deli," got directions, sprung for a cab (regular, not streak) and went inside. Her first act was to thank God it wasn't an Indian restaurant, as there was a "Hello Delhi" in Los Angeles that she made the mistake of dropping in once and "her stomach didn't know from dat curry spices!"

The deli was a curious place. The front of it was completely white bathroom tile, with some black tiles mixed in. There was some Hebrew written on the window in Gold (she hoped it meant

Kosher) and some of the tiles were blue Jewish stars, reminiscent of the Israeli flag. Tentatively, Pearl hooked her bag around her elbow, and pushed through the stainless steel and glass swinging doors. The place wasn't too busy, and so she sat down at one of the tables. It was early Fifties Formica trimmed with aluminum, reminiscent of the table she had in her house in the early Fifties, with red naugahyde and chrome chairs. On the table sat a jar of Kosher pickles in brine and pickled tomatoes, sugar jar, salt, pepper, *regular* mustard (not that hot French stuff that she hated, it was practically anti-Semitic). Fairly clean flatware setups were strewn beside paper napkin holders. Also on the table was a plastic pitcher of ice-water with those plastic cup-cone holders and a stack of paper cones. Pearl had definitely been to this Deli before.

The first pass by the one and only waitress was simply to toss two menus in front of Pearl, the Breakfast and the Lunch. Pearl was completely used to this kind of drill having haunted practically every deli in the Los Angeles area and San Fernando Valley for years. She quickly located the sandwich she was looking for and, without looking up yelled, "Miss I'm ready over heah!" This was proper protocol in a deli, where it might be frowned upon in any other type of restaurant, or a deli not familiar with proper deli protocol.

A hefty woman wearing a light blue waitress outfit complete with starched napkin pinned to her breast and also donning a plastic name pin stating "Bubulah" came over to the table. Whipping out her order pad and, of course absolutely not looking at Pearl, she grabbed a pencil from behind her ear. Bubulah's hair was piled up in dog-turd curls on her head, and in the center of each curl was carefully placed a small plastic daisy. The lipstick, like Pearl's, went stylishly a good quarter inch over the upper lip line, flared at the ends, and Whoopie Red, of course. Bubulah smelled like "Jungle Gardenia" or "Raid" but Pearl was used to it, having gallons of both herself at home for festive occasions.

"So talk to me," was Bubulah's opening line.

"Dis coaned beef, oveh heah. It's not too fat, is it?"

"One lean coaned beef sandwich, Number Tree. Anyting to drink?" The waitress was still not looking at Pearl.

"Yeah. I tink I'll have a Chocolate Egg Cream, but don't make it too tin [thin], and gimme some extra seltzah on the side." Without a beat, the waitress walked over to the next table and began taking their order.

"Talk to me" she snapped.

"Ill have the ham sandwich . . . "

At that very moment Bubulah was back over at Pearl's table, this time looking her straight in the eye in an extremely confrontive manner. "Whatsa matteh? You don't tink I know how to make an egg-cream? Toity yeahs I been workin' heah, and I don't need you to gimme lessons. Whaddaya tink about dat?"

"So make, make!" This did not faze Pearl at all, being completely used to abusive New York waitresses. "If you would start, I would have my sandwich sooner, no? By the way, dats a very nice handkerchief deah. Did you do dat yuhself?" Pearl knew what to say.

"Of coase, dahlink. Pure Egyptian cotton (you should pardon the expression!) I wouldn't put nuttin' else on my chest. Yuhs order is already in. You want to save room for seven layer cake? Fresh today it's made, gorgeous and delicious. I'll put a piece away." And with that the sisterhood of flared-lipstick Jewish women remained ignited.

Pearl opened her bag to pull out her compact and check to see that her lipstick was, indeed, properly flared. After adding yet another thick coat, and making the obligatory lip stretches and faces, she clapped her compact to, looked up and gasped. For sitting in front of her was her late husband, Maury.

"Hello beautiful. Whats going on?" Maury was a tall, big man with broad shoulders, craggy features, and bald on top with wisps of hair around the ring-side. He had a moustache, which Pearl adored. She always told him that his "tick" [thick] mustache was so masculine. And Maury's size made Pearl feel feminine. I mean, she wasn't exactly a petite woman, about five foot six, and pretty big-boned. Maury's long arms and big hairy chest had always been perfect for Pearl to bury her head in.

"My God. My God! What is going on heah!" Pearl was tearing up at the sight of Maury. She didn't remember him this way. No. He lost so much weight and size those last two years with the cancer, she hardly recognized him. But the picture in her mind was always the big burly guy sitting in front of her.

Pearl remembered when they were "dating" in New York. Maury had a full head of hair then, was trim and muscular, playing football for New York University in New York. He was to inherit his father's retail clothing business, and so they planned to marry after Maury graduated. When Maury's father finally died, and everyone realized that the store was basically bankrupt, Maury took Pearl (who was pregnant) and his and her mother (their fathers were now both dead) to California where he opened up a pattern-cutting facility downtown, employing cheap Mexican labor. This business was lucrative, and kept them smack dab in the middle of the middle class for many years. The business saw both Pearl and Maury's mothers into old age and death, and left enough after Maury's untimely death to keep Pearl in a decent apartment and the health care paid for. Pearl did odd jobs here and there, and donated time at the Senior Citizen Center. She still went to the garment district for discount clothes (there were still some old contacts alive there) and it was from there she was traveling when she landed on the infamous subway car.

"What are you doing here, honey?" Maury was asking all the news.

Pearl related the entire story since Maury's death up to and including the subway incident to Maury. She still could not believe. But the person. It *sounded* like Maury. It *looked* like Maury. And right now, it was close enough for Pearl. This was the closest she felt to home since she couldn't remember when.

Pearl and Maury talked, mostly reminiscing about old times, going way back to the New York days. At several points during the conversation, Pearl teared up, and Maury even kissed her on the cheek. He held her hand.

Maury said, "It's so wonderful God has given us this second chance!"

"What do you mean, Maury, second chance?" Pearl was perplexed.

Well, here we are together again, honey. It's what you dreamed of. It's what you hoped for. It could never happen down there again. I was gone. But here we have a chance to live our lives again. God is giving us a second chance! We can be together again."

Pearl was momentarily tempted. Yes, what was waiting for her back there at the subway station? Memories, bingo, a few trips downtown, and lumbago? She could easily do without all of it. But something wasn't right.

"You could give up the singing group. I mean, they could get somebody to replace you. And we could make a new life here, indefinitely."

Pearl was an instinctive person. She wasn't analytical. She went on hunch, vibes, feelings. And something here was amiss. Pearl looked down into her bottomless coffee cup and teared up again. She knew what she was wishing for was not the reality. She had figured out what the catch was.

"I don't know who you are, sweetheart. But you are *not* my Maury. Maury was of the Earth. Maury was level headed. Maury was a religious man. He knew that passing from Earth was just that. Your time is up, and there's no going back. And he would *never* insist that I give it up. No, Maury would want me to fight for living my life to the fullest, to explore whatever mystery awaited me and, when my time came, to meet him in the ever-after. No, sir, you are not Maury."

"Besides, Maury would *never* ask me to give up my friends. He knows they are the most important thing to me. In fact, whatever, he would want me to stay with them, because he knows it's what *I* really want. He was not a selfish man, even when it came to the two of us."

"I thank you for your time, sir. You did re-light a memory in my heart that is very dear to me, and if you were trying to be cruel, you didn't succeed. My memory of my beloved husband is too strong, even for someone of your power. I know I have to go back and live the rest of my life. It is what Maury would want."

Pearl got up, grabbed her bag and shouted "bye" to Bubulah, who nodded in an all-knowing way. She didn't even have to ask Pearl if she wanted a carry-out. She threw Pearl a kiss.

Pearl donned the large pocket book, thrust her shoulder up against the door and pushed it open into the noisy traffic. No way, shape or form. Pearl would not be tempted. She never looked back.

28 - THE TRIALS AND TRIBULATIONS OF MAKEBA

The "Second Place" win only reminded Makeba of the sad lack of blacks who ever prevail in white-run contests. She conveniently forgot that the Mariachi that did win was comprised of third-world Latinos who probably originally came from shacks South of the U.S. border. But Makeba was, like many other American Blacks, much too busy contemplating her own distresses to think about that. In fact, Makeba was historically a strong purveyor of the crazy and unsupported notion that, somehow, the plight of the Blacks in America was qualitatively worse than the plight of anyone else. In other words, "my hate is worse than your hate." Makeba could remember herself thinking when Gay rights was an issue in California elections, "How dare those faggots think that their discrimination is in any way related to our discrimination." In fact, in a discussion with Nardo, Makeba finally found out where the word "faggot" came from. It was *much* worse than the word "nigger" which was simply a manifestation of ignorant whites who couldn't properly pronounce a Spanish word, "Negro." Nardo said that at a Gay, Lesbian, Bisexual and Transgender conference, he learned that the phrase "flaming faggot" had its roots in the Spanish Inquisition (screw that Ferdinand and Isabella, anyway) where the "crime" of homosexuality was punished by the victim being hung up by the hands and having flaming logs rubbed against the body until there

225

was no flesh left. Makeba had become nauseous when this story was told to her. She rapidly dropped the word "faggot" from her repertoire.

She had also had a talk with Pearl who told of atrocities of the Jews in the Camps which even Makeba could not trivialize as "not as bad" as the Black slavery plight. In essence, Makeba's great high IQ brain was finally breaking through and realizing that the plight of *any* group, whether Black or Gay or Jewish or Latino deserved a sacred and serious consideration, especially when the excuse for the monstrosities was the destruction and annihilation of one sector of people by another. Makeba's "our hate is best" theme finally rapidly crumbled, and the stupid remnants of it, to wit, her feelings that Blacks never won any contests was soon overcome by more reasoned and intellectual thinking. "It's good they won," she thought to herself, even though she wanted to win, no matter what color she was. Besides, Pearl and Jake weren't saying "Jews never win" and Nardo wasn't screaming, "Gays never win." She decided against making up silly excuses for them not winning First Place, and actually tried to figure out why they hadn't won. Not that she expected it. She just was feeling the "we came so close" syndrome and was rapidly tiring of the whole R.O. nonsense, having to earn and spend time and credits, and who the hell did these people think they were anyway, putting them through all this? At least her thought was about putting *them* through all this, including herself in a group. Makeba was making some progress.

"De lady she need five minutes to he'self," said Makeba, as she dressed early one morning and sneaked out of the motel room where the group was now staying. Maybe she could find a park or something. She just needed some quiet time to let all these new experiences settle in her soul. She put on the turban for the first time since the Mystery of History. But this time it was because she chose to do it, not because she wanted to hide behind it.

Makeba slowly tiptoed out the door, trying not to wake Pearl and Norma. She didn't realize that both Pearl and Norma were already out on their own adventures, and that she was actually being courteous to piles of pillows. It's the thought that counts, however. She even got some R.O. time for it, just a little.

Makeba breathed in the wet early morning air. Even though these islands always produced a dawn or dusk effect with the mild salmon glow from the main planet, sometimes the air was brisker than others, usually in the early "mornings," which, of course was more governed by *time* than light or dark. It must have been similar to the Midnight Sun in the North of Earth, Makeba was thinking, when she even had an opportunity to contemplate such things. She was very tied down with the tasks at hand here.

After walking about a mile, Makeba came to what she thought was the city center. She saw a small river running under the main street, a six or seven lane divided road, with some old trolley or railroad tracks running down. Makeba looked down from the bridge to the river. It looked like recent rains (or something) had swelled the river into a larger rushing body. Under the bridge for few hundred feet, the river was running down, and she could make out the sounds of white water rapids in the distance. She took out her glasses, and could barely see the telltale whitecaps about a quarter of a mile from the bridge. She knew from experience in Northern California, that when the snows melted, the smaller rivers became extremely dangerous, and even the best swimmers couldn't maneuver the raging waters.

Makeba looked back up towards the traffic on the bridge. Things were picking up as the rush hour, such as it was, set in. She noticed across the bridge a jogger on the other side of the street. As the jogger came closer, Makeba recognized the handsome Latino face of the lead singer of Mariachi Verde on the other side. She quickly dealt with her thoughts of jealousy. She hadn't had an opportunity to meet Angelo, but Norma told her that they had a great conversation, and Makeba recognized that Norma was duly impressed by the golden skin, black straight hair, and flashing white teeth of the singer who looked like an Aztec god. At that moment, Angelo recognized Makeba (how could you not!) and waved to her, finally slowing his jog to a stop. "Wait! Wait!" Angelo was calling to her from across the street but Makeba couldn't make out what he was saying.

"What? I can't hear you! What?" Makeba returned the call. She then saw Angelo wave her to stay put, and he began looking both ways to negotiate the now heavy traffic across the wide street on the bridge. Makeba's better judgment rang a warning bell, and she attempted to yell to him to wait on the other side, so they could both cross at the lights. Angelo, however, was already onto the street, and she didn't want to distract him from what was turning out to be a fairly dangerous journey. As he made it to the center divider, Makeba waited for him, but grew uneasy with the amount of traffic and noise.

At once, Makeba's worst fears were realized. As Angelo approached on her side of the street, he tripped. Makeba could finally see that his running shoe had become caught in one of the long-unused railroad tracks sunken into the street. She saw him pull his foot over and over, and saw that he couldn't get out. No traffic was stopping for him. Then she saw the Mac Truck traveling much too fast directly toward Angel. He pulled and pulled his foot with his hand, but in vain. The horrible wail of the air horn from the truck sounded, and the squeal of the brakes gave way to the white cloud of burning rubber as the tires locked. Angelo was standing when the truck hit him, full force.

As if in a dream, Makeba watched his seemingly lifeless body knocked in the air, and over the side of the bridge in front of her. She looked in horror as Angelo's body hit the rushing water below. "Help! Help!" Makeba screamed. A crowd quickly gathered, but seemed paralyzed. No one took any action. For the first time, time seemed to drag endlessly, and slow motion ensued. "Somebody call an ambulance! Quickly, somebody call an ambulance!" Makeba's instincts took over.

"He's gone. There's nothing anyone can do for him now." Makeba recognized this voice and looked up into the handsome face of the Bartender from her pursuits during Mystery of History. Makeba wondered what *he* was doing here, so out of place, but quickly flashed backed to the dire emergency at hand.

"No, *call an ambulance, NOW!*" Makeba was not listening to this man. In fact, Makeba rarely listened to anyone in an emergency. She had always counted on her quick thinking and that alone. She always made her own decisions, even if they were based on someone else's thoughts. At times like this, her every move was the result of her own considered and immediate analysis.

"He's not dead, not here anyway," said the Bartender. Makeba remembered that this was the man who put her straight about her life, and so she was tempted to listen to him, but she knew that she hadn't much time to act.

"Besides, with Angelo out of the picture, your group now goes to Inter-Galactics. Isn't that what you want?" Although that is exactly what Makeba had dreamed about not an hour before, a loud alarm bell went off in Makeba's head. The same man who made so much sense to her before now seemed to be rationalizing her into ignoring her instinct. Instinct. Hadn't she learned that instinct was the most important voice to listen to? Although this was the Bartender, what he was saying made him into a different person than he was before. Makeba noticed a man holding a cellular phone. She grabbed it and dialed 9-1-1.

"A man has been hit by a truck and knocked into the river on the bridge on the main street. There is injury. Get here as soon as possible!" Makeba only glanced back at the smiling Bartender as she kicked off her shoes, climbed up onto the concrete bridge railing, and jumped the tall jump deep down into the river after Angelo. Water rescue was not one of Makeba's strong points, although she had seen several of them live on television, and knew how to swim with the current, letting the current force take her where she needed to go. She located Angelo floating lifelessly a long way from her, but she maneuvered to the side of the river where the current was strongest, and began to catch up with him. She had to reach him before those impending rapids, or there would be no hope - for either of them. The traffic noise had given way to the roar of the river. Makeba's turban was still on her head, she always wrapped it tightly. She was gaining on Angelo, but would she make it before the rapids?

Makeba saw a rock a long way in the distance in front of them, jutting out of the water on the side of the river. If she could grab Angelo and steer toward the rock, they would be able to avoid the rapids. As she got closer to the rapids, she noticed that they ended in a falls, to she knew not where. Putting her hands straight in front of her, she began using her arms as oars, and slowly but surely, she was able to grab onto Angelo's limp arm. With all her might, she yanked Angelo's arm, sticking her feet out in front of her and, getting her arms around Angelo, she turned her back to the rapidly-approaching rock, and they both slammed into it. Makeba's back was on fire, but she didn't notice it. Instead, she pushed her feet against the rock, and was able to shove Angelo into a corner where the current was mild. Although the bank was steep in most places, by this rock, there was an eddy where she saw she would be able to drag Angelo. Even though Makeba was injured herself, she pushed Angelo onto the narrow bank, struggling to pull herself from the water, and began to look at his injuries.

Makeba was thrown back into her Black Panther quasi-paramedic and trauma training (which she never thought she would have used) where they learned battlefield medicine techniques for the "imminent revolution." It never happened, but Makeba remembered the training. Seeing an inordinate amount of blood coming from the head wound, she ripped off her turban, and tore it, fixing a bandage as she was taught. Angelo was turning bluish-white, which meant he wasn't breathing.

Makeba first held her head to Angelo's chest where she received some bad news. Angelo's heart had stopped. Immediately, Makeba laid out Angelo flat on his stomach, first pushing hard on his back to flush the excess water (from her Senior Life Saving training at the South Central LA YMCA). She knew that the water had to be removed from the lungs first. After getting a substantial amount out, she turned Angelo's body over, put her two fists together, and slammed them into his chest, to attempt to get his heart started. It did not start. Then she cleared his throat passageway with her finger, and began mouth-to-mouth. One-two-three-four-five breaths. Wham! The fists again came down on the chest, this time she pushed heavily on the rib cage. One-two-three-four-five. All this was instinct.

By the time the ambulance arrived, Angelo was coughing and his heart had started again, although Makeba could not tell if he was conscious or not. The paramedic told Makeba, as he was dressing the large scrape on her back, that without her, Angelo would certainly not have survived. After a check was made, it was determined that Angelo had only a minor leg injury, and would probably fully recover.

Makeba was helped to the top of the river bank, where the crowd from the street had moved and had grown. She looked for the Bartender, but he was not there. She did notice the man with the short dark beard, his hands in his jean pockets, walking away. She hadn't noticed him before. Makeba also didn't notice that her R.O. now displayed 11 credits and was blinking on and off. She had received credit for Instinct Over Intellect. It had nothing to do with saving the life of Angelo.

Angelo was loaded in the ambulance. The paramedic almost insisted that Makeba come to the hospital to be checked because of her back, but Makeba would have none of it. Struggling to her feet, she wrapped up the remaining soaked portion of her now-ripped turban, thanked the man, and began to walk back towards the main street. Makeba looked back at the ambulance pulling away. However, in a blinding white streak of light, the ambulance was gone. Maybe it was like one of those streak limos or something. Makeba was much too tired to think about it, or anything that happened. She just made it back to the motel where she collapsed onto her bed, falling into a deep, well-deserved sleep.

29 - NORMA'S CHOICE

Norma was awakened by the light tapping on the door. She threw on her robe quickly, seeing that both Pearl and Makeba were sound asleep, and they looked like they needed it. Tiptoeing to the door, Norma undid the inside locks and slowly pulled the Motel Room door open. She was surprised to see Jesus (pronounced "Hay-soos"), the leader of Mariachi Verde, in a very agitated state.

"We cannot find Angelo. I think he has been sent back to Plane of Origin!" Jesus was beside himself, since the rest of the group had not yet finished time and credits enough to return. Jesus spoke Spanish to Norma, who understood well. "Is there someplace we can go?" Norma, always ready to help, agreed to go to the park. She asked Jesus to wait, and then slipped quietly into her closet and carefully shut the door behind her so as not to wake the tired twosome sleeping. Slipping on her coat, she exited the closet and sneaked out the door. Soon she and Jesus were walking down the thoroughfare in front of the Motel.

"Yesterday, Angelo went to jog, as he does every day. I heard that there was an accident and he was taken away. We don't know what is wrong with him. We cannot find him, and no one will tell us where he went. I asked the director of the Inter-Galactics from the Super Region what to do. He says 'Angelo is gone. You must make other arrangements.' I am very concerned. Angelo is a dear friend of mine. I am worried for his safety. I also worry for my group. Without Angelo, we have no lead singer. With no lead singer, we are out of the running for Inter-Galactics, and we have no hope to gain our remaining credits together."

Norma understood all too well. The five of them had the same conversation the night they came in Second Place at Super Regionals. What were they going to do? They had invested all of their time into the competitions, and would basically have to start over again at Locals, and God only knew when those would be. But there was something in Jesus' manner, something that Norma knew was about to be spoken, something that she dreaded hearing.

Jesus stopped and turned facing Norma. There was an obvious lull in the traffic. The salmon light shone in his face, like a stage light. A corona encircled his head. "I want you to be our lead singer." These were the words Norma had feared. "I want you to take Angelo's place in our group for Inter-Galactics. You can do it. You have the voice and the presence to front our group. Without you, there is no one else on Chronos to take Angelo's place. Without you, we are lost. We are without a means to get back to our Plane of Origin. If you come with us, we will win. We will all earn enough credits to return to Plane of Origin." Jesus was extremely convincing, out of necessity.

"But what will happen to our group? What will become of my friends.?" Norma vocalized the immediate thoughts she was having. She knew that La Quinta would not survive without her — that the group might disband and be tossed to the four winds and that she might never see them again. On the other hand, if she did not go with the Mariachi's, she would be sealing their fate.

"Your group will not be able to win the Inter-Galactics anyway this time. It is futile. The Sweepstakes is never awarded to a first year group. They will have to make their way up again next season." Jesus made sense, but that did not alleviate the sinking feeling that Norma felt deep in her stomach. On the one hand, she would have an easy ticket back to Plane of Origin, singing with the Mariachi Verde and receiving enough credits to return. She only thought of the possible empty subway car, with her alone riding in it. There was a clear choice before her. If she left La Quinta and sang with Mariachi Verde, she would have a ticket home. If she refused, and stayed with La Quinta, Mariachi Verde would not be eligible to attend Inter-Galactics, and La Quinta would attend as substitute, being first in line and probably not winning, and probably not gaining enough credits. So it would invariably be Mariachi's last chance to return to Plane of Origin, or La Quinta's first try, in which case, heaven only knows what would happen.

"I have to think about it. I have to pray. I cannot give you a decision right now."

"But do not wait too long. We have to inform the authorities as soon as possible." Jesus kissed Norma's hand and then turned to go away.

"I will tell you by this night," Norma called after him. And with that, Norma was left alone in the park, by the side of the river.

The sound of the rippling water was soothing, but did little to quell the tempest inside of Norma. She was now faced with a decision that would impact, not only herself, but all of her friends, and her compatriots as well. Norma began aimlessly climbing up the mountain trail toward the source of the river, into the glades. After climbing above a small, smooth waterfall, she came upon a glassy pond. It was a beautiful spot with a dark green pool covered with lily pads, where the water collected before once again tumbling down the mountain to the river in the park. Norma wanted to rest, so she found herself an ample rock to sit on to contemplate the matter at hand. "Oh dear Lord, please help me to think of the right road to take," she prayed to herself. At that moment, she heard a rustling in the bushes and heard a great shrieking cry. Norma immediately turned to see what noise was breaking the stillness of the moment. She gasped as she beheld a great peacock with its tail flared out, shaking and rattling. Around the peacock's neck was a necklace shining bright with coins stamped from a pink ore. They resembled the brand new shiny copper pennies which her father had given her to reward her for doing a good deed.

The great peacock turned and faced Norma. She beheld its magnificent presence. The feathers were shining in gold and silver, bejeweled with what seemed diamonds, rubies, emeralds and sapphires. On the peacock's head was a crown of platinum. As the salmon light struck the peacock, Norma was forced to shield her eyes. Out of nowhere, the peacock began to speak.

"I am called Fame. People know me from one end of the universe to the other. If you choose me, you will have your rewards. You will be known throughout the galaxy. If you choose to sing with the Mariachis, you will have many who adore you. You will have riches. You will stay only in palaces. You will travel only Royal Class. You will meet the kings and queens of the universe. I am called Fame. I am bright, I am fire, I am a blinding flash. Choose me."

Norma was completely taken aback. She did not know what to do or say. Here was one of her choices set clearly before her. If she choose to sing with the Mariachis, she would have everything she ever thought she wanted. She would not be poor. She would earn her credits. For a moment, and only a moment, she forgot Pearl, Makeba, Nardo and Jake. For a split second, she thought only of the ease with which she could accomplish her goals.

Out of the stillness, Norma's trance was broken by the distant yelp of a small dog. As she looked up again at the Peacock, the light had changed. The copper coins were no longer bright, but appeared tarnished. The gold of the tail had turned a dull bronze, and the jewels looked like so many bits of glass without the light to help them.

Without thinking, Norma got up and bowed to the Peacock. "What you offer is tempting, but I cannot leave my friends with no way out." With that, Norma turned from the Peacock, looked up the trail, and hiked on, taking herself further up the mountain, past the second waterfall.

As she cleared a stand of trees in a flat area, she drew in a breath. Before her was a still pool fed by a large waterfall. The pool was midnight blue, and the light bounced off it, sparkling like stars in the black velvet sky. Norma noticed a large old tree stump which had been hewn down. Tired, she sat on the tree stump to catch her breath.

The rustling of leaves once again caught her attention. Norma whipped her head around to see a small furry dog coming up to her.

Norma was a lover of animals. She now knew where the barking had come from. The little dog came right over to Norma and sniffed her hand, and Norma began to pet it. Norma noticed that the dog wore a collar, and that the collar was studded with shining silver coins. As Norma inspected the collar more closely, she was startled. Out of nowhere, the dog began to speak.

"My name is Loyalty. Wherever you are, I will be there. Unlike fame, a blinding flash, I am constant. I never waver. No matter what consequences present themselves to you, I will share them. My rewards are slow, not quick. I do not unfold my entire treasure at once, but only over a long period of time. If you choose to stay with La Quinta, you will have chosen me. I am for better and for worse. My name is Loyalty. I am constant. Choose me."

"But if I choose you, what happens to the others? What happens to Mariachi? What happens to those who have worked hard before me to succeed? Jesus tells me that La Quinta doesn't have a chance this year. And what happens to my dreams of being in Mariachi?" Norma was totally perplexed. She was torn between the two choices before her more than ever. And, worse yet, her distress over the choice had slowed her to inaction. She didn't know what to do, so she would do nothing. In tears, Norma sprung from the great stump, and began running further away from Loyalty and up the mountain trail, toward the source of the river.

Norma had no concept of how long she had been running, her tears blinding her, branches snapping this way and that, brushing in her face and the roar of the river becoming more deafening with each step she took. Finally, able to stand it no more, Norma fell down in a heap in the thick undergrowth, and there seemed to fall into a dream.

When she awoke, it was to a familiar sounding voice. Norma opened her eyes and saw a pair of shiny black shoes with buckles on them. She looked up a little, and found the bottoms of a black robe, and gold cords around them. Strong but gentle hands picked Norma up and she found herself staring into a kind familiar face.

"Padre!" Norma wiped away the tears from her eyes. "Padre, I didn't think I'd see you again here!"

"I am always here for you, Norma. I am never away."

"Padre. The most awful choice has been foisted upon me. I am made to choose between my friends and my compatriots. I am made to choose which will be successful. This horrible choice has been set upon me, and me alone. I am made to believe I am the only one who can save them, but I can save only one."

"Ah." The Padre smiled benevolently. "You have decided that you can only save one, and so you have decided to put to yourself a terrible choice. Come with me my child, and I shall tell you of a parable. With this story, and your will and prayers, the answer to your dilemma will appear to you."

With that, the Padre took Norma by the hand and led her through the Piney grove. As they cleared the trees, Norma beheld a sight more beautiful that any she before saw. A large lake loomed, surrounded by green lush trees with plumeria, ginger and orchids growing from every crevice and cranny. The perfume of the blossoms was overwhelming. As Norma looked up at the head of the lake, she saw a great waterfall, wide and at least a hundred feet tall, with the billowy cascades creating a beautiful cloud at the far end of the lake. The lake was relatively still where she and the Padre stood. The Padre took her by the hand to lead her further to the base of what seemed to be a great pyramid, of the type she had seen in the Aztec and Mayan culture. It was a great step pyramid, covered now with the vegetation of years, and inscribed with intricate carvings hidden by eons of weather and growth.

The Padre led Norma to the base of the pyramid. It was then that she noticed that his belt was made of shiny gold coins, also Aztec in their look. The Padre sat Norma down at the bottom step next to him and this tale unfolded.

"A man passed over the portal of time and space, and left his earthly body to the place of no time and space. He found himself on a road and soon it was dark. In the distance, he saw some small wooden buildings, and as he approached, he saw that there were two inns. Out of one Inn, bright lights streamed, and the seeming screams of laughter and merriment abounded. Out of the other Inn, only a small light shone in the window, but there was no laughter or noise. In fact, the man was not sure that anyone was in the second Inn."

"He was immediately attracted then to enter the first Inn, the one of the bright lights and loud sounds. As he walked through, he heard merry music and saw in front of him a great table filled with the most luxurious of foods, cornucopias, and bounty. Seated around the table were many people. As the man approached, his attraction to this place was shattered. For what he had initially beheld as laughter were in actuality, screams of agony. Each person's hands were bound and to each hand was tied a long spoon - a spoon long enough to reach the food and the bounty. But, alas, there was no way that the person could get the spoon to turn around to put the food in his mouth. There was no way to cut the large fowl or the meat, no way to eat the abundant fruit which fell from the cornucopia. The man looked closely at the faces of the people seated around the table. In horror, he realized that they were screaming in pain, they were starving. The man, who had been invited to be seated at the table, ran in terror out the front door and catching his breath, looked toward the second, quieter Inn.

Cautiously entering the second Inn lest he behold another ghastly sight, as he slowly proceeded through to the large dining area. Once in this area, he became shocked to find that the scene was almost identical to the one he had just left. A great table, full of bounty was laid and the table was lined with people. But there was a marked difference. Although these people had the same implements bound to their hands, they were happy, quiet, well fed, and only murmured thanks to God, intermittently. As the man watched further, he noticed that the fowl had been sliced, the fruit made into edible portions and the meat cut. But most importantly, the patrons of the Quiet Inn were feeding each other. Although the spoons did not reach their own mouths, they thought only of feeding the other patrons, and therefore sat in comfort and meditative silence. It was there that the man learned that the same facts, circumstances and people can lead to diametrically opposed results depending on whether those people realized that the sum of them was worth much more that the total of the individual parts."

Norma sat in awe, staring at the great waterfall at the end of the pool. She did not hear the Padre get up and quietly slip away. When Norma once again became conscious of her surroundings, the Padre was gone.

Norma was a little dizzy from the perfume of the flora, and the crisp smell of the mist from the waterfall. Not quite out of her daze, Norma located the path down the mountain, taking one last look at the great lake and the pyramid. As she passed the second pool, there was no sign of the dog; at the first pool, the Peacock had disappeared. But by the time Norma got down to the park level again, she knew what her choice would be. Norma turned to take one last look at the path from which she had just emerged. It was gone, there was no sign of it. Norma walked slowly and deliberately back to the Motel. It was time for another meeting, this time with both La Quinta and Mariachi Verde. Norma had found possible redemption for all of them.

30 - CLOWNS AND SALSA

Norma did not think it would be difficult to convince the groups that they should meet and discuss their merger. The sum being greater than the total of its parts – this was a theory that both groups had learned since arrival on Chronos – and maybe it was meant to be. The fact that they had a semi-language barrier did not hurt, since both Norma and Nardo spoke Spanish and Jesus spoke a little broken English. Both groups didn't have a lot of time for the kind of background chatter they were leisurely able to afford among their own groups in prior times. Norma discovered that the Mariachis were from somewhere in Mexico, but she didn't know where, when or how. The mystery of Angelo was also not solved. No one seemed to have any information on where he went.

There was a man with a dark beard on this Island who knew, and wasn't telling. Abraxas wasn't feeling great about himself these days, and neither were the people who had spent so much time on hiring him to do this job. So far, with the exception of Angelo, he had been foiled at every juncture. Oh, well. He still had many tricks in his jeans pocket . . . many tricks. These novices were no match for Abraxas. He had toppled them all the way from naïve to sophisticated and intellectual, and he wasn't going to let this "Subway Car Earth Trash" get the better of him. He was already on to his next scheme. His next idea was brilliant, if he did say so himself. And it was so easy. Quick, time-sensitive, and infallible. It had never failed to work in the past. Abraxas paid a visit to some other long-timers. Although he would pay dearly for this one, his reputation would be saved. He called his sticky-sweet clients and told them to prepare for the next competition, the Inter-Galactics, no holds barred. They were, of course, ecstatic, and began to do so with reckless abandon. They would spend every minute earned on this. They would finally have their chance.

Norma and Nardo had arranged to borrow chairs from the Motel for the meeting. Since Angelo's disappearance, the people back in Rim-of-the-Stars, not knowing what to do, told La Quinta that they should stay in the City pending the resolution of the issue on Inter-Galactics. Since Mariachi Verde might not be able to go, La Quinta would have to prepare for Inter-Galactics, just in case. They were not aware of the meeting that was about to take place.

Mariachi Verde now had nine members, without Angelo. Two fiddles, three trumpets, a guitarron, a marimba and two Spanish Guitars, so the little Motel room was very crowded. Norma had ordered soft drinks for everyone, and seemed extremely determined as she stood up and exposed her plan of merger. The only thing that stood in their way was the prospect of having to clear the merger with the Inter-Galactic Authorities. In the end, Norma's common sense arguments to them saved the day. After all, they were both from the same Super-Region, First Place and Second Place. If one didn't perform, the other one would anyway. And the groups were allowed to change both people and compositions prior to Inter-Galactics, so long as a substantial number of the same members performed. The new, merged group met all of these criteria, and Norma, having done her homework, was prepared to answer questions regarding these matters to the whole group of which there were many.

The group listened intently to Norma's idea and the only dissent was the distant wail of Pearl kvetching, "Oy vey, I hope I don't havta loin anotheh tambourine pahhhht!" Makeba smiled at her and winked, not having the slightest compunction about teaching Pearl a new part. Makeba loved these challenges. And after the spectacular swimming rescue, which by the way was covered in all the local rags, Makeba's confidence was at an all-time high. She actually gave her name as Makeba "Mona Lisa" Edwards to the newspaper just for kicks, hoping against hope that maybe somebody, somewhere would remember Mona Lisa Edwards from the Berkeley incident and wonder, "Is that the same person? It *must* be." Yes, Makeba's confidence had been fully restored, and had she looked at he R.O. occasionally, she would have realized how well she was doing in the credits department. Unfortunately, none of them had time to check R.O.'s. It was a luxury they could no longer afford.

Norma continued the meeting with the combined groups, first delivering the English, then the Spanish version. She felt like a stewardess for Mexicana Airlines, but Nardo felt she handled it brilliantly.

After a quick, unanimous vote, the group was ready to begin. Norma had already found a place to practice - an old church recreation room in the area where they could plug in and play as loud as they wanted during the day or night, and all they would have to do would be to clean the place up. And cleaning it needed. Having been sadly neglected for many years, the chairs were in disrepair, the old stage and lights were falling down, the curtains were filthy and needed to be rehung and balanced. Here's where the combined team soared in competence. The Mariachis (there were also two women in the nine, a guitar player and a fiddle player) could help fix up anything, being quite used to renovations in Mexico, since things there had to last a long, long time. They scrounged some paint and equipment.

The girls (pardon the expression) concentrated on the curtains, completely washing the place down. The old chairs were first fixed by Jesus, who was a carpenter by trade, with the help of the other Mariachi men. Then they were painted spectacular white, and the old recreation room at the church began to take on a new brilliance. By finagling an electrician to work for almost nothing, the sound system and lights were repaired to better than before they broke, the stage was re-sanded and varnished by hand. Soon the recreation room was spic and span.

In the meantime, the combined group had regular business meetings. "Our next order of business is the name of the group," said Norma in her determined voice.

"What about keeping Mariachi Verde?" exclaimed Jesus in a kind of protest.

"Shouldn't it be something new?" said Jake.

"We already have the costumes, which cost a lot of time. We should probably build on what we have." Jesus was sort of adamant on keeping the name.

"Why don't we try something unique and different?" Jake was speaking up, thinking about the fact that the queer and diverse combo of La Quinta had been their trademark. People responded to and related to the sort of goofy-looking group with a good sound.

"Well," Norma said, translating everything, does anyone have any ideas for the name of a kooky Mariachi band?"

"What rhymes with Mariachi?" Makeba was thinking now. "I can't think of anything in the *world* that rhymes with Mariachi."

And she was practically right. For ten minutes, everyone sat there with dumbfounded looks on their face trying to think of something that rhymed with Mariachi.

Pearl finally broke the silence. "The only ting I can tink of dat rhymes wit Mariachi is 'Pagliacci', you know, from the opera oveh deah."

"Pagliacci. Pagliacci was the sad clown in the operas, wasn't he Pearl?" Nardo had looked up from deep thought.

"Yeah. He was supposed to be happy all the time, but instead he cried."

"Pagliacci Mariachi. I don't think so," said Jesus. "It just doesn't make any sense. People have to know what you are talking about."

A slow smile broke out over Nardo's face. The apotheosis of new costumes was forming in his mind. A Mariachi group singing great and serious Mariachi style tunes, but which broke all the rules. The Pierrot diamond patterns of the traditional clowns spun in his mind.

"That's it! Pearl thought of it! That's what we should do. We have nothing to lose. We're a crazy-mixed up group of all kinds of people, and we need some kind of image that can tie us together. The idea of the sad clown is perfect, especially for this place. I mean, aren't we all performing and entertaining, while underneath we're sad because we want to go back home? This is something *everyone* will relate to." Nardo was ecstatic.

Jake chimed, "I agree. Our group got where it is by being unique and by stressing the strong points of the individual members. We've got a group that doesn't fit into any category. Why should we try to conform?"

Jesus excepted. "But these people seem very traditional. Traditional groups have constantly won, over the years."

"Not our group," opined Makeba. "We rocketed to stardom by stressing our uniqueness. Call it strange, call it whatever. The crowds loved us because we *were* us and we didn't try to conform to some standard. We let the nature of the group derive from the character of its individual members."

"We're still going to play Mariachi music, aren't we?" Jesus wasn't yet convinced.

"Yes, of course. That's what most of us are used to. But we have other influences we should add. That way nobody can copy us. That way, we have our own particular or, if you will, peculiar, style." Norma had caught onto the idea.

"Well then," compromised Jesus, "How about MARIACHI PAGLIACCI? Let's do it the Spanish way, at least, and have the adjective at the end."

With that, the group was off thinking. They began trying various styles of music, some worked and some did not. They never let the West African/Latin influence go, and laid down the interlocking rhythms underneath. Makeba taught the new rhythm section who learned of a new dimension in music. Nardo was playing special licks on his flute to match the interlocking rhythms - rhythms he had learned in Indonesia from Balinese Gamelan music, which was also played with interlaced beats. Jesus on lead guitar could play the formal Spanish *Rasgueadas* from Flamenco, and the rhythm guitarist taught Jake, an apt pupil by now, how to play the Malagueña rhythms correctly.

Nardo and the ladies immediately got to work on the costumes. Starting with the bases of the kelly green Mariachi uniforms, Pearl, Nardo and Norma began to work their "seconds and scraps" magic once again. Nardo designed huge Maria Clara dresses for the women, full skirts with ruffles and whatever sparkles and rhinestones they could artfully apply. Of course, they were all in the Pierrot diamond clown patterns. The headdresses were amazing. The sombreros were practically gilded when Nardo finished with them, and Makeba's turban shone like a great jewel. Pearl's hair was pushed on top of her head and an ample cascade of silk flowers formed her diadem. The two women in the old Mariachi had straight skirts, bejeweled of course, with the same silk flower treatment. The rest of the band was in the Bolero jackets, but now decked with glitter and sparkle diamond patterns. And in front of this great madness was Norma.

Nardo felt that Norma's appearance should stand out, and by underplaying her outfit, she did just that. Nardo fashioned a Gaucho outfit for her in Kelly green. Down the sides were solid diamond-rhinestone stripes, and the bolero jacket disclosed a beautifully tailored ruffled shirt. Norma's hair was pulled back, showing her practically flawless face, and a she donned a corona of loose diamond-rhinestones which, individually hung, followed her every movement. Shiny black knee high patent leather boots completed her outfit.

As far as songs for performance went, Norma and Jesus immediately got to work, what with time being so short. Jesus was an excellent musician and, after much discussion, Jesus asked Norma was she was most passionate about.

Norma could not hold back her tears when she related the story of the Television studio to Jesus, and the underlying story of her "coming of age" in East L.A.

"But, mi amiga. That is what you should sing about!"

"But . . . I can't. It's too personal!"

"Not about the assault, mi amiga! About your conquest of life. About your revelation. It is only when you write and sing about what is closest to you that you will communicate with the people!"

Norma considered this carefully. Here would be an opportunity for her to turn the ugliest moment of her life into something beautiful. At that moment, she knew Jesus was right. "But how do we say it?"

"Ah, my poor little conquerer. Conquistadora pobrecita. She cannot express what she feels. Jesus will help you."

And with that came the inspiration for the original song, "CONQUISTADORA POBRECITA," the poor little conquerer. Jesus took his guitar and began with some excellent and, of course, flashy flamenco guitar work. And from his mouth came the song . . . beauty born out of ugliness. Without stopping, he sang this chorus with a Salsa/Tejana/Africana mix:

CONQUISTADORA POBRECITA
PARA LA VIDA TENGO YA UN RAZON
CONQUISTADORA POBRECITA
DAME UNA JOLLA PA' MI CORAZON

Poor Little Conquerer
For life I now have a reason
Poor Little Conquerer
Give me a Jewel for my Heart

The response of the group to the song was phenomenal. Although Pearl was still distraught about having to learn another interlocking rhythm, Makeba soon found a part for herself and Pearl which interlocked with the corresponding guitar rhythms and the flavorful Indo-Caribbean sound of Nardo's flute.

Although Norma would sing the chorus by herself, the men would respond in traditional Mariachi harmony, and Makeba would follow-up with a blues riff which was, in all probability, loud enough to balance her against the rest of the group without a mike.

The group practiced diligently every night and worked during the day. Between their locals, the Super-Region supplying them with time for their R.O.'s for living expenses, and the free rehearsal hall, they were the best kept secret in the Galaxy. Or was it. The new custodian at the church quietly closed the door, and smiled to himself as he rolled his pail and mop back to the Janitor's closet. He wiped his hands on his jeans. The group was rehearsing all-out, unaware of the "secret admirer" lurking in the church. And anyway, they didn't care. Tonight was their night off. Norma and Jesus said that they had to have every seventh evening off. Most of them had plans, either together or separately. Jake had his own plans, or did someone have plans for Jake.

31 - THE SEDUCTION OF JAKE: JUST THIS ONCE

Jake unfolded and read the neatly-printed napkin once more which he had carefully concealed from his music-mates. Meet me at the Savoy-Tivoli. I am in the penthouse. M." Although the message had been passed to him during the awards ceremony at Super-Regionals, Jake did not have to think twice about who this was. It was the blond "Madonna" he had met at the Banyan Bar. And now he would have the chance to accept the romantic evening that he missed at the Banyan Bar.

He was on top of the world. And, though he dearly loved the group and what they were doing, he needed a night to himself. A night to himself as a man. This was his golden opportunity, and he was going to grab it.

Jake hailed a regular cab. He didn't want to waste the money (time) on a Streak Limo. They were expensive, and he'd rather spend the time in the cab, enjoying the ride and jabbing with the cab driver. "So where are you headed?" The cab driver spoke with his head straight to the window in front of him, never turning it.

"I'm headed to the Savoy-Tivoli."

"Ooooo. Ritzy hotel, the Savoy. You got lots of time to

spend?" The cab driver obviously had this conversation many times with riders.

"This is a special occasion." Jake was taciturn about the particulars.

"I can show you a place where you can have plenty good time!" The cab driver laughed, and turned back toward Jake, narrowly missing a car in front of him. Like most cab drivers, he leaned on his horn hard, fast and first. That was how you told another driver it was their fault, whether it was or not.

"No thanks," Jake thanked the swarthy driver. Where had he seen that face before? Oh well, everything was beginning to look familiar to him. He let it pass.

"You sure you don't want nothing to make you feel better? I know where I can get some. Hey, it's your night off. Live a little. It can't hurt."

"How did you know it was my night off?" Jake queried.

"Why else would you be out. Going to the Savoy. It has to be your night off." The cab driver laughed. Jake passed it off again.

The doorman opened the cab door and the cab driver stated a price. Jake looked over at the meter, absolutely flabbergasted that he had not gotten the price *before* making the cab ride, a mistake he hadn't made in years. But he hadn't taken a cab in years. He noticed that the cabbie had a cloth over the meter, and insisted that he remove it. The doorman walked over to the driver's side, reached in and pulled off the cloth, exposing the meter. The meter showed about one-half the amount the cab driver was demanding.

"You got extras," said the cab driver.

"Extra this," and Jake handily flipped him off, permitting only the precise amount of the meter to be deducted from his R.O. He then tipped the doorman the cabbie's tip, the doorman opened the huge glass doors, and handsome Jake strode into the vaulted, Rococo-ornate lobby of the Savoy-Tivoli. Jake was in jeans and this was definitely not a "jeans" establishment. Before Jake could even move, a Hotel Concierge was upon him, asking him his business.

"Can I help you sir," the well-suited Asian woman said to him with a nice smile, supercilious though it might be.

Jake pulled the napkin from his pocket. It wasn't really a class act, but Jake hadn't thought about a nice place like this in a long time, and the nicest thing he had to wear were his costumes, a little overdone for anywhere but the stage.

"Ah, come right in Mr. Silver. You are expected. I will unlock the express elevator to the Penthouse for you." The tune of the Concierge had transformed immediately, and Jake was led through a gilded door into a special lobby, where a small but fantastically carved wooden elevator was awaiting him. There were no buttons inside. The door closed, and Jake's heart leapt.

For a moment he thought, "Where the hell am I going?" and was truly scared. But a few seconds later, the door opened into a private elevator lobby, and in front of him was one door marked "Penthouse 1 - Waterloo." Jake rang the doorbell.

The scent of balmy ocean and plumeria swept out of the door as it cracked open. "What does this remind me of?" Jake tried. Then he remembered as peeking out from around the door, Jake stared down into the big blue eyed, blond haired friend with whom he had danced at the fragrant Banyan Bar. It was Madonna.

As the door opened, Jake's eyes widened. There, at the top of the hotel, Jake looked out onto the city of lights below. The lavish suite decorated in French Provincial antiques spread out before him, in tones of amber, gold and orange calcite. There was some soft, sexy early Eydie Gorme music playing lightly in the background, room service had already been ordered, and two meals and a candlelight dinner were sitting there under large silver covers.

"C'mon over Jake. I'd hoped this moment would come before you left. And now it has." Madonna took Jake's hand. Madonna's hand was very soft and white, with bright red nail polish to set off her otherwise alabaster skin. Never taking her blue eyes off Jake's own blues, she lovingly led him to the big bay window overlooking the bejeweled city below them, and in the distance loomed space with its pearl-studded lapis expanse. Jake melted as he sat down on the luxurious high backed love seat, done in a soft pearl damask, stuffed with goose down. He had remembered these hotel rooms from earlier times when his agent was frivolously spending his money on them. Unfortunately, he never stayed in them himself. Only that agent. Oh, well, thanks to the revelation at the Hot Tub, he was over that now. And into the moment.

A magnum of expensive champagne in a large silver bucket was the only thing which broke up the view. Madonna immediately poured out two Lalique crystal flutes of it.

"Why are you being so opulent?" asked Jake, perplexed. This was far from the down-to-earth Madonna he had met in the Banyan Bar. Not that he cared. In fact, he was caring less and less. "Why ask questions?" he thought to himself. "Jake, just go with the flow, for a change."

"I wanted it to be a very special night. I . . . I've never done this before." That statement would turn out to be true enough. Madonna lifted Jake's champagne flute to his lips.

"Alcohol," thought Jake. "I haven't had it since . . . well since the day of the subway accident." Even though Jake called it an "accident," he knew damn well it wasn't. "Oh well, one glass of champagne can't hurt. After all, I've been working like a dog since I got here. A lot of people drink one or two glasses of champagne, and they're not alkies." Jake flashed back on going home after AA meetings in Hollywood and snorting lines of coke. Somehow, he had separated in his mind drugs and alcohol. Since he got here, however, he had seen the light, especially traveling with a completely tea-totaling and drug-free group. "I guess if you put yourself in situations of non-distraction, it's much easier." Jake had learned not to put himself where the drugs and alcohol flowed freely, and was able to break himself of the habit here. Of course, sticking with the Subway Brigade helped immensely.

But something was amiss. Madonna hadn't been drinking at the Banyan Bar. Of course, there was no cause to. She was "on duty" and he really didn't know her habits. "I don't think I should. I mean, I have a problem with it." Jake put up a little fight.

"On, come on. Just a little sip. I mean, everyone takes a sip of champagne on New Year's Eve. Well, isn't this our New Year? Jake, when will we ever get this opportunity again?" Madonna was still holding the crystal flute to Jake's lips. She still had her blue gaze transfixed on his. The luscious little-girl lips were in the most subtle sexy pout. She smelled clean and wonderful. Jake took a sip, and so did Madonna. Putting the flutes down, Madonna leaned over to Jake and planted a soft, luscious kiss on his lips.

It had been so very, very long since he had been attractive to a woman. Her eyes told the whole story. The two embraced, and softly made out on the couch. Madonna's soft tongue made its way into Jake's mouth and the kisses became full and sexual. As they came up for air, Madonna again offered Jake "just one more sip" of champagne. Soon, the flutes had been refilled once, and then again.

Jake was beginning to feel very light headed. "Maybe we should eat something. I'm starting to feel the champagne . . . a little." Jake was feeling the champagne, all right, as well as his oats. Madonna threw her head back, shook the platinum blond hair, and laughed.

She got up and went to the candlelit table, pulling the lids off simultaneously. "See . . . I remembered!" Jake approached and saw that there were two gorgeous plump hamburgers and fresh French fries, just the way he liked them. This was something else he had not had since the night of the Banyan Bar.

The two ate, reminisced over times at the Banyan Bar. Jake related to Madonna the rest of the story, going through the mansion, the masque ball, the hot tub, the purloined Book, the purple farts bus and the competitions, and brought her up to date. She listened intently, never looking away from his eyes. During the meal, Madonna served a ruby red cabernet, and Jake partook . . . just this once, mind you.

The sexy music played on, and after dinner and excellent coffee, the two stood up and embraced and kissed. Jake was much taller than the minute Madonna, but she was a woman in every sense, smell, feel, taste. Yes, Jake was feeling his oats. Without warning, Madonna had slipped her minimal slip dress off, and was standing there in soft mauve bikini underwear, with the silk dress now a pool by her feet. Jake's eyes widened, among other things. A slight breeze was blowing her hair from somewhere, as she laughed and tossed her head again, wetting her ruby red lips with her tongue.

"I'm ready, Jake. Just one more thing. One more thing to make it perfect." Madonna pointed out a standing dresser on the side of the room. As Jake walked over and approached it, he saw what he had not seen in years. An ornate, mirrored tray was striped with lines of the white powdery substance. On the mirror was a silver coke straw. "I've already had mine, Jake. Just one line, that's all. It'll take the edge off. Just this once."

Jake thought, "there's really no edge to take off, now," feeling no pain from the wine and champagne. But he remembered how the drug would enhance geometrically the effects of sex. And especially sex with this beautiful woman. Jake was torn. He was able to convince himself of the "just this once" argument for the wine and the champagne, and had sublimated his pangs of guilt for those, but was he ready to do this again? Full bore drugs? Because that's what it was. Fully slipping back into the old habits.

Jake turned and looked at Madonna standing there like a statue of Venus, still not removing that hypnotic gaze from his eyes. "Oh well . . . Oh Hell, why not." Jake turned toward the dresser and slowly picked up and considered the silver coke straw. "Why am I doing this?" But things had gone too far. He turned once more to see the statue standing there. Then slowly, he began to lean over in front of the dresser mirror, down to the mirrored tray with the coke straw up to his nose.

As he glanced in the mirror to see the vision once again, he was halted in his tracks. There in the reflection of the mirror stood a well built, stark naked, hairy bearded man, dark and swarthy. The man in the suit at Super Regionals. The Janitor. The Cab Driver. Jake's face first paled, then turned bright red. The image in the mirror was *not* the image of the girl he was expecting. Jake finally realized that all along, this had not been Madonna.

"I'll KILL YOU!" Jake threw the coke straw at the mirror, and blinded by rage, whipped around and grabbed the throat of whatever was there and began to squeeze with his eyes shut tight in anger. He cracked them open only a little, and saw that his hands were around the neck of the beautiful woman, who was grabbing his arms, unable to breathe. Even all the rage of wanting to kill his manager, all the frustration of his career, and now the trickery, the debauchery, the larceny played by whoever this was . . . even all of this couldn't turn Jake into a killer. The vision's eyes were blue and wide, Jake threw her on the bed, as he wended his way back toward the front door of the suite. "Treachery . . . treachery." Jake strode out of the suite, hammering his fist on the elevator button. When it came, he got in and was breathing hard. On the way down, he buried his head in his hands in shame. Shame that he had almost been coaxed into the unreal, the same place his problems had all started on Earth. He clung to one thought and one thought only. "I never took the drugs." It was there that Jake swore an oath to himself that he would never be tempted by "just this once" any more. Jake pounded the elevator with his fist. He had not been this angry with anyone since the Lilywhite manager incident. But this time, as he finally realized, the anger was directed toward the right person . . . himself. *He* was fully responsible for each and every moment of his life, no one else. It was a lesson forever etched on his soul, beyond intellect. These are the lessons that change our lives.

Jake wondered when the elevator was ever going to reach the lobby. He was tired and light-headed from all the champagne and wine. It was all he could do to keep his eyes open.

Up in the room, Abraxas went up to the dresser mirror, still panting and gasping for breath. Thoroughly disgusted, he threw the mirror tray across the room, shattering it. He had failed once again. He cursed his silly antics with the brakes on the Purple Farts bus, his failure as the Bartender to dissuade the heroics of Makeba, his flop at the delicatessen with Pearl, and his fanciful Peacock and Pooch which did not stop Norma from making the right decision. He was not dealing with his normal moronic idiots, although that's exactly what they looked like for all intent and purposes. "Never underestimate the competition," was his rule, and he had broken it now, four or five times. Well, there was still one left. One more that would be the *piece-de-resistance*, one still in the hopper. Yes, still one more chance to undo this team, to crack whatever they had going for them. "This time I won't be so fancy. This time I'll go for the throat." Abraxas looked at his very handsome face and muscular body in the mirror. "I know what he wants."

32 - STREAKING

The Inter-Galactics were finally here. Pearl thought to herself as the Streak Limos were being loaded, "So much junk and tchachkes. I liked it better when it was just one guitar," thinking back to the simplicity of the ordeal at the Blue Barn compared to this. This competition business was extremely grueling.

Of course, Nardo and Pearl had gotten the costumes together and they looked immaculate, but not before several hang-ups. Materials not matching. Having to order and send for. Nardo advanced much of the time to pay for the additions, always believing he would be repaid immediately by the group. And then there was a big to-do about that. "Why didn't we vote on it? *How* much did you spend? You should've told us!" Oh the problems with democracy in a performing group. Nardo, who had always worked alone as a drag queen had certainly figured out one thing.

"Art is a dictatorship," he mused. You couldn't get any true art done on compromise. At best you would end up with mish-mash, as Pearl called it. In her heart, Pearl agreed. She knew what Nardo's vision for the costumes were and was extremely content to be a follower, especially when she trusted his talent.

"When everybody throws their two cents in, you get something dat makes no sense," Pearl philosophized. She had also advanced time for the costumes, but with a little more life-experience than Nardo, was cognizant that she might not recover it, although she would register in her mind which members made the biggest stink. And once listed in Pearl's register, one was not easily removed.

In the final analysis, the Subway Brigade quickly came to its senses, and Norma was able to talk the Mariachis into splitting the costs which only made sense. That way, each would feel it only a little, not one sacrificing a large chunk for the good of the whole. It was back to the parable of the two Inns. That's how Norma was going to run this thing, and she wasn't afraid to use her unexpendable position in the group to enforce it.

"Conquistadora Pobrecita" was sounding excellent. Although the group themselves became used to the sound, the mix was so unique, the song was strong, the back-up vocals, the rhythms, everything fell together to make a great thing. And Jesus was a perfectionist. Although the group itself was a crazy combination, Jesus put each element artistically together, filled in the holes where needed, wrote parts, and he and Norma made certain everyone could do their parts blindfolded. The church rec room had served its purpose, and the group was as ready as it would ever be.

Jake, unfortunately, showed up just before the Streak Limos were going to pull out. Nardo and Makeba were going crazy trying to locate him, since he had left no message about his whereabouts, a left-over appendage from his days of carousing and so forth, they supposed. Nardo had fully packed for him, and when he finally showed up, five minutes prior to the Streak Limos leaving, he surprisingly looked none the worse for wear. In fact, Nardo for the first time noticed how really good-looking Jake was, his natural coloring and sparkling blue eyes. Nardo was in the habit of not letting himself get involved in the looks of other men, especially straight men. He knew his unfortunate weaknesses in that department. And any such attachments could only lead to disaster, as they had in the past. Nardo quickly pulled his eyes away, and asked Jake to help him load the trunks onto the Streak Limo.

The group had decided that the Mariachi group would actually go ahead to the theater, wherever it was, and set up, get the costumes ready, and so forth. Since each Limo held only up to eight or nine passengers, the Quintet decided they would follow in the second limo. After all, it would just be a matter of seconds. In fact, Nardo was excited about finally being able to take the Streak Limo, as they had been heretofore relegated to the slower and less dependable Purple Farts bus.

The costumes, instruments and all accoutrements loaded on the first Streak Limo, Jesus hugged the girls, the men all shook hands, and they said a prayer in a prayer circle, something Norma had demanded. "I don't care where we are, we can use the extra insurance," and everyone agreed. Pearl, of course, cringed when, at the end, the phrase "we say this in the name of our Lord Jesus Christ, Amen" was used, but being Jewish Pearl was extremely stable in her knowledge that "Jesus was a Jew, and he neveh converted!" In this way, she could rationalize the prayer's ending along with the rest. Jake, however, did not flinch.

After the first Limo had streaked, Norma got everyone up into and situated in the plush Limousine. There was a bar, a television (no Jacuzzi, Nardo thought, thankfully for Jake, knowing of his "swim" with the wretched old men), and the driver told them that the trip would take less than four seconds. Makeba finally realized that the Streak Limo was superior to the Purple Farts bus on Chronos since *time* was so important and the Streak Limo had it all over the regular bus. In four seconds, they would be at Inter-Galactics. Makeba's mouth was becoming a little dry as she became more excited.

The electro-mechanical sound of the doors double locking echoed throughout the limo. A dark glass separated the front seat from the rest of the passenger section in the rear. The Quintet was very quiet, each thinking over the past however long it had been on Chronos, and hoping that the Inter-Galactics would finally give them, all of them, the time and credits needed to return to Plane of Origin. The group had never worked so hard in its collective lives.

A digital sounding bell rang, and the seatbelts automatically clicked into place. Nardo and Norma were sitting on the back seat, and Pearl, Makeba and Jake were on the side seat. Soft music began to play, and lights that slowly changed color began their sequence. Nardo could not make out the driver through the very dark glass separating the front from the back. However, he could make out the "lights" on the dashboard. This was no ordinary limousine in the earthly sense. It looked far more like science fiction, with holographic indicators of all hues, and especially a hologram of the Limo itself, with destination plotted out. Nardo didn't understand it, so he closed his eyes and left the driving to the unseen driver. Anyway, Nardo had more important things on his mind . . . costumes, makeup, flute part, back-up vocals. He brought himself back to the rice drying on the roads outside of Manila. This was his respite. In his daydream, he pulled down a fresh mango, which reached from the heavens to the ground, and plucked it. In his mind, the pungent flavor of the mango filled his brain.

An unfamiliar whine began, ostensibly the limo's streak engines starting. When they were at a reasonable pitch, the digital bells sounded again. Nardo opened his eyes and saw the lights in the "cockpit" flashing at odd times.

At once, the group was surrounded in a blinding light, fully certain that the next thing they would see would be the theater at Inter-Galactics. The blinding flash subsided, and the group became perplexed. Outside the Limo, they were floating once again through space, like they first had on the subway car, and the large salmon globe they had encountered took up much of the sky. Norma quickly glanced at her watch. Four seconds had come and gone.

"Where *are* we?" said Makeba. "I thought he said four seconds." Jake immediately began pounding on the dark window. Mysteriously, no driver was anywhere to be found in the cockpit. The Streak Limo was free floating in space and, worse yet, it was passing the salmon globe destined for who knows where.

"Oh my God. Oh my God!" Pearl began to get scared and hysterical. Makeba reassured her.

"Nothing is wrong. We can't lose our cool over this." Makeba's instincts began to rise.

"Lose our cool? We're floating a million miles from nowheah over deah. Oh my God!" Pearl was becoming undone.

Jake acted. "Gimme something hard. We've got to break through this window and see if we can get up to the driver's seat here!"

Makeba took off her high heeled pump, mysteriously restored after the much touted "broken heel" fiasco in Mystery of History. "Will this work?"

"I'm afraid not. This is safety glass. We need something hard like a stone." Jake was looking furiously around the Limo.

"What about this?" Pearl was eyeing the three beautiful cut crystal decanters which held some sort of liquor.

"Perfect!" said Jake. And Norma began pouring the contents of the decanter into the other decanters. When she was finished, she handed the empty decanter to Jake.

"All right. Everyone at the back of the Limo and cover your eyes!" It seemed that Jake was taking over. With almost superhuman strength he heaved the decanter as hard as he could.

The sound of splintering glass was heard all over. The decanter had done its job. Jake picked up the decanter, still in one piece and began knocking the loose glass out of the window. The salmon globe was almost completely past the Limo now, and the Quintet was destined for points unknown. "Ladies, do the best you can with those cloth napkins, and get those shards out of the way. Norma, you come up here with me."

Nardo watched as Jake threw his jacket over the sharp edges of the glass still sticking up and climbed over the front seat, braving what was certainly a circle of knives. After he got there, he quickly turned around, holding his hand out to Norma and helping her navigate over to the front. The limo was still streaking at hyper speed, and the salmon planet was becoming smaller and smaller. "Norma. See if you can figure out what these dials mean and the digital readouts. I'll try to turn this around some way." Jake was busying himself, scanning the steering mechanism.

Norma looked at the panoply of lights and dials in front of her. She had not had much training in computers and the like, other than accounting and word processing packages. However, she quickly looked and noticed that the labels on the limo "dashboard" were symbols and not in any particular alphabet. Jake was trying to turn the wheel, and figure out the controls, which seemed to cause him to be perplexed him more than the cockpit of a stealth fighter would have. No matter how much he turned and twisted the controls, the limo streaked steadfastly on. "Maybe it's on auto-pilot or something like that? See if you can find anything that resembles auto-pilot." Norma quickly began looking around. All the "buttons" were actually part of a large screen in front of her. There were at least one hundred choices. Methodically, she began looking at them. The whine of the limo began to develop into a high scream. Norma was becoming increasingly nervous.

An alarm began sounding, and next to one gauge, a light began to glow red. Norma was still trying to find anything which resembled auto-pilot. The alarm began beeping faster. The light was glowing bright orange. Another alarm began to sound. "This doesn't sound good," yelled Jake over the whine.

Meanwhile in the back, Pearl and Nardo were trying to clean up from the broken glass. Makeba wanted to help out in front, but knew her girth would not make it through the front window. The best she could do was keep out of the way.

Norma was trying to make heads or tails out of the strange markings. Alarms were screaming, and numerous lights on the "dash" were flashing faster and more furiously. "Hurry, Norma. Just find something! Press something!" Jake's tone seemed to be total panic, as he yelled above the excruciating whine. The lights next to the gauge, which Norma figured was something to do with temperature, had turned from orange to a blinding white. Something had to be done now. They clearly had only seconds.

All of a sudden, Norma's quick eyes spotted a single isolated and unobtrusive digital toggle with two dashes on one side, being the side the switch was toggled, and two zeros on the other.

In a flash, Norma switched the toggle.

"OY MEIN GOTT IN HIMMEL!" yelled Pearl as the limo lurched savagely. Norma noticed that Jake's pushing and shoving of the controls were having an effect.

"That's it!" he shouted. The horrible whine of the engines began a decrescendo and the pitch gradually dropped. One by one, the alarms seemed to shut off, and the temperature gauge returned gradually to orange, red-orange, red, purple, blue and finally . . . off.

"Wow," said Makeba. "How did you ever figure that one out?"

Norma finally gave herself the opportunity of catching her breath. "Well," she said, "I looked for anything that looked like 'on' and 'off'. Then I noticed the switch with the dashes and the zeroes and I thought to myself 'sleep and wake . . . closed eyes and open eyes' so on a guess, I switched from 'closed' to 'open' eyes, and that turned out to be the auto pilot switch.

Jake seemed to finally get some control of the ship. Nardo remembered Jake telling him that he had to learn how to fly a plane once for a movie that he did. That being the Quintet's last great hope, Nardo invested all his wishes on that.

The limo had quieted down, but seemed to be floating aimlessly now. Although Jake was able to maneuver the limo back facing the now very distant salmon dot, he was having more problems.

"We've got to make this thing go back, at least to where we came from."

"Norma, can you figure out where the program is on the screen?" Makeba was looking at the endless stream of "switches" and "dials." Norma's quick eyes again began to peruse the dials. Jake was looking, too.

From the back, cringing, Pearl slowly crept up to the window to share the space with Makeba. Nardo also poked his head up there. For a moment, the five of them stared, perplexed, at the maze of lights.

"It's right deah . . . oveh deah!!" Pearl screamed, as Makeba bashed her head on the top of the window. Fortunately for her, her turban stopped any glass shard from coming through.

"Which one, Pearl?" queried Norma.

"OVEH DEAH! Dat's the one what looks like a circle with an 'X' through it at the top!"

"How do you know that," asked Nardo.

"Because, dat's the sign for 'round trip' on my Senior Bus Pass! It looks like a circle wit an 'X' but really it's a round arrow pointing to itself! I know, 'cause I asked the driveh, Joe. He's a friend of mine, Joe is, 'cause I take the same bus so many times."

The group studied the symbol. Sure enough, it certainly could be an arrow pointing to itself. "Well, at this point, we should try something!" said Jake. "Strap yourselves into the back seat and hold on."

Jake was back in control again. Nardo, Makeba and Pearl went back to their seats and buckled up. Jake and Norma strapped into the front seat.

"Here goes nothing." Jake leaned over and touched the button under the appropriate symbol. A read out popped up which seemed to indicate a ten-second delay. 10-9-8-7-6-5-4-3-2-1.

The limo then seemed to right itself and, as if it knew what it was doing, pointed itself directly toward the salmon ball. The engines began to whine again. Pearl grabbed the seat in front of her. Nardo's throat lump was choking him. The hearts of the Quintet were pounding in synch. The whine of the engine once again reached fever pitch. The limo lurched, and the familiar blinding white light flashed inside.

The next thing they saw out the window was the parking lot at the motel again. This time, there was a crowd of people outside the limo. Someone opened the driver door. "What happened?" the familiar voice of the Purple Fart bus driver asked.

"I don't know what the heck happened, or what happened to our driver." Jake was noticeably shaken.

"Well, move over. I've always wanted to drive one of these things. We've got to get you to the amphitheater. You're late already!" The driver pushed Jake over to the middle seat, taking care not to cut himself on the thousands of glass shards. Norma accommodated. With knowledge, the driver began pressing various buttons and switches on the screen. "We're off!" he yelled, and with that, the limo engines whined, the flash blinded, and the group found itself at the back lot of an immense outdoor amphitheater. Somehow, it was dark, and the lights, like a great night baseball game, glared in their eyes.

The limo doors opened automatically, and the driver shouted, "Get out and get into your costumes!" As the group emerged from the vehicle, Norma noticed Jesus and two women, dressed in the new Mariachi Pagliacci costumes running towards them. In a flash, Norma was in her costume, and Nardo, already in his, was pulling her hair back, and applying her makeup. He quickly finished, and made up the rest of the group as they were ushered through a long underground corridor, up stairs, and on to a dark portion of the stage. Pearl picked up the tambourines, handing one to Makeba, and stage hands led them to their spots. No one noticed the very disappointed Sugar Twins who passed them in the corridor on the way down. Evidently, the Twins had some prior notice that the Subways might not show.

No one had time to think. The group before, a large gospel group, was finishing, and the faraway sound of the full amphitheater's applause was eerie in its roar. "Ladies, Gentlemen and Entities of all kinds. Let's give a warm welcome to the representatives from Super Region One . . . 'MARIACHI PAGLIACCI'!"

No sooner than the announcement had finished, the clarion sound of a lone trumpet began the triple-tongued introduction to

"CONQUISTADORA POBRECITA." Over the trumpet, Norma's now gladiator-force voice, with all the strength of a tenor, began the pickup to the first verse, and then they were off. The mix was perfect. Pearl's tambourine was interlocked with Makeba's cabasa in exactitude. Now and then the angel tones of Nardo's Indo-West African flute licks peeked through the simple melodies and harmonies. And, of course, Makeba added the soulful cry of the woman who had finally come to terms with who she was. By the time the group had climbed to the final chorus, the eerie sound of the crowd singing along was spooky.

"CONQUISTADORA —— PO-BRE-CI-TA!!" The crowd had already learned the melody, and was on its feet clapping to the Latin-African rhythms. The group on stage was completely immersed in its performance, and didn't notice that, at that moment, their new star burst forth on the intergalactic horizon. As Norma rolled into the "stretto" portion, signaling the coming end of the piece, her arms slowly raised, and each and every arm in the audience raised absolutely simultaneously.

In a roar that dwarfed all other roars, the crowd erupted, stamping their feet and whooping and hollering. The Quintet went into a dream state. Being the last act, in the nick of time, it was nothing more than a wish fulfilled, but not yet fully appreciated when the announcer screamed "MARIACHI PAGLIACCI" as the Inter-Galactic First Place winners for the season. A fantastic trophy including a hologram of the galaxy which floated where the angel usually stood was handed to Norma. The group had achieved the impossible, winning the final award. No one knew what awaited them on the other side of the trophy. Makeba quickly glanced at her R.O. It had eleven and one half credits on it. She turned to Pearl. Pearl's had eleven credits.

"We're on our way home," wished Makeba to herself, secretly tiring of the constancy of the effort. Makeba turned to Jake who was walking next to her. She didn't notice his R.O. pinned on his costume. "Maybe he lost it?" she asked herself. Oh well, the crowd was pushing in. Tele and Holo vision cameras were blinding them. Whatever, she would have to remember to tell him later. There was no time for anything now.

33 - BE CAREFUL WHAT YOU WISH FOR

It seemed like weeks later that Nardo first realized what was happening to the group. They were immediate Inter-Galactic celebrities. They were booked promptly to perform huge shows at huge arenas. They performed constantly on Television and Holovision. They had dolls and merchandising contracts. Exposés of the group appeared in tabloids, of course having absolutely nothing to do with reality. Nardo longed for some time to himself. He noticed that Jake had emerged as the clear leader of the group and, although Norma and Pearl had figured out the Streak Limo codes, Jake's "take charge" attitude and new confidence was extremely impressive, especially to Nardo who had problems with controlling any life other than his own. Jake and Nardo had been paired off, sharing their hotel rooms and whatnot. Nardo thought to himself, "He sure has changed," remembering the quasi-homophobic homeless man he first met. Jake paid a lot more attention to Nardo than he ever had before. There was a change in him. Ever since the limo incident, he seemed to be a different person. But then, Jake was paying a lot more attention to the whole group, and he and Jesus had split up the authority and responsibility for the group's heavy travel, performance and other schedules.

More than once Nardo had seen Jake come out of the shower, flashing the big blues and the bright white smile at him, half naked.

Each time, Nardo's shields had gone up and, although civil, he could not let himself become involved. Besides, now he was completely in charge of costumes and makeup, and that was proving itself to be a full time job. The group almost never wore exactly the same costumes more than once.

But the MARIACHI PAGLIACCI theme had caught on, and there were now added to the dolls and merchandising, cards, stuffed toys, computer games and no telling what else to deal with. When the group performed on Tele and Holo, Norma, Jake and Jesus were the usual spokespersons.

Hotels were now all of the highest class. Gone were the days of the Launch Pad. Meals were whatever they wanted, steak, lobster, caviar, escargot or anything else. Even Streak Limos were becoming too slow for them to keep their busy schedules.

It started happening while they were staying at the GRAND INTERGALACTIC, reportedly the best hotel in the quadrant. Jake and Nardo were sharing a suite, which was fine, because Nardo certainly enjoyed not being alone, the Mariachi players wanted to stay together, and the "girls" always shared a suite. Nardo had fought his way back to the hotel. He wanted to shop for some additional material for costumes, but now that he was so recognizable as "that short cute gay guy" by all of the fans, he couldn't go out without being accosted by autograph seekers, Paparazzi, and the like who were intent on vulturing the story of the new "gay" icon. The group had a seventh night off, and Nardo was glad of it.

The crowd had followed him into the lobby, and was physically grabbing at him. Although he was trying to escape, there was nowhere for him to go, and the service elevator was definitely out of reach. Someone grabbed the back of his shirt and pulled hard. He knocked his teeth on a microphone which had been shoved in his face. The press of the crowd became overbearing, and Nardo was reaching only chest high to some of them. He looked up. The room began to spin.

Suddenly a pair of strong arms encircled his waist. Nardo didn't have the strength to resist. He was light headed and faint. "Hold on buddy. I'll get you out of here." He heard a familiar voice breathe directly in his ear, and in a moment, he had been whisked out of the crowd, through a door to the service elevator. Nardo turned as the arms loosened, and found himself in the elevator with Jake's arms around his waist. Nardo looked up into Jake's eyes and for a moment, the shields were down. He noticed the beautiful square jaw and mildly cleft chin, the perfect sandy brown hairline, and the steel blue eyes. Jake added his spectacular smile to the combination. Nardo's legs gave way under him, but Jake caught him. "Whoa. Steady there! That'll teach you not to go out by yourself. I could've gone with you." Jake's voice was soft and alluring. Of course, Nardo had not, this last time, collapsed from dizziness. His shields were getting slower, especially in the Jake department. He instinctively remembered how dangerous this was. Dangerous to attach yourself to a known straight man. But, at this moment, Nardo didn't have the strength to fight it. He allowed Jake to keep his arms around him all the way up to the suite.

Smiling down at him, Jake picked up Nardo like so much cat, and placed him softly on the bed. "You should get some rest. You'll need it." Nardo was drinking in the nurturing tone. He realized, maybe for the first time, that Jake was the best friend he had here. Yes, certainly the best friend. And he swore he would do nothing to endanger that friendship. Jake put his large masculine hand on the side of Nardo's shoulder and smiled. "Sleep, buddy. Sleep." Nardo turned his head to the side. Everything was so confusing. The crowds, the schedule, the unending bustle. His shields were definitely coming down. He vowed to keep them up. Yes, he had to keep them up . . . if he only could.

34 - NARDO'S SACRIFICE

The next few weeks presented Nardo with a roller coaster of excitement. Never before had he so much attention drenched on him all at one time. He was now a "star" of the first degree, like Elton John, Freddie Mercury, Boy George. He was this week's latest, and he was loving every minute of it. He was badgered, exposed, run after, hounded . . . and for once, he loved all the attention. Nardo, of course, never let down his guard.

The entire troupe was moving so fast. It was funny. Everyone forgot the Streak Limo incident, putting it off to an accident, or simply the Sugar Twins desperate to play at Intergalactics.

"I really feel sorry for them, in a way," Norma sympathized. "I mean, they were here first, and we won."

"A stroke of pure luck," chimed Pearl, "who was really more interested in finding a game of Super Nova Mah Jong, something a little less strenuous than a full time career as a Pop Star.

However, now they had no privacy. Throngs of people were all trying to take them apart, bit by bit — managers, publicity agents, critics, and all the rest of the vultures commonly found in the entertainment business. When you're nobody, you can't get arrested. When you're somebody, they flock to you like junk spam e-mail to a new web site. Now, they are all driven to staying away from crowds. No longer can they go shopping, or do anything without getting mobbed. They tried to disguise themselves, go incognito, but to no avail.

And the competition was looming. Groups were beginning to copy them. New groups were coming out, and trying to replace them at the top of the charts.

Makeba cursed as she read in the entertainment rags where a new group called "Dulcinella Pulcinella" and another called the "Get Down Clowns" had new record deals. She thought to herself, "this can't be good." Some of the papers even began calling them "legends" which is another word for "over the hill" in showbiz talk. Can you imagine? A *Legend* in less than one year?

And then there were the vicious rumors begin spreading about each of them and all of them. They were bombarded with cameras, and Makeba slowly came to realize that the fame and celebrity that she wished for was not what the expected fantasy promised. "In fact, I liked it better when we were facing the little adversities rather than this out-of-control fame and fortune." The amusement park ride was beginning to lose its luster, and Makeba noticed the same pall falling over almost all of them.

On the other hand, Makeba was finally together in herself, although she still could not figure out why the Bartender had tried to stop her from saving Angel. "Life is extremely perplexing," she would think to herself, her Jamaican-Ghetto English being almost completely forgotten by this time.

Nardo and Jake became inseparable during this period. It was almost as if Jake had taken on the role of Nardo's protector or big brother. They did everything together, eat, share rooms, work out (yes, Nardo even began aerobics). He didn't want to get too muscular in case he ever went back to drag. Nardo would admire Jake in the weight room while Jake pumped iron and Nardo did stretches. No one would dare say anything to Nardo for two reasons: First, he was a *major* celebrity and second, he had a very strong friend who would protect him. These were some of the happiest days of Nardo's life.

But slowly and ever so subtly, the shields were dropping even more. Nardo sighed as he looked at Jake wiping the sweat from his large pectoral muscles with a gym towel. With all the good feelings, with all the success, with all the trappings of wealth and happiness, Nardo couldn't figure out why he felt like there was an empty hole inside of him. And the more apparent the celebrity became, the more stark the hole became to him. Something was missing. Something fine. At times, he never felt more lonely in his life, and the empty feeling began to creep over him, and slowly take over his being.

Nardo remembered the night which he later would referred to as the "turning point." The group had finally demanded a hiatus. "But this is the high season! We'll lose trillions!" The roar of the vultures resounded. But Norma, Jesus, Makeba, Pearl and finally Nardo and Jake demanded that they take a break for about two weeks. "Don't expect to be stars when you get back!" The publicity agent was really a Gorgon when she wanted to be, but finally Norma talked to them (with Makeba sitting and making stern faces on the sidelines) and the managerial group decided that they could move things and give the group the two weeks off they desperately needed.

Jesus and the Mariachi group decided to take their vacation in a city called Seven Wells. It was a desert city that had been transformed into a spangling city of lights and twenty-four/seven action. Although Jesus was not interested in the gambling, and neither was the rest of the group for the most part, there was lots of entertainment and a diversity of beings to meet, with loads of color and excitement. It would be nice to go to a show without the horror of having to perform it. They would, of course, be recognized, but they would also receive VIP treatment. In addition, there were spas, massage, pools, and general relaxation facilities.

The Quintet decided to go off on its own, and with the Purple Fart bus driver, they Streak Limoed to a beautiful mountain resort by an idyllic lake, called the "Aerie Lodge." An Aerie is an eagle's nest, and this very exclusive and small resort was perched high above the lake splashed between verdant hills and mountains, with a suspended cable car going down to the lake and funiculars to take you to the little town for shopping and whatnot.

Each room was beautiful, had its own hot tub smack dab in front of the view, and all rooms were suites and had a spectacular view of the lake. The resort had a small staff which was extremely competent, but there was almost one staff member for each guest. There was a five-star restaurant which melded the local fare into fantastic French cuisine. They even had some bridge games for Pearl.

"Tanks God fuh something, oveh deah!" Pearl had been dying. Although there was no kugel, Pearl did fine on the éclairs, Madeleines and Napoleons, and didn't care if she gained weight or not.

However, she made it perfectly clear when she found out that "escargot" was really snails, that she had reached her Hebraic limit. Although not kosher herself, even she terminated the gastronomy at some point. When Makeba finally talked her into eating one, she spit it out promptly and continuously swore, "That little monsteh kept rearin' its ugly head in my stomach fuh monts afteh dat!" She immediately washed it down with a Napoleon and great French roast coffee.

The mountain air at the Lodge was not only medicinal, but seemed a little thin, and everyone noticed the lightheadedness it produced.

One night, after a beautiful day on the lake fishing with Jake, the two were walking around town, with Nardo explaining some of the particulars of Chinese embroidery to Jake, who seemed to listen with gusto. Eventually the two of them found themselves paired off in the Aerie restaurant. Although Jake wasn't supposed to drink at all, they split a nice bottle of wine, which mellowed them both out. After the lovely dinner, they went up to their room and sat listening to music. The group had decided that no work was to be allowed during their Sabbatical, and so Jake and Nardo sat looking at the never-ending dusk, with the twinkle of the town lights spread below them.

Uncharacteristically, Jake softly suggested that they take a Jacuzzi in front of the window with the view. Nardo said, "That sounds wonderful. Okay, you can go first."

A mellowed Jake looked directly at Nardo and said softly, "why can't we go together?" Nardo became light-headed and began to swoon. Why was Jake doing this, to torture him? "He must figure it's harmless." However, with his shields almost completely down, Nardo agreed, against instinct. After all, nothing was going to happen. Jake was straight. He knew this intellectually. And he could stand twenty minutes in the tub. Besides, they were closer than ever, now. Like brothers.

In the dim light of the antique filled suite, Nardo saw Jake emerge like a statue of David from the bathroom. Nardo's eyes were wide as he slipped off his slight polo shirt and twenty-six inch waist shorts. How could he not succumb to this heaven which was about to happen? Nardo saw the Adonis approach him flashing that bright smile, and he was in Jake's arms, who gently lowered him into the hot tub. Nardo closed his eyes, and felt Jake climb in behind him, and then Jake's great legs wrap around his slender body.

Nardo dared not open his eyes. He felt Jake's strong hands on his shoulders, and felt Jake's massive hands perform a heavenly undulation of the muscles in his neck, back and shoulders. The magnificent manipulation lasted for what seemed a glorious eternity. Soon, Nardo felt Jake's warm breath on his neck, as he was softly kissed. Nardo breathed deeply and sensed Jake's masculine smell. He was falling, falling. Without any overt sexuality, the empty hole in his soul was full. He felt complete, and was bathed in sensuality. Nardo felt Jake's powerful arms again encircle his body, and the two fell into a blissful spell, as the hot tub bubbled, and soothed, around them for what seemed an eternity.

On its own volition, the motor of the Jacuzzi stopped, and the two were wakened by the sudden silence. Jake slowly released Nardo, got the towels, and the two got out of the tub and warm in their luxurious robes, sat across from each other on the overstuffed couch in the dim candlelight, sharing a bottle of late harvest Riesling, a sweet dessert wine.

Nothing was said for almost a half-hour, it seemed to Nardo. Nardo's eyes closed and opened intermittently as he drifted in and out of heavenly bliss. When he opened his eyes, he noticed a glint by the light of the flickering candle on Jake's cheek. Jake was crying.

Nardo looked again closely to confirm what he thought he saw. "Jake. Jake," Nardo said softly. "What's wrong?"

"Nothing. Nothing I can tell you, buddy."

"But that's impossible. You can tell me anything. We're . . . friends. We're almost brothers."

"I'm afraid to say it. It's something that I can't even come to terms with myself. No, no . . . I won't ruin it. I won't say something that will ruin what we have."

"Jake. Come on. Nothing you can say to me will change anything. Nothing. Now tell me. Let me be a friend to you. Grant me this. Be the family that I am missing."

"Well . . . I . . . I think . . . I think I've fallen in love with you." Jake turned his teary eyes up towards Nardo. Nardo saw now, not the invincible Adonis, but the poor little fallen angel, his wings folded and smashed there on the couch in the candlelight. Jake began to sob.

Nardo's heart was filled with sympathy, pity, and the purest of loves in this moment. He got up and walked to Jake's end of the couch, sitting down, and hugging him. What a feeling this was, finally, to hold him dear. Nardo whispered, barely audibly, "I love you too, Jake. I love you too." The two sat wrapped in each others arms, as Jake continued to sob.

"But that's not everything!" Jake pulled away from Nardo, his tortured face only inches away. "I really screwed up, Nardo. I really screwed up again."

"What do you mean?" Nardo had absolutely no idea what Jake was referring to.

"I've lost all my credits!"

"What?!"

"I'm telling you, I've lost all my credits!"

Nardo was amazed. "But how? How did that happen?" Jake pulled his R.O. out of his robe pocket. Although he had a lot of time racked up, there were no credits in the credit read-out. Nardo was dumbfounded. "My God! Tell me what happened!"

Upon his question, Jake began relating the story of Madonna and the hotel room, the booze and the drugs, embellishing a little on the true story, and conveniently leaving out the part about Abraxas. Nardo held Jake's hand as he listened intently.

"I guess I must have screwed up royally, because when I looked at my R.O. when I got home, all my credits had been taken away." Jake began crying uncontrollably, while Nardo hugged him and soothed him. "I'll never get home. Never."

"Don't worry about it Jake. Don't worry." Nardo sat up. He had come to a decision. "I love you, Jake. I will fix it." Nardo went to the closet, opened it, and pulled out his R.O. It was showing twelve full credits, enough to return to Plane of Origin. Nardo sighed as he looked at his R.O. It had been such a long haul to earn these, so hard. "Unity in the face of crap," Nardo quoted the Purple Farts driver to himself.

But Nardo was not afraid. Why shouldn't he? After all, he was successful in this place, like he was never successful on Earth. He was a star. He felt that he could make a success of his life here. But looking at Jake, he felt Jake wasn't as strong as he was. He felt Jake would never have his inner strength — the strength that comes from surviving as a flaming little faggot from day to day in a world where the penalty could be death at any moment. Nardo breathed in.

"I give you all my credits, Jake. I don't need them. I don't want to go home." This was killing Nardo inside, since he loved Jake and knew if Jake got the credits, he would go back to Plane of Origin, without him. But this was a sacrifice Nardo was willing to make.

"You will?" Jake stopped crying.

"Yes."

"But what will you do?" Jake seemed concerned.

"I . . . I will stay here." Nardo explained that he could live here, that he now had the strength to do it. At first, Jake absolutely refused. But after some coaxing, Jake finally relented and Nardo gifted the credits to Jake.

Nardo saw Jake's eyes light up as he looked at his R.O. "There here. Twelve credits. How can I ever thank you?" And Jake ran to Nardo, and hugged him. Nardo looked at his own R.O. The credit column was empty. Nardo exhaled deeply. A new empty hole was brewing inside of him.

Then the two retired in each other's arms to the four posted Rice bed, and Nardo drifted off to sleep. He was very tired, and would have to contemplate his action when he awoke.

When Nardo opened his eyes after a long needed restful sleep, Jake had gone. He was nowhere to be found.

35 - A FINAL ACCOUNTING

"Abraxas. Damn him. Abraxas. I should have known! I should have warned you!" The General Manager of the hotel was genuinely appalled at his own lack of perception. Things like this happened at other people's hotels, but not his.

Under the watchful eye of the General Manager, Nardo had been tricked by Abraxas into giving all his credits to him. Nardo was completely smashed inside. The four sat quietly at breakfast, not eating. "Where is the dignity?" cried Pearl. She wasn't used to people violating other people's space. It was against her religion. Makeba suggested they find Abraxas and kill him, but Norma toned her down. They all looked in astonishment at Nardo's empty credit column.

"And, if that was Abraxas, where the hell is Jake?" Makeba roared, as though, some how, but she didn't know how, this was all his fault. "When did they make the switch?" And thinking back to the streak limo, and how different "Jake" had been acting, and the disappearance of Angel, and trying to figure out where they both went, Abraxas' treachery was clear. Nardo didn't even have the strength to chastise himself.

As if Jake would fall in love with me, he thought. "It's not Jake's fault," whispered Nardo somberly. "It's not anybody's fault." But everyone knew how hard Nardo had fallen for the false Jake. They could feel it. The little man from the country of rice and mangos was crushed.

"We'll each give you some of our credits, so we can even them out," said Norma. Pearl and Makeba quickly agreed. "Then we'll work again, and earn enough to leave." All had twelve credits racked up, and each was willing to give to Nardo in his hour of need.

All were becoming weary of Chronos. This "Buying Time" certainly had its drawbacks. Pearl knew she would never take her "free" twenty-four hours a day back on Earth for granted.

Nardo grabbed everyone's hand in the middle of the table in great appreciation. "No." He refused it softly. "No, no. Last night I had a revelation. I like it here better. Even with all of this disaster, I am a success here." Nardo went on to explain his reasoning. No matter what anyone did, they could not talk him out of it.

The quartet, sans Jake, decided to go back and see if they could find Jake in the city where they had last been. The Purple Farts driver came up with the old bus, and they decided, for old times sake, they would bump and grind down the mountain in the old bus, uncomfortable though it was. They all climbed into the bus with their suitcases. This time they were the only passengers. All were quiet and somber. The bus driver looked at them in the rear view mirror, and slowly shook his head. The news of the larceny of Abraxas had reached him, and God knows who else.

On the third try, the bus finally started and began rambling down the narrow road from the Aerie. Norma looked up at it in the salmon light and knew she would never see a more beautiful place. What a shame it had to end like this.

Without warning, the familiar blinding light filled the Purple Farts Bus. "I thought dis bus couldn't streak oveh deah!" exclaimed

Pearl, wondering why they had puttered so long in it when all the time it could streak. It was an answer she wouldn't receive . . . this time.

36 - WILSHIRE STATION

"Explanations! Explanations very, very cheap!" A cry they had not heard for infinity re-entered the lives of the quartet. They looked cautiously outside the bus, and they were at their initial mustering point. The bus door opened, and there, in all his glory, was Jake!

"My God, Jake!" Makeba was completely startled. They were all glad to see him, but Nardo, understandably, developed throat lumpitis and kept his distance. Jake related to them that he had been "detained" after the elevator incident in the Madonna hotel, and couldn't get back to them. He told them that it only seemed like seconds, however, before they all showed up.

"So the entire episode from the Streak Limo, through Inter-Galactics, through Nardo's ordeal . . . that was Abraxas, not me!" Jake looked up at Nardo as he spoke. A deep sorrow poured over him, and as Nardo exited the bus, Jake put his arm around him, squeezing him.

"I should've known. You can't change from gay to straight. What made me believe that you would change from straight to gay? It's all my own stupid fault!!" Nardo broke down.

Jake and the rest re-offered to donate credits to Nardo, but he refused. To make things worse, the bus driver reluctantly informed them that Nardo's credits had probably disappeared from Abraxas' R.O. because you can't trade credits and make it stick *unless the recipient would have had the power to earn the credits themselves*, a reminder from their first explanation. Abraxas had not even profited from his treachery. He did it only for the "kill." So basically, Nardo had thrown his credits to the wind.

The group noticed that they were parked right next to the familiar subway car. "Get in. Get moving people! Get in the car. How much time do you think we have?" The long lost voice of the Nancy Kulpesque woman who had first handed out the R.O's cut through the continuum, as she spoke in Initial Capital Letters: "Everyone With Twelve Credits, Back On The Subway Car, Now!!"

Nardo and the rest all looked sadly at each other. Tears filled everyone's eyes.

"We love you very much," said Pearl. "You want some Napoleon I saved? I got some pills?" This was the best Pearl could do, besides the earnest hug and kiss she gave to Nardo.

Makeba hugged Nardo next. "Are you sure you won't take the credits?" Nardo assured her not to worry. Was that smoke in Makeba's eye?

Norma couldn't say anything, and was a mess. How could she say good-bye to her little friend? She held on to him for all he was worth.

Jake picked up Nardo as he hugged him. He knew that Nardo had fallen in love with "him" and was so sorry. But he also knew and understood that Nardo had been willing to give all his credits to Jake, albeit a false one. "Bye, my friend." Jake actually had tears in his blue eyes, too, but Nardo noticed that these eyes were true and blue, not like the steel blue eyes of Abraxas.

The loudspeaker on the grounds kept squawking various things, and the din of the mustering grounds was as obnoxious as always. The familiar buzz of the loudspeaker blurted, "Attention. Attention. We have a Gift Lottery winner. We have a Gift Lottery winner!"

The Quintet was barely paying attention, but snapped to when the winner was announced. "For his selfless donation of 12 credits, this time unit's winner is . . . LEONARDO DE LOS SANTOS!"

Nardo's R.O. immediately began beeping. As he looked in amazement, he saw the credits rack up from zero to twelve. The group was flabbergasted and ecstatic. The joy was greater than any joy they had experienced in combination since arrival. Jake picked up Nardo and put him on the subway car.

"But I thought I would stay here!" Nardo was more surprised than anyone. He had completely forgotten about the Gift Lottery, although he had heard the announcements from time to time at the library, on TV and holo and throughout. He never imagined he would win.

"Well, y' can't get out of living life that easily," said the butch woman, as she grabbed the R.O.'s out of each of the Quintet's hands. "Didn't y' learn anything while you were here? Pshew! Y' can't get away from your obligations. Y' can only stay here if you absolutely can't make it on Plane of Origin. You *gotta* go back, Mister!" And with that she was gone and the subway doors whooshed shut.

The subway car jolted, lights flashed, and they were soon once again floating beside the large familiar salmon globe. All were silent. As they cleared the gas planet, the subway car began to shake as if there were major clear-air turbulence, then more violently, then another blinding light, then total darkness. All of a sudden, the whining changed into the sound of a subway track, a tunnel of light appeared in front, the train slowed to a traditional stop, and the WILSHIRE STATION sign was visible outside the train car.

The seating arrangement of the car had, however, changed. What was happening? As they looked around, they saw that Pearl and Makeba were now sitting next to one another, with all of Pearl's stuff on the next seat. Jake, looking homeless and bearded once again, was sitting next to Norma, and Nardo was sitting facing them.

"Wha . . . Wha happened? This I don't need." Pearl was grabbing Makeba's arm, and Makeba put her hand on Pearl's leg to steady her. Both women noticed that Pearl's packages had been strewn all over, tchachkes were broken, and the floor was basically a mess. "By the way," Pearl ventured to Makeba. "My name is Pearl. Pearl Pelzman." Grabbing her purse with her arm, she thrust out her hand to shake Makeba's.

"I'm Makeba. Well, really Mona Lisa, but my friends call me 'Makeba'."

"Mah . . . wah?" Pearl was making attempts at international diplomacy.

"Mah-kay-bah. It's the name of my favorite folk singer.

"Mah-kay-bah. We'll it's nice to meet you . . . finally, Mah-kay-bah!" Pearl looked disheartendly at the strewn packages.

"We'll have to do something about that," offered Makeba, and the girls began the task of collecting tchachkes and assessing damage. "Godammit! The heels broke off my shoes!" Makeba noticed that her spiked heels were without. It was now clear. Nobody remembered a thing. Or did they? Chronos wasn't even a splintered memory. In fact, nobody remembered anything except that the car had started to shake like a martini tumbler and, after the tremor, the car pulled into the next station.

Pearl, who had previously silently viewed the others from

afar and practiced her own form of xenophobia with "strangers on a train," was concerned that Makeba had hurt herself. Makeba thought to herself that she needed to help Pearl, in distress since the packages were strewn all over the car. "Can we clean this up?" queried Makeba as she instinctively climbed onto the floor. Makeba and Pearl teamed up to collect all the items, some broken.

The other three were pulling themselves together after the debacle. "Was that an earthquake, or what?" Jake was voicing everyone's concern about the violent shaking of the subway car. "Is everything okay? Oh yeah, my name is Jacob. Jake Silver." Jake's beautiful smile shone through his scruffy "Foghat" beard.

Norma nodded to Jake. "I'm Norma Jardines. But, is everybody is all right?" asked Norma and everybody, checking around, upon finding all appendages in good working order answered affirmatively. She looked at a disheveled Jake. "This poor man," she thought. "And I though we were poor." Without even thinking she asked Jake, "Where are you sleeping tonight?" A changed Nardo's head popped up as he looked directly at Jake. Norma continued, "What are you *eating* tonight?"

"Wilshire Station trashcans, I guess," Jake said, brushing his dirty clothes off. He scanned the trashcans as a matter of habit to see if any fresh paper plates or bags were left.

Norma was quick to put the issue to rest, although this was never out of character for her. However, inviting strangers into her own private world was a new response. "No, you are not. You are not eating here tonight, Jacob Silver. I am making a traditional Mexican dinner tonight." Including Nardo, she asked, "Would the two of you like to join my family for dinner? We live close to the Station." Turning to Nardo, she managed to coax his name out of him, and the trio all shook hands. With not much pushing, Nardo and Norma talked Jake into the new eating arrangements. For the first time in years, Jake saw a little light at the end of his tunnel. Nardo felt that he was no longer intimidated by life's situation, for some inexplicable reason. It certainly seemed to Norma that added to her palette was a deep compassion through a new wholeness in herself.

Nardo looked carefully at Jake. Whereas at the start of the Subway trip, he would have avoided looking at almost anyone, inside Nardo grew a deep sympathy for Jake now. Somehow the fear had left him. Nardo thought about Jake sleeping in the Station again. He thought of the cold floors and the dirty blankets and people shunning Jake. It would be so easy for him to say, "Look. I have an extra bed in my apartment. You could come and clean up. You could get a good night's sleep." But this wouldn't happen yet. Not just yet anyhow. But who knows what could happen after a great traditional Mexican dinner? Nardo's courage was beginning to bud. He again looked up at Jake, a good head taller, as he helped the homeless drug-bedraggled man amble off the train, while Norma took Jake's few pitiful possessions with them. "Bye. It was nice meeting you. I'm glad you're all right. See you tomorrow!" was Norma's refrain to Pearl and Makeba as the three waved to the "clean up" crew and started up the extra-long escalator to the street at Fairfax

"Bye! Take care!" responded Pearl. "Boy oh boy, dat earthquake was too close fuh comfort, oveh deah!" she said to Makeba. Without explanation, gone was any xenophobia between the two. Makeba's restored sense of self, and Pearl's expanded view of global diversity definitely lingered even though the specific memory of Chronos had been completely eradicated.

"I'm so nervous, my heart is racing." Pearl took out her panoply of pills, and without thinking, offered the mixture to Makeba.

"Thanks, but I'm all right," declined Makeba gratefully. "Say, did any of your expensive things get broken?" Makeba held up a broken faux crystal frame to see if it could be repaired.

"Nutting dat can't be replaced," Pearl mused. Norma's invitation to the guys lit a fire under Pearl. What the hell. What's the harm in asking? After all, being in an earthquake together. That qualifies as a friendship making event. She cautiously approached Makeba. "Look. I got a kosher chicken at home from Sam, the Butcher. He saved it for me. It was on sale, but I got to eat it now. Day old, y' know." Pearl hesitated ever so slightly. "Do … uh …. ya' wanna come oveh fuh suppeh … maybe?"

Makeba straightened her turban and stood up. She smiled at Pearl with a newly discovered kinship. Why had it taken so long to even learn her fellow riders' names? But Makeba had never been shy. "Let's go girl. I can make a jerk chicken with peanut sauce like you never knew."

"Jerk? Whazzat, jerk? As long as it's not too much of a jerk!" Pearl punned. "Like my brother-in-law, Sidney. Now theah's a real jerk!" The two women grabbed up Pearl's packages smiling, rolled their heads back and roared as they climbed on the escalator and rode towards the bright light of day.